THE FRENCH PARADOX

THE FRENCH PARADOX

Ellen Crosby

**SEVERN
HOUSE**

First world edition published in Great Britain and the USA in 2021
by Severn House, an imprint of Canongate Books Ltd,
14 High Street, Edinburgh EH1 1TE.

Trade paperback edition first published in Great Britain and the USA in 2021
by Severn House, an imprint of Canongate Books Ltd.

severnhouse.com

British Library Cataloguing in Publication Data
A CIP catalogue record for this title is available from the British Library.

ISBN-13: 978-0-7278-9101-3 (cased)
ISBN-13: 978-1-78029-758-3 (trade paper)
ISBN-13: 978-1-4483-0496-7 (e-book)

All Severn House titles are printed on acid-free paper.

Typeset by Palimpsest Book Production Ltd.,
Falkirk, Stirlingshire, Scotland.
Printed and bound in Great Britain by
TJ Books Limited, Padstow, Cornwall.

For Cathy Brannon, who helped my first book find a publisher in London twenty years ago, and Rosemarie Forsythe, whose intriguing suggestion that I write about the Old Mistresses, research assistance, and multiple 3x5 notecard illustrations of my plot, led to this book.

'I pray you, do not fall in love with me, for I am falser than vows made in wine.'

– William Shakespeare, *As You Like It*

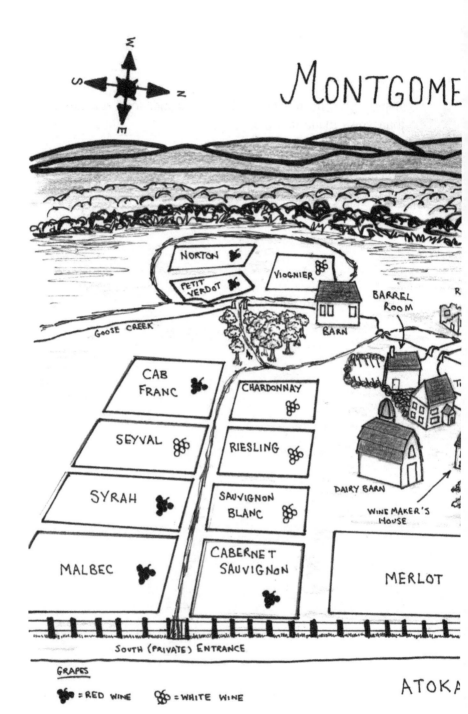

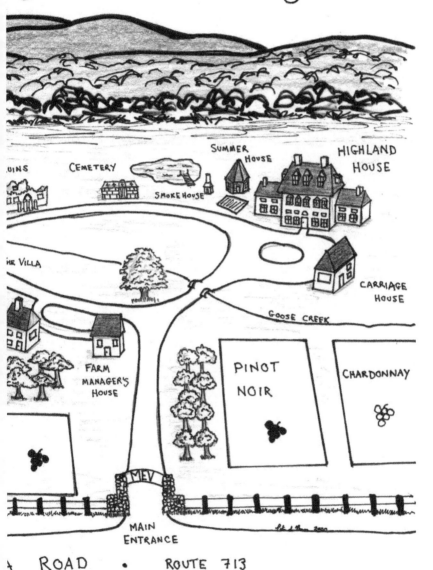

PROLOGUE

found out about my grandfather's affair with Jacqueline Kennedy Onassis when I read my grandmother's diaries – ironically over Valentine's Day weekend. No, I had no idea. Yes, it was a shock.

Grandmama was so matter-of-fact describing their relationship that she could have been reporting on the weather or what she ate for dinner that evening. Plus she implied – with the blasé nonchalance French women possess when discussing *l'amour* and cheating – that such liaisons are what any woman living with a man deals with sooner or later, as normal as breathing. Though reading between the lines I got the impression she felt more envious of Jackie, one of the most iconic and glamorous women of the last century, than angry at my grandfather for being so captivated by her.

The affair took place in 1949, a year Jacqueline Bouvier later described as the happiest of her life. That autumn she sailed from New York to France along with thirty-four young women from Smith College to spend her junior year in Paris studying art history and literature at the Sorbonne, the Louvre, the Institut d'études politiques (better known as Sciences Po), and a former porcelain factory in Montparnasse where Smith had its classrooms. On the last night of the voyage to France, the ship's captain asked the Smith students to sing '*La Vie en Rose*' – and for Jackie to sing a verse by herself. The song pretty much summed up the year to come for a privileged group of American teenagers, or perhaps the hoped-for year that awaited them in the most beautiful and seductive city in the world. Not to mention the tantalizing prospect of romance, love and maybe a little discreet sex in the place that wrote the book on it. As for Jackie, it didn't take long after arriving in Paris before she fell head over heels in love with the City of Lights, all things French – and my grandfather.

To be fair, my grandparents weren't married at the time or

even formally engaged, although they had been seeing each other and my grandmother, at least, had assumed theirs was a serious relationship. Which was probably why Pépé kept his on-the-side dalliance a secret and Grandmama wrote that he did a bang-up job because she never caught on. It wasn't until years later that she found Jackie's letters – my grandfather had kept them all – which she read with the benefit of clear-eyed hindsight and the wisdom of a wife of nearly thirty-five years. I was almost certain she never told my grandfather she found out about him and Jackie; I wondered if Pépé ever guessed that she did.

By the time I learned about the affair, it was decades too late to ask her. Nor could I ask my mother, who had also passed away, though she must have known since she was the one who hid the journals in an innocuous-looking box from Galeries Lafayette, one of Paris's main department stores. It was tucked away in a dark corner of the attic at Highland House, my family's home for generations and now my home; I found the box after I finally got around to replacing a light bulb that had burned out ages ago. When I took off the lid, the journals – half a dozen well-worn burgundy leather volumes smelling of mustiness and old memories – were lined up in chronological order in two neat rows.

My grandfather had met Jackie by chance at the Louvre. Jackie dropped her gallery map. Pépé picked it up. They started talking and later went for drinks at a café in the *Quartier Latin*, the student district near the Sorbonne. Even though my grandfather was fluent in English, their conversation was in French since Jackie had signed Smith College's pledge to speak only French for her entire time in Paris, even among her classmates.

There were more meetings at art galleries and museums, places Jackie loved and couldn't get enough of visiting, trying to absorb everything she could. But there were also what seemed to be heavy make-out sessions in parks, gardens, and other out-of-the-way places. According to Grandmama's journal, that's as far as it went. If there were any hotel room trysts or back-seat-of-the-car steamy midnight lovemaking sessions, Jackie didn't allude to them. Still, it was obvious there was passion, flirtation, moonlight poetry, champagne-fizzed dancing at nightclubs, and plenty of, well . . . opportunity. Whatever really happened, Jackie had been discreet in what she revealed in her letters.

It was also clear their relationship would never survive her departure for America the following spring. Pépé wouldn't follow her to the States; she would get on with her life once she returned home. They were both wide-eyed realists about their future. I did know – because my mother told me – that my grandparents had dined at the White House on several occasions when John F. Kennedy had been president and my grandfather was France's young, brilliant Deputy Head of Mission at the embassy in Washington. My mother also hinted that Pépé had played a role behind the scenes in the complicated diplomatic negotiations between Jackie and the French Cultural Minister whom she managed to persuade to allow Leonardo da Vinci's *Mona Lisa* to leave the Louvre and travel from France to the United States in 1963. I suspected the irony wasn't lost on either Jackie or my grandfather: the Louvre was where they first met. I wondered, as well, what their relationship had been when she was First Lady and he was the number two diplomat at the French Embassy, meaning he ran the place when the Ambassador wasn't there.

I kept what I learned from my grandmother's journals to myself, not even sharing the revelations about my grandfather with my fiancé, Quinn Santori, just like two generations of women in my family had done before me. My mother hadn't told my father, either. She wouldn't. I knew that with absolute certainty.

Don't ask me why I didn't tell Quinn. Maybe it was because it was Jackie, who had come often to Virginia to ride and hunt because of the privacy, discretion, and uncomplicated acceptance she found here. No paparazzi lurking around corners waiting to ambush her. And perhaps, also, because she had been a good friend of my mother's, someone I had known as well, although I was just a little girl.

Much of what I remembered was embodied in a photograph of Jackie seated on a wicker sofa on our veranda. I sat cross-legged on the ground in front of her and she was smiling, her arms wrapped around me, her chin resting on top of my head. Me with a gap-toothed smile, since two front teeth were missing, bandages on both elbows after I skinned them falling out of one of our apple trees, and my mother, on the chair next to us, grinning as well.

Both of them still in riding clothes after a morning hack: jodhpurs, boots, sleeves rolled up, shirt buttons undone, flattened helmet hair. A teapot and two cups and saucers sat on the glass-topped coffee table. A small glass for me, probably lemonade. No other glass or teacup for a fourth person so I wondered who had taken the picture. Both Mom and Jackie looking relaxed and happy. The kind of photo you frame as a souvenir of a happy time.

My mother kept it in a place of honor on the desk in her study off the master bedroom. Now that room was mine. I'd seen the photo so often it was difficult to separate what I really remembered from what I imagined about that sweet, sunny spring morning.

Maybe it was because Jackie's affair with my grandfather completely upended my rock-solid faith that my grandparents – unlike my parents – had been genuinely in love, each other's soul mates. After my grandmother died, my grandfather had kept company with his friends from the old days – *les vieux potes* – his buddies from the Resistance, colleagues from the French diplomatic corps, friends who would come over to drink his finest champagne, smoke cigars, and watch France try to win Six Nations rugby or the World Cup. If he ever went out with another woman, I never knew about it unless it was because she needed an escort and he did it as a favor to a friend. Not even a whisper of romance with someone new. Had I been naive to believe – to *want* to believe – my grandmother had been his one and only?

And as these things sometimes do, the story of that complicated year in Paris had suddenly come full circle. Jackie's junior year abroad had recently become a hot topic of conversation around here – in Middleburg and Atoka, the next-door village where I lived. In a few days several paintings Jacqueline Bouvier had bought seventy years ago when she was an exchange student – apparently for a song – would be on display at The Artful

Fox, Middleburg's newest art gallery. Not only was everyone in town interested in the exhibit, it had attracted national attention because of the fascinating backstory of how she had acquired the paintings. With her discerning eye for art and beauty, Jackie had chosen oil paintings by a little known – at that time – French artist named Élisabeth Vigée Le Brun, who had been Marie Antoinette's portraitist. Two of the paintings were of the French queen. Now they were worth a fortune because Vigée Le Brun had been re-baptized in the art world as one of the 'Old Mistresses' – female painters who were contemporaries of the 'Old Masters'. They were just as talented as the men but never got their due for the very reason that they *were* women. After the exhibit was over, their current owner, Cricket Delacroix, one of Jackie's close friends from that year in France, was going to donate Jackie's Old Mistress paintings to the National Museum of Women in the Arts in Washington, D.C.

And my ninety-three-year-old grandfather was flying here the day after tomorrow to attend the exhibition and celebrate Cricket's ninetieth birthday at a party to which it seemed everyone in Middleburg and Atoka had been invited.

Pépé was the only one who knew the real story of what happened between him and Jackie, who could fill in the gaps and blank spaces, the little stutters and ellipses that I had detected in the pages of my grandmother's journals.

But after all these years would he finally reveal the truth about his relationship with one of the most private and secretive women in the world if I asked him? More important, did I have any business prying, just because I had found out about the affair? Pépé knew me so well and I am the worst liar in the world. Would he figure out there was something on my mind when we visited that exhibit together – and maybe he'd ask *me* what was going on?

I was dying of curiosity to know more about the star-crossed love story between my grandfather and Jacqueline Kennedy Onassis, one of the most beautiful and fascinating women of the twentieth century.

Who wouldn't be?

ONE

'Then there are the death threats.' Parker Lord sipped coffee from a to-go cup with a Cuppa Giddyup logo on it. He added, half-amused, 'Although some of my reviews are far worse. "Best ecological use for this book: line your cat box or your hamster cage with the pages and recycle."'

'Wait a minute,' I said. 'You're getting death threats?'

He had been kind enough to bring me a coffee as well, though by now mine was tepid. The two of us had been standing in my backyard for the last half hour talking about roses, azaleas, camellias, irises, and exotic breeds of tulips on a chilly mid-March day. The pale yellow sunlight gave off no warmth this early in the morning and the washed-out brownish-yellow grass left over from winter was cold and wet under my work boots. A gust of wind whipped the bare rose bushes and rhododendrons until they shook in a forlorn-looking garden my mother had planted decades ago. The first day of spring was in a few days, but just now it felt as if winter might have one more trick up its sleeve. I pulled my hoodie tighter around me.

My conversation with Parker had somehow shifted from his recommendations for what to plant, prune, or give up as a lost cause so our gardens would look like one of those perfect, everything-gloriously-in-bloom gardens you see in magazines in time for my outdoor wedding in May. Now we were talking about his new book, *The Angry Earth*.

'Not exactly *death threats*.' He made air quotes with the fingers of the hand that wasn't holding his coffee cup. 'Just comments or rants on social media – you know, *trolls*, or whatever you call those disgusting people – who want to stir folks up. *Provocateurs*,' he added, pronouncing the word with a French accent flavored with a healthy dollop of South Carolina drawl.

'Have you done anything about it?'

He shrugged. 'Bullies are usually cowards, Lucie. My editor

and publicist are trying to get the most egregious comments removed.' He gave me a sly look. 'Although *The Angry Earth* has now shot up to the number-one slot on *The New York Times* bestseller list for non-fiction. It's an ill wind, you know?'

'You think that happened because of the death threats?' I asked.

'I think the negative publicity hasn't hurt,' he said. 'Truth be told, there are people who say I'm fabricating this whole controversy myself.'

'You mean, it's fake?'

He gave me a noncommittal look and remained silent. It took a moment to sink in that his detractors might be right.

'So are you?' I asked. 'Making up these awful comments and rants yourself?'

I wanted him to say no.

'Darling,' he said, 'you don't bring a spitball shooter or a slingshot to a gunfight. I don't plan to sit on the sidelines. At least folks are talking about the book, about this subject. I'm glad it's controversial. People need to be disturbed. They need to be upset.'

'Parker, are you serious? A person with your reputation doesn't need to be getting involved like that.' I stared at him. '*Why?*'

I looked at this man whom I'd known almost all my life. Parker Lord was probably one of the best-known and most revered landscape designers in America. He had worked for the White House, the Capitol, the National Arboretum, Mount Vernon, Monticello – if the garden was historic or a national landmark, he had probably been involved with it. Years ago he apprenticed with Bunny Mellon, who, along with her husband Paul, had been legendary philanthropists and arguably Middleburg's most famous and generous residents. Bunny had designed the White House Rose Garden in the 1960s at President Kennedy's request; later she planned the gardens of the Eternal Flame at Arlington Cemetery for his memorial.

Parker had also been a close friend to my mother, who died when I was eighteen. Years earlier she had accompanied him as his translator when he went to study the gardens of Versailles and Monet's Giverny. The two of them had traveled throughout

France to visit as many of its most beautiful gardens – classified as *jardins remarquables* by the French Ministry of Culture – as they could.

The Angry Earth had been published in early January and it had been a contentious subject of debate, to put it mildly. Parker had been interviewed everywhere – all the major news shows, high-profile book reviews in the media, NPR, Oprah, late-night television; the British media had also taken an interest and there would be an overseas book tour down the road. He'd been excoriated as a phony by naysayers and lauded as one of the voices of sanity by supporters for speaking out in the ugly, bubbling stew of science, politics, and mud-slinging that was the climate change debate.

The biggest outcry from his critics was that with this new book he was fearmongering, scaring people with nightmarish scenarios about how bad things were going to get as climate change became more and more extreme. He painted a bleak, terrifying picture of the cascading consequences that would befall us as the result of man's behavior. Rising seawater permanently flooding coastal towns and drowning islands, relentless wildfires, crippling hurricanes, heat so intolerable it would make certain places uninhabitable, countries going to war over water rights, and not enough food.

Parker practically snapped at me, repeating my question. 'You want to know *why* I'm getting involved, *why* I'm playing hardball? Because climate change is real, that's why. And plenty of people – including some of the idiots down the road in Washington – think it's fake, made up. Bogus science.' He pointed a finger in the general direction of Washington, D.C. and his face reddened in anger. 'Look what happened right here in our backyard last December. The Christmas tree farm in Middleburg had to close its doors after selling only a couple hundred trees over Thanksgiving weekend because a fungus killed all its Fraser firs and Scotch pines. And do you know the cause of that fungus?'

I nodded. I did. And I had commiserated with the owner of the farm who told me last month that he had to cut down thousands of trees and burn them. My heart ached. Christmas trees.

'I know the cause. Warmer temperatures. Global warming,' I said.

'Damn right.' He stared at me, suddenly contrite. 'I'm sorry, sugar. I shouldn't be taking this out on you. But I can't understand how so many people – especially folks in a position to do something – can ignore what's happening to this planet. Can ignore the goddamn *science*. And what the consequences will be if we don't act before it's too late.' He took a long sip of coffee. 'That is, if we haven't already passed the point of no return.'

The point of no return. I shuddered. What would that world be like? How hot would it be? How bad would it be?

'We have vines that are dying all of a sudden and we don't know why. It could have something to do with last winter being so warm, but who knows?' I said. 'Josie Wilde is coming up from Charlottesville in a few days to have a look. I hope they're not too far gone to be saved.'

'I heard Josie was working with you. She's the best. Doctor Grapevine,' he said. 'Best viticulture consultant on the East Coast. Hell, best viticulturist anywhere. She doesn't take on just any vineyard. You must have impressed her.'

We had. Josie knew my winemaker Quinn Santori and I wanted to up our game, make better wine than we already did at Montgomery Estate Vineyard, especially because of Virginia's growing reputation as a top wine-producing state, a place with so much potential to be even better. I had persuaded Josie we would do whatever it took, follow her advice and recommendations religiously. Quinn, who was from California, had been reluctant to cede so much authority to someone else, but I was working on him. He would come around.

Now, however, we needed her help for a different reason: the alarming rate at which rows of Merlot vines were dying for no apparent reason. We didn't know whether it was a vector – a predator or pest – or some weird, random thing, maybe the consequence of a pesticide or fungicide reacting in a way it wasn't supposed to do. Whatever the cause, I worried it might have been caused by the unusually warm winter we had just gone through in Virginia. Or to put it simply, one of the consequences of climate change.

The breeze kicked up once more. 'Do you want to go inside?' I asked Parker. 'It's chilly.'

'I'm OK,' he said. 'Why don't we sit on your veranda out of the wind and we can finish going over these plans for your wedding garden? Which is what we should be talking about. Not global warming or my book.'

We walked across the lawn and climbed the steps to the long, columned veranda with its west-facing view of the Blue Ridge Mountains. Parker slowed his stride because I still needed to use a cane, the result of a car accident a dozen years ago that left me with a limp and a deformed foot.

He tried to take my elbow, a proper Southern gentleman who wanted to assist a lady, until I said, a bit sharper than I needed to, 'Thanks, but you don't need to do that. I can manage.'

He withdrew his hand. 'Just like your mother. Stubborn as all get out.'

'I'll take that as a compliment. Have a seat.'

'Don't mind if I do,' he said. 'I'll take the glider.'

I sat in the love seat opposite him. We hadn't yet put out the seat cushions since it was still too early in the year, so I sat on the bare wicker sofa and he sat on the metal glider. Which was probably pretty cold, though he didn't let on.

'So.' Parker set a scuffed leather backpack on the glass-topped coffee table between us and unzipped it, pulling out a sheaf of papers that he waved at me. 'Are we all set? Here's a list of the plants I'm recommending for your gardens based on what we discussed and a plan for where everything goes. You can order them from wherever you want and I gather your crew will take care of planting them.'

'We'll order everything from Seely's,' I said. 'Just like we always do.'

Parker leaned back in the glider and pushed off, rocking back and forth with one foot. 'Sure,' he said. 'Seely's, or wherever.'

'What do you mean "Seely's, or wherever"? When have we ever gotten our plants from any other nursery?'

Seely's Garden Center, on the outskirts of Middleburg, was an institution. My mother had bought all our plants from Noah Seely ever since she moved to Virginia after she married Leland, my father. I still went to them for anything we needed.

'Fine, but don't mention my name to Gabriel,' Parker said.

Gabriel Seely was Noah's oldest son and he had slowly been taking over the family business now that Noah was semi-retired.

'Why not?'

Parker grimaced and gave me a you-don't-want-to-know look. But he was going to tell me anyway.

'I'm PNG at Seely's,' he said.

Persona non grata.

'You seem to be on everybody's naughty-not-nice list at the moment. It's a good nursery, Parker. What happened?' I said. 'This time.'

His eyes flickered with ironic humor.

'This time,' he said, 'I had a little run-in with Gabriel. I found out he falsified results for the post-doc research project he's been working on with New Dominion University.'

'What research project?'

An arched eyebrow. 'Didn't you know? He got a grant to analyze how plants react under stress. He's focusing on glutathione, the antioxidant a plant creates when it's not doing well – although I suspect you are aware of that. Anyway, if a plant realizes it's created too much glutathione, it knows it's in trouble, so it sends itself a message to self-destruct. Kind of plant seppuku – you know, samurai honor dying.' He grimaced at his little joke. 'Like I said, you're familiar with glutathione because you find it in grapes.'

I did know about it. Though in winemaking glutathione plays a different role as a natural grape antioxidant that protects the aroma and flavor of white and rosé wines and prevents premature aging.

It sounded as if Gabriel was going down a different path, though, and that his research didn't have anything to do with wine.

'What happened?' I asked. 'Gabriel's a straight shooter, a smart botanist. He doesn't do stuff like that, make things up.'

Parker shrugged. 'That's what I thought, too. However, he wrote a paper, which is about to be published for peer review in *The Journal of Plant Pathology*, claiming he's been able to determine when a plant is dying, or about to die. What's an even bigger deal is that he says he also figured out how to manipulate the DNA structure of glutathione in a plant. In other words, he can play God and stop it from going into a death spiral. Keep it alive.'

'He can fool a plant into believing it's not dying? My God, Parker, that would be incredible.'

'Wouldn't it? A total game changer if it were true. Imagine the potential for being able to save a dying species, possibly mitigating or blunting the impact of climate change. Unfortunately, Gabriel is only at the earliest stages of experimenting with this and he's neglected to mention that fact. That's problem number one.' Parker ticked it off on a finger. 'And problem number two, which is worse, and for me, utterly damning, is that the results he's gotten so far have been . . . shall we say . . . massaged.'

'You mean he faked his results? Gabriel? He wouldn't.'

'He did.'

'I don't believe you.'

'You should.'

'How did you find out?'

He gave me an enigmatic look. 'I'm not going to burn my source, because his project has the potential for enormous commercial value – if his ship comes in, so to speak. I'm talking about Big Serious Money. Except that day is a long, long way down the road and Gabriel needs more cash to continue his research. Of course no one wants to throw good money after bad and investors want the big payday, the sooner the better. So he needs to make his early work look promising, to persuade current and future investors of the potential for a significant return on their investment.'

'Have you confronted him about this?'

Parker put his feet up on the coffee table, crossing his long legs. Then he tugged on a lock of his white hair. 'Age confers wisdom, and at sixty-eight I'm plenty wise,' he said. 'Plus, I'm no longer willing to suffer fools gladly. I just haven't got the time or the patience. I told Gabriel what I found out and that he needs to come clean about the real results. That right now it's just smoke and mirrors.'

'What did he say?'

'In the nicest possible terms, he told me to go do something anatomically impossible to myself. In the presence of a lady, I'm not going to repeat his exact words.' He gave me another twisted smile. 'Ash wasn't too happy about any of this when I told him. He and Gabriel are pretty tight. And he, uh, is one of Gabriel's financial backers – which I found out after the fact, by the way.'

'I'm sure that didn't go over well at all,' I said.

'No.'

Parker's husband Ashton Carlyle was a horticultural consultant, advising most of the major commercial farms in the region and many of the big estates that had their own fruit and vegetable gardens, telling them what to plant and what to do to make sure those plants grew and flourished. I'd hired him at the request of my cousin Dominique Gosselin, owner of the Goose Creek Inn, to put in a vegetable garden here at the farm with the plan that Dominique would buy the produce from me and use it in her menus. What she didn't need we would sell. We also wanted a cutting garden and a green-house to grow flowers for her tables and to use at the winery.

'Ash is getting all the plants and seeds for our new garden from Gabriel,' I said. 'He and Dominique are coming by tomorrow to make the final decisions on what to buy. He's also got our soil sample results back from Virginia Tech.'

'Make sure Josie sees Ash's plant list. You want to be certain nothing you put in is going to be a host for a pest that could kill the vines. That's the last thing you need.'

'I will,' I said. 'Now we need to talk about your fee for the wedding garden.'

He waved a hand at me. 'Don't insult me. You've always been like family, Lucie. You know how I adored your mother. My only requirement is an invitation to the wedding.'

'Of course you're on the list. There was never any question.'

'I thought I might be.' He smiled and swung his legs off the table. 'I ought to be going. Cricket asked me to stop by and check on some problem or other in her butterfly garden. It's probably nothing, but I think she just wants reassurance. Or, more likely, company. I assume you're going to her birthday party? And the gala at The Artful Fox?'

'We are,' I said. 'Harry invited Quinn and me – looks like she's going all out for both events. Dominique's catering everything so I've been hearing about it for weeks. What about you?'

A look of annoyance crossed his face when I mentioned Harriet, Cricket's daughter. 'Same,' he said. '*Cricket* invited me.'

'Why the pissed-off expression?'

'Because of Harry, why else? It was her decision to change the international premier of those paintings from the National Museum of Women in the Arts – where it should have been held – and have it at The Artful Fox instead. You know why, of course. She wants to promote Jackie's book. Except now she's acting as if it's *her* book.' He sounded resentful.

'*Jackie's book*' was a series of papers, notes, an outline, and even a few partially written chapters for a book on the subject of Élisabeth Vigée Le Brun – the Old Mistress artist whose paintings were being exhibited at The Artful Fox – and her relationship with Marie Antoinette as her portraitist and friend. Harry came across this gold mine while she was looking through her mother's photographs and papers to put together a collage of the last ninety years for Cricket's birthday: two unmarked boxes Jackie had left Cricket along with the paintings which, for unknown reasons, had been relegated to the attic at Mon Repos and never opened. Apparently the book had been a passion project of Jackie's during the period she worked as an editor in New York at Viking and Doubleday, except she never finished it. In 1994 she had died of cancer at the age of sixty-five.

However the *real* treasure was a private journal containing Jackie's introspective, deeply personal thoughts about herself and the two fascinating women she was writing about: Marie Antoinette, France's most famous – or infamous – queen, and Élisabeth Louise Vigée Le Brun, the most celebrated and sought-after female artist of her time, who later fell into total obscurity. Harry, who'd bounced around the world as a freelance journalist in between three disastrous marriages, decided she could finish Jackie's book with help from her mother, Jackie's dear friend, who would provide unique insight into the life of an iconic woman about whom the world remained obsessed to this day. The diary was a bonus. As a result, the new book – now Harry's version of Jackie's book – would be about Vigée Le Brun and Marie Antoinette, but Harry would also be channeling Jackie, a well-known Francophile who was as important, influential and fascinating as her two subjects.

To everyone's surprise, but also *not* to everyone's surprise, because after all this was Harry, Cricket's beloved only child, Cricket had been fine with the idea of her daughter finishing the book. What had not been fine was the reaction of folks around here of a certain generation who had fond memories of Jackie, a Middleburg habitué since the days of JFK's presidency until her death. People who knew such a private woman would not want Harry Delacroix turning Jackie's scholarly research into some kind of breathless, sensationalized exposé. I could imagine the titles:

The Woman Who Accompanied JFK to Paris: Jackie's Love Affair with France.

Secrets Revealed: Jackie in Her Own Words.

The Queen, The Artist, and The First Lady: The Story Jackie Never Told Us.

Parker's reaction over Harry taking on this project was one example of that kind of outrage and ire. I knew he had known Jackie; for one thing, she and Bunny Mellon had been great friends. Bunny had helped Jackie design the gardens for the home she bought on Martha's Vineyard after Aristotle Onassis died. Parker might even have been involved in the project.

'Did you know her well?' I asked. 'Jackie, I mean.'

His smile was full of melancholy and nostalgia. 'Oh, my, yes. I think I always felt protective toward her, too – though she was a fiercely strong woman.'

'Did you meet her when you were working for Bunny Mellon?'

'Lord, no. It was years before that. I met her in New York before I went into landscape design. Back when I wanted to be a writer.' He saw my astonished expression and smiled. 'Oh, yes, I did. Writer with a capital W. A *literary* writer. Jackie had just moved from Viking to work as an editor at Doubleday when my first book landed over her transom. She never wanted anyone to know this, but she edited it as a favor, made it so much better than it was. Then she refused to let me thank her in the acknowledgments and wouldn't take any credit for all the work she did.'

I tried to recall all of Parker's books, all bestsellers. Which we owned. 'I guess you don't mean *Designing Eden*. That's the first book I remember.'

'No, this one was called *Porch Wisdom or Things My Momma Taught Me*. The subtitle was *Stories of the South*. The only people who bought it were family members and close friends. I gave your momma a signed copy – it might still be collecting dust somewhere on one of your bookshelves if Leland didn't chuck it out or donate it to the library after she died. It got a few good reviews, but nothing that set the world on fire.' He added in a soft, faraway voice, 'Jackie told me it was wonderful.'

I couldn't remember ever seeing this book on any of our bookshelves. Maybe Leland had pitched it after Mom died, especially because he hadn't approved of her having male friends. Even gay male friends. Though he had his share of girlfriends and my mother had put up with his shenanigans.

'Were you in love with her?' The question slipped out before I realized whom I was asking. But still. Parker spoke of Jackie like someone who had fallen under her spell.

'How could I not be? Though since I'm gay, not in the romantic sense, obviously. I found her utterly captivating. She was . . .' He seemed to be searching for a word. 'Mesmerizing. You couldn't help but be enchanted by her.'

I thought of my grandmother's journal and all the between-the-lines things that hadn't been said about Jackie and my grandfather. Mesmerizing. Enchanting. Parker just admitted he'd been in love with her. How could Pépé not have been as bewitched?

The wind gusted again, rustling Parker's papers in my hand like dried leaves. He stirred.

'I'd better go see Cricket,' he said. 'Before I forget, do you want me to have a look at those dying vines of yours? I'm not trying to bigfoot Josie, but I might be able to provide some insight. Especially if it's something to do with pests that inhabit other plants or trees in the vicinity of your grapevines.'

'That would be great,' I said. 'It's the Merlot block in the south vineyard. The fastest and easiest way to get to them is to park at the winemaker's cottage and walk. You'll see them right away. They'll be the dying ones. Hopefully they won't already be dead.'

'I'll find them,' he said. 'I heard your sister's living in that cottage these days now that Quinn isn't there any more. Moved home from New York with a new boyfriend. An Italian, a lot older than she is. Art restorer.'

Parker probably knew Mia's boyfriend Sergio's shoe size as well, but he was too polite to say.

Small town.

'That's right, they moved into the cottage last month. Sergio works out of the house; Mia got a job at The Artful Fox and she's renting studio space in the back of the gallery. She's painting, but she also got her first commission. Harry just hired her to paint a mural in the solarium at Mon Repos that she wants finished before the Garden Tour at the end of April.'

'I heard about that mural,' he said. 'Sergio, huh? An art restorer. What's his last name?'

'Ianelli.'

Parker's face crinkled into a thoughtful expression. 'Sergio Ianelli. That rings a bell. I believe I knew him when I was living in New York. I might even have used his services. Or maybe I met him at an art gallery, someplace arty, you know, a party or a *vernissage*.' He frowned as if he were still trying to remember. 'Yes, I'm sure I knew him. And there was something . . .' He trailed off, still frowning.

'What?'

'I don't know. I'll have to refresh my memory. This would be thirty, thirty-five years ago.' He stood up. 'When it comes to me I'll let you know. These days my memory isn't what it used to be. I think it's because I'm trying to juggle too many balls. Look, sugar, I'm not sure when I'll be able to get by and take a look at those vines. If I get a chance I'll do it at the end of the day. Otherwise, my next available time would be the day after tomorrow, probably in the afternoon. Do you want to meet me out there? I'll call you or text before I show up.'

'I can meet you this evening,' I said, 'but on Wednesday afternoon I'm picking up my grandfather at Dulles. He's flying in from Paris for Cricket's birthday and the party at the gallery.'

Parker's eyes lit up. 'Luc's coming? I didn't know that. Cricket must be over the moon,' he said. 'She absolutely adores him.'

'He's looking forward to seeing her, too.'

'About time she had a chance with him, even if they are both in their nineties.' He gave me a roguish, lascivious grin. 'She's waited long enough.'

'Parker!'

'Oh, come on. I'm talking about a crush goin' on seventy years. Cricket knew Luc only had eyes for Jackie from the beginning, from the year they all met in Paris.' He shrugged and said, sounding wistful, 'Though that's no surprise. Jackie, well, she was a knockout even then. All you have to do is look at the photos.'

I sat up straighter, alert and at attention. 'What are you talking about?'

Did Parker know about Jackie and my grandfather?

'Darling,' he said, 'surely you knew about your grandfather's, uh, relationship with Jackie? Or to be more precise, their affair. This can't be news. Your mother knew and so did your grandmother.'

'How did you find out?'

'Your mother confided in me,' he said with a guilty smile. 'We'd, uh, had a few glasses of wine one afternoon. Your father was off hunting. She'd just found out about them herself after reading your grandmother's diaries.' He gave me a shrewd look. 'Which presumably you've read as well.'

'Only a few weeks ago. I'm still sort of in shock,' I said. 'Does Cricket know?'

'About the diaries? Not from me,' he said. 'Maybe your mother talked to her, but I wouldn't know about that.'

He came over and brushed my forehead with his lips. 'I'm off,' he said. 'Tell Luc I'm looking forward to seeing him, will you, darling? And I'll let you know about those vines.'

After he left I took his drawings inside and brought them upstairs to the desk in the study off the master bedroom. I had moved my mother's photo of her, Jackie and me from the desk to the top of a bookcase. I went over and picked it up.

Maybe I didn't need to ask my grandfather about his relation-ship with Jacqueline Kennedy Onassis, because there was someone else who could tell me about the two of them, had probably watched them fall in love, and was shrewd enough to figure out what was going on when it was right in front of her eyes. Especially if she also had a crush on Pépé.

A woman *knows*. *I* would know. So would Cricket.

My sister had told me in an offhand way that I was welcome to stop by Mon Repos and check out the mural she was painting in the solarium.

Maybe I would do that – and maybe I could have a chat with Cricket, who had wanted to know about my grandfather's plans when he arrived here the day after tomorrow. Jackie had trusted Cricket enough to leave her not only paintings, but that deeply personal journal, along with notes and an outline for a book she never finished. So it made sense, it seemed to me, that Jackie would have confided in Cricket about Pépé.

My grandmother's journals told only half the story of Pépé and Jackie's affair: Jackie's side.

But Cricket knew all of it. And maybe she'd be willing to talk.

TWO

Mon Repos, the Delacroix home, was located in Upperville, a sweet blink-and-you-miss-it village that was even smaller than Middleburg. It was also a Virginia historic landmark and the home of the oldest horse and colt show in the US.

Cricket's home was like many of the grand estates in this part of the Piedmont: wrought-iron gates and imposing stone pillars at the entrance to a long driveway that was more like a private road. A small sign with *Mon Repos, Built in 1804* hand-lettered in beautiful calligraphy hung next to one of the pillars. The main house and its outbuildings – guest houses, spring house, pool house, summer kitchen, greenhouse, stables, equipment barns and the like – were down the road out of view.

Though I have lived here almost all my life, I find this corner of Virginia to be breathtakingly beautiful. Even with so much wealth and affluence, it is still small-town America, where villages dating to the founding of the country are tucked among rolling hills and winding country lanes marked by signs that read 'Scenic Virginia Byway' or 'Civil War Trail'. This is land once surveyed by young George Washington; 250 years later it is still a farming county as well as horse-and-hunt-country. Thoroughbreds that will be future Derby and Olympic champions are bred and raised here and fox hunting is a way of life. Expensive horses and Angus cattle graze in pastures crisscrossed by post-and-board fences; farmhouses with hipped-roof barns and sentinel-like silos anchor fields where corn, grain or hay grow.

All of it framed by the aptly named Blue Ridge Mountains, a peaceful low-slung range that has been here longer than the Rockies and were grandfather-old when the Alps were formed. We may get teased about our mountains looking like speed bumps or the worn-down nubs of an old man's row of teeth,

but no one can dispute that the Blue Ridge – part of the Appa-
lachian chain – are *old*.

In spring – which is our loveliest season – trees like cherries,
Bradford pear, saucer magnolia, and dogwood come into bloom
before everything else so that for a few glorious weeks all
you see are lacy flowering trees in every shade of pink and
white in gardens and yards, along roads, or an occasional outlier
springing up in the middle of still-bare woods. This year,
however, the calendar and Mother Nature weren't on speaking
terms, so vestiges of winter vegetation that refused to surrender
still remained and the flowering trees were a few days away
from exploding into bloom.

It was also the time of year when the local news was all
about Washington, D.C.'s annual state of blossom-watch frenzy:
a politically polarized city that most days couldn't agree on
which way was up suddenly swept up by the romance of tiny
pink flowers and a huge guessing game: on which day would
the Tidal Basin's famous Japanese cherry blossom trees be at
peak bloom?

I turned the Jeep off Mosby's Highway at the entrance to
Mon Repos, where the gate was wide open. Although I could
have called in advance to ask if it was all right to stop by to
see Mia's mural and chat with Cricket Delacroix, around here
everyone sort of lives in everyone else's back pocket. No one
thinks twice about leaving a basket of zucchini and tomatoes
from their summer garden on your doorstep because they're
literally drowning in vegetables or just checking in if word has
gone around that you're under the weather or need to borrow
a piece of equipment for some minor construction project. We
show up for neighbors. We take care of each other.

As for how the word got around about what was happening
and to whom, all of it emanated from Atoka's General Store.
Thelma Johnson, the owner and a sassy octogenarian who kept
her fingers on the pulsing nexus of our little corner of Loudoun
County, Virginia, was aided and abetted in this endeavor by
the Romeos, whose name stood for Retired Old Men Eating
Out, which was who they were and what they did. They were
also retired old men *drinking* out, frequenting local restaurants
and watering holes for hours each day where they hoovered

up tidbits of information they then passed on to Thelma over coffee and donuts at her store the next morning. Although nobody ever called them the *Romdos*.

I parked in the circular driveway in front of a fountain where two winged cherubs frolicked on a large half clamshell. Cricket and her late husband, a French financier whom she'd met on another study-abroad program in graduate school, had been art collectors for many years; I knew the fountain had been imported from Italy and had once graced the gardens of a villa owned by the Medicis.

A maid answered the door and asked me to wait until she informed Mrs Delacroix and Ms Montgomery that I was here. The opulent foyer was decorated with antiques from the period of one of the French kings – which Louis I could never remember – and the walls were filled with an overabundance of museum-worthy oil paintings. On closer inspection, the place seemed *un peu triste* as one says in French – a bit sad and forlorn. The blue and white toile wallpaper was peeling in a few places; cracks ran through several of the black and white harlequin-patterned marble floor tiles. A large mirror in an ornate mahogany frame that hung over a console table herringboned with rare woods showed black streaks on the silvered glass, signs of age. One day the house would be Harry's; I wondered whether she would try to restore it or perhaps make changes that would better suit her taste so the place would look less fusty in a preserved-in-amber way.

I heard the maid's footsteps clacking on the tile as she returned to the foyer. 'Mrs Delacroix would like you to stay for tea,' she said, 'after you've visited the solarium. It will be served at three o'clock in the drawing room.'

She glanced at the antique tall-case clock that stood in a corner by way of subtly ensuring that I knew precisely how much time until I was expected for tea. I followed her gaze. It was ten to three.

'Thank you very much. Please tell Mrs Delacroix that I'd be delighted. Will her daughter be there?'

The maid's face creased in annoyance, but it was such a fleeting thing that I wondered if I'd really seen it. Then she was all professional composure and control again.

'Not today. She's not at home.'

'I see. Well, I'll be along shortly.'

'Very good. In ten minutes, then.'

The solarium was at the back of the house, a bright, cheerful room with floor-to-ceiling windows and glass-paned French doors that had exposures to the east and south. Furniture covered with Provençal fabric looked as if it belonged on a sundrenched patio or terrace overlooking the Mediterranean on the Côte d'Azur. If Cricket's house was a bit down-at-heel, her gardens, which were on full display through the windows and French doors, were – there is no other word for it – *glorious*. Parker had implied that Cricket had him on speed dial to come by for the least little issue pertaining to her flowers, plants, bushes, and trees. Consequently her gardens had the high, holy imprimatur and unmistakable stamp of a garden designed by Parker Lord.

My sister was kneeling as I entered the solarium, her long blonde hair done up in a high bun to keep it off her shoulders and away from her face while she worked. Mia was the beauty of the family and just now a shaft of pale gold afternoon sunlight pouring through a southern window caught her profile so perfectly that she looked like an angel lit from within. Her faded blue jeans were paint-stained and ripped at the knees and there was paint on one of Sergio's oversized navy sweat-shirts, which was missing its sleeves. Underneath, a black camisole was cut low enough to reveal a fire-engine-red bra. More paint stained her hands and she was barefoot. At the moment she looked half her age, about twelve years old. A paintbrush was clamped between her teeth like a horse with a bit in its mouth and she was frowning in concentration as she worked on an elaborate-looking flower that appeared to be part of an ornate arabesque design.

What didn't belong in the peaceful scene was her music, played through a speaker plugged into her phone: Billie Eilish – the Grammy-winning green-haired kid who, along with her brother, was the latest and youngest of the James Bond franchise of movie-title singer/songwriters – singing about what a bad girl she was. I was dead certain my sister wasn't aware I had just walked in, but all of a sudden the hand that wasn't holding the paintbrush turned off the speaker and her words were filtered through the other paintbrush in her mouth.

'Hith-hod-ham-mur-haul-is-gun-hake-for-eh-ah.'

I walked over and removed the paintbrush from her mouth. 'There are teeth marks on this handle. Did you just say "This goddamned mural is going to take forever"?'

She grimaced and nodded as she sat back on her haunches. 'I could die here. I swear to God I'll be an arthritic old woman still working on this. It needs to be finished by the middle of April, before they start getting the house ready for the garden tour. Maybe I should move in until I'm done.' She tilted her head, closed one eye, and stared at the flower she was working on. 'Actually I might do that.'

'I thought this mural was going to be some abstract thing, you know, that reminded you of a garden. This looks like you've gone all William Morris Art Deco.'

'Morris was Arts & Crafts and he was textiles. Art Deco was later in the early twentieth century.' She took the paintbrush from me. 'I was hoping you'd say Alphonse Mucha. You know, the artist who designed the posters for Sarah Bernhardt's plays in Paris in the 1890s that were so famous? Mom used to have a coffee-table book on Art Nouveau that had a lot of Mucha's work reprinted in it. Unfortunately it was in French so I just looked at the pictures since my French was never that good. But I always loved his work because it was so romantic.'

'I remember that book. Didn't Mucha paint women who had flowers coming out of their hair and in their gowns?'

'That's him.' Mia wiped a smear of green paint off her thumb on to her jeans. 'Plus he did a lot of commercial work for companies like Moët & Chandon, Nestlé, and a bunch of others. You see those posters reprinted all the time. My favorite is a series he did called *The Seasons*, which is what I'm going for here – four seasons, four walls.'

I glanced around the room and returned my gaze to the half-finished wall she was working on. It looked like she was somewhere in the middle of spring. Three more seasons to go.

'It's going to be gorgeous, Mimi, but it's a lot of work. Why didn't you choose a simpler subject? Or fewer seasons?'

'It wasn't my call or even my idea.' She rose from a

cross-legged position in one swift, graceful move without using her hands and stood in front of me. 'Cricket wanted something Picasso-esque, all modern and spare lines and splashes of color. Harry wanted to evoke Mucha – the flowers and the pastel colors but without the women. She's in love with his posters, plus she lived in Prague for a while where the Mucha museum is located. I think she has some kind of romantic association with either Prague or Mucha, although she didn't say and it's just a guess. Anyway, I thought I could pull it off in time, but it's going to take way longer than I expected.'

'So Harry won. Mucha over Picasso?'

'Yup, she's calling the shots now that she's home again. Same old bossy Harry. She was in here this morning, bugging me again about when I'm going to be done.'

'What about Sergio? Can he help you out?'

She gave me an incredulous look. 'Lucie. It's not paint-by-numbers. This is mine. It's my commission. No, Sergio can*not* help.'

'You don't need to bite my head off. It was just a suggestion.'

'Sorry. I'm pretty flipped out right now, is all.'

'Well.' I shrugged. 'No one's going to die if it isn't finished, you know.'

'No, but Harry might commit murder if it isn't. This year is the centennial of Historic Garden Week so you know what that means. It's a big deal.'

Historic Garden Week, which went on for eight days throughout Virginia, was billed as 'America's Biggest Open House'. The money raised by the admission fees supported the renovation and preservation of Virginia's historic gardens, places like Mount Vernon, the Pavilion Gardens at UVA, and the Woodrow Wilson Presidential Library. People went all out, spent absolute fortunes to get their homes and gardens ready for the tour. It *was* a big deal.

'That sounds like Harry. Go big or go home. Why didn't she ask you sooner?'

Mia puffed out her lower lip and blew upward, trying to get a stray piece of hair off her face without using paint-stained hands. 'Because she's such an airhead, that's why. She doesn't ever think these things through. But she's paying me a ton of money, so no way was I going to say no. Even if she is driving me crazy.'

'It looks gorgeous, Mimi. You'll get it done.'

'I hope so. Unfortunately Willow expects me to help her get the gallery ready for the Old Mistress paintings. She's in way over her head with reporters calling twenty-four-seven asking about it. Plus now Harry wants to use excerpts from Jackie's diary and have them displayed next to the paintings.'

'*What?*'

Mia looked pained. 'Damn, I don't know if I was supposed to say anything about that. Harry's publicist might not have announced it yet.'

'Are you serious?'

She nodded. ''Fraid so. She's planning to photocopy passages from Jackie's diary, blow them up, and hang them next to the Vigée Le Brun paintings as wall text. She's keeping the excerpts she's chosen a secret until the exhibit opens.'

'Excerpts that have something to do with the paintings?'

'Nope. The really personal stuff. Harry says it'll shock a lot of people when they see it.'

'Jackie would have hated that. Harry ought to know better, and if she's going to be totally tone deaf, Cricket should tell her. She might shock some people, but she'll offend everyone who knew Jackie and knew how she valued her privacy.'

And was so beloved here in Middleburg that the town had dedicated a small pavilion to her memory in a pretty little garden tucked away in the center of town.

Mia gave a one-shoulder shrug. 'I don't think she cares. She says there's some good stuff in that journal, things people didn't know.'

Like maybe whether our grandfather, who was having an affair with Jackie and had taken her to art galleries and museums on numerous occasions, might have been there the day she bought them. Was that what Harry meant by 'it'll shock a lot of people'?

'Maybe those unknown things should stay unknown. The journal was *private*,' I said and Mia's eyebrows went up when she heard the anger in my voice. 'I'm surprised Jackie left something that personal with those notes and papers about her book. I'll bet it was an oversight. Everything else of hers is at the Kennedy Library in Boston under lock and key.' Though that was probably not entirely true, because as far as I knew Pépé still had the letters she'd written him. Unless he'd destroyed them after she died, which was another possibility. 'What do you bet Jackie didn't realize that journal was there when she gave everything to Cricket?'

My sister shrugged again. 'I have no idea, but Harry believes it's finders, keepers. And Jackie's been gone, what, almost twenty-five years? Harry's going to go through with it, Lucie. You can be as outraged as you want, but the bottom line is that it's going to help sell her book.'

'Of course it is.'

'I'll get to see everything on Thursday when we set up the gallery. I'll let you know what she uses if you keep it to yourself. Now I'd better get back to work.' Mia picked up her paintbrush and I felt a stab of guilt when I thought about the other diary she didn't know anything about: our grandmother's.

I didn't want her to be blindsided.

'If Willow is stuck for people to help her set up the gallery, I can do it,' I said. 'I know how to use a level and hang a picture. That way you can spend the time painting here instead.'

And I could see the wall text before Mia did.

My sister's eyes flickered momentarily to my cane and then she looked away. My mouth tightened, but I didn't say anything.

My accident and the fact that I walk with a limp is a subject she and I do not talk about any more than we talk about that day she and our mother were out riding and Mom's horse Orion threw her jumping over a low stacked stone wall. She died in the ambulance on the way to the hospital. Mia said a rabbit spooked Orion, but when they'd left the barn one of the vineyard workers heard her and Mom arguing over Mia's latest bad boy boyfriend. Whatever really happened, it was Mia's word against no one's. She said it was a rabbit.

Then my sister ended up dating another bad boy: my ex-boyfriend, the one who'd been driving too fast on the rain-slicked day his car crashed into the stone wall at the entrance to the vineyard. He walked away. The jaws of life pried me out of what was left of the passenger seat of the car. A few years later when I came home from convalescing in France to take over running the vineyard after Leland died, he and Mia were an item. I wasn't sure whether I was more pissed off because he was my former boyfriend or because, by now, with Mia being eight years younger than I was and him two years older than me, he was borderline having sex with an underage teenager.

Of course Mom had started the whole ball rolling – falling for the good-looking dangerous guy with the slow hands and fast car that you already knew was going to be trouble – when she'd married Leland. Later she found out just how bad his drinking and gambling habits really were. Not to mention his womanizing. And she still stayed with him.

The Montgomery women. Somehow we always wanted to save the wrong guy.

Then I met Quinn and he saved me.

The clock in the foyer chimed three.

Mia cleared her throat. 'Look, thanks for the offer, but Harry's so paranoid about the exhibit staying a secret until the actual opening, I don't think Willow would say yes to you helping. Anyway, Sergio's going to be there so it will go faster.' She gave me a knowing smile. 'Although now you're probably dying to know about the journal excerpts, aren't you?'

'You bet I am. The whole world is going to be when word gets out.'

'I think that's the idea.'

'When is Harry's publicist going to announce it? Middleburg will be crawling with journalists and paparazzi when that happens.'

'Like I said, I have no idea. It might have already happened for all I know. I kind of lose track of time when I'm in my cocoon working.'

'I'll leave you to it. I'm invited for tea and tea is served at precisely—'

'I know,' she said. 'Three o'clock. You'd better get going. If you're late she'll give you the look. Trust me on this. Harry's gone a lot these days and I think Cricket's lonely. She'll be thrilled to have you to talk to.'

'When Pépé's here, he'll keep her company,' I said.

'She's counting on it,' Mia said. 'His visit is the only thing she's been talking about for the last couple of days. I think she's sweet on him, Luce.'

'Ms Montgomery?'

Mia and I looked up simultaneously, guilty expressions on both our faces as if we'd been caught picking blossoms off one of Cricket's prize miniature orange trees that scented the room. It was the maid. 'Miss Lucie, I mean,' she said. 'It's three oh two.'

'I'm coming.' I turned to Mia. 'Let me know if there's anything I can do. Come by for a meal some time, why don't you? With Sergio, of course. You need to eat.'

'Thanks, but probably not until after I'm done here,' she said. 'Besides, Sergio knows how to cook. Actually he's a great cook, so we eat really well. He has dinner ready when I get home every night, no matter how late it is. I don't have to do anything.'

Mia's idea of a three-course meal used to be two beers and a bag of chips. Emphasis on the beer.

'Lucky you,' I said. 'Where did he learn how to cook?'

Mia had volunteered almost nothing about his background, except to say that he came from northern Italy – Bologna, specifically – and had immigrated to the States when he was in his twenties. His family back home, what jobs he'd had, where he'd lived, were all subjects she never discussed. Nor did he.

She gave me a bland look and said in a flat, this-ends-the-conversation voice: 'Italy.'

'I gathered.' I returned the look and ignored the tone of voice. 'I meant, how did he learn to cook so well? From his mom, a girlfriend . . . cooking school?'

She pulled on the bun in her hair, tightening it with a hard yank. 'I don't know. We don't talk about that stuff. We don't talk about our pasts.'

'Where he learned to cook is a taboo subject in your relationship?'

'Lucie . . .'

So far we hadn't had a single argument since she'd moved back to Virginia. It had to be some kind of new record.

'What?' I said.

'Don't start.'

I started. 'Why don't you know about him? Why all the secrecy?'

'It's not that any of it's a secret. It just doesn't matter.' She added with a note of defiance, 'Besides, I don't care, either. Why do you?'

Because it *did* matter. You couldn't really know a person without knowing where they came from, who influenced them, what they'd accomplished. A relationship couldn't just be *tabula rasa*, a blank slate. Start from today and never look back. Sooner or later the past was going to catch up with, or more likely crash into, the present.

Unless you wanted to erase it, or at least part of it. Unless you had something to hide.

I didn't want this to turn into a full-blown shouting argument but I didn't want to let it go, either. 'You don't care? Does he have kids, a prison record, a wife back home in Italy? Is he in the witness protection program? Jeez, Mia. You have to know *something* about him. So do I. You two are more or less living with us now.'

'I don't have such a great résumé myself, if you remember, Lucie. In and out of trouble in school. I lived in the principal's office when I wasn't suspended for something. Drinking, some drugs. Nearly went to jail for killing someone while driving drunk.'

'*That* was someone else. Not you. You were set up.'

'It took our family lawyer to get me off,' she said with bitterness. 'My friends weren't exactly Scouts or honor students. As for New York, there's stuff I never told you and Eli. And I still don't want to talk about it.' She waved the paintbrush. 'I love Sergio. He loves me. There doesn't need to be anything else. It's *enough*.'

'Mia—'

'I mean it. And now you're even later for tea with Cricket. You'd better go.'

I turned and left without speaking. Before I got to the door, Billie Eilish was playing again. Louder than last time. I didn't know whether she'd resumed painting or was still standing there watching me leave. Either way, I wasn't going to turn around to find out.

Maybe she thought our conversation was over, that she had managed to deflect my questions.

But it wasn't. The next time I saw Parker I was going to press him to tell me what he knew or remembered about the mysterious Sergio Ianelli, plus I was going to look him up myself first chance I got. Because now I was more curious than ever about him. And why my sister was so adamant that she didn't need to know anything about who he really was and where he came from.

Or maybe that's just what she wanted me to believe.

THREE

Cricket Delacroix, at ninety, had the regal bearing and ramrod posture of a woman who had lived most of her life on her own terms and still knew exactly what she wanted and what to do to get it. You didn't trifle with her. This afternoon her snow-white hair was pulled back in an elegant chignon, she wore bright-red lipstick that looked like a slash of blood against her porcelain skin, and what I knew was a couture suit, probably Chanel. I was still in the jeans I'd been wearing for this morning's meeting with Parker, though I had swapped my burgundy Montgomery Estate Vineyard sweatshirt for a green cashmere turtleneck that Quinn said made my green eyes turn the color of dark emeralds.

'Lucie, my dear.' Cricket held out a bejeweled hand as I walked into the drawing room. And she gave me the look. 'I wasn't sure you were coming. I don't like my tea to get cold.'

'Cricket.' I crossed the room and took her hand, shaking it gently and trying to stuff my conversation with my sister into the back of my mind. At least for now. 'Thank you so much for asking me to tea. You look lovely.'

'I've been told I'm still well preserved for someone entering her tenth decade,' she said in a prim voice. 'At least the furniture is older than I am. But thank you for the compliment. And do sit down.'

Like the foyer, the furniture was antique – English and French – and more art hung on the walls, though these paintings were more personal. An enormous portrait of Édouard, her late husband, handsome in a beautifully cut double-breasted pin-striped gray suit, seated in a burgundy velvet wingchair with his hands folded in his lap, a serious expression on his hand-some face and one of their beloved Jack Russell terriers at his feet, hung over the fireplace. Cricket's portrait, to the left of his, was the complete opposite of Édouard's. Where he was staid and dignified, she was smiling, languishing in an upholstered armchair, her eyes teasing, dressed for a party in a full-length mink coat that fell open to reveal a stunning red satin evening gown with spaghetti straps and a sexy décolleté. It must have been the days before PETA, when a fur coat was *the* thing to wear. She looked as if she were in her mid- to late-thirties, which meant the painting had been done in the 1960s.

Just now Cricket herself was sitting in the place of honor in the room, a royal-blue tufted damask sofa, where she presided over a sterling silver tea set, delicate floral-patterned Limoges cups and saucers, and a plate on which slices of homemade pound cake had been arranged. I took the matching love seat opposite her.

'Would you mind pouring, dear?' she asked. 'Just a slice of lemon for me. I hope you like Earl Grey.'

I poured our tea and used an engraved silver cake server to place a piece of pound cake on a plate, which I handed her along with a fork and napkin. Then I took some cake for myself.

'I was just texting with Luc,' Cricket said, dabbing the lace-edged linen napkin at imaginary crumbs on her lips. Her lipstick had left bright-red kiss marks on her teacup. 'He promised to stop by and visit me on his way from the airport. I didn't think you'd mind. We're both so anxious to see each other.'

I wasn't sure whether I was more surprised that my grand-father knew how to text or that he and Cricket were making plans that involved me without telling me. She figured it out right away and arched an eyebrow that had been mostly drawn with eyebrow pencil.

'Don't tell me you don't think the old folks know how to text? Or call or send photos on WhatsApp?'

'I . . . no. I just didn't know my grandfather knew. And of course I'll bring him here to see you after I pick him up at Dulles.'

'Yes, well, of course you will. He is coming to see me, after all.'

I sipped my tea and gave her a benign smile, deciding not to add, 'And his grandchildren and great-granddaughter.' Instead I said, 'He didn't want to miss your birthday. Nor the exhibit. It's very generous of you to donate the Old Mistress paintings

to the National Museum of Women in the Arts. Was this something you discussed with Jackie before she passed away?'

'We never got around to it,' she said. 'I was with her that
day in November when she fell off her horse while we were out
hunting, you know. They discovered the cancer when the doctor
at the clinic here was checking her out, making sure she had
no injuries.' Cricket set down her cup and saucer on the coffee
table and closed her eyes. In a heavy voice she added, 'She went
back to New York and six months later she was gone. She was
only sixty-five.'

'I know. I remember my mother being in floods of tears
when she found out.'

Cricket opened her eyes again. Hers were full of sadness.
'Everyone was shocked. It happened so fast.'

'Were you with her when she bought those paintings in Paris
the year you were studying there?' I asked. 'Or was it my
grandfather?'

Cricket sat back on the sofa, folded her hands in her lap as
if she were praying, and gave me a long, assessing look. 'What
are you really asking, Lucie?'

You don't trifle with Cricket Delacroix.

'I found my grandmother's diaries in the attic not too long
ago.'

She didn't look surprised. I couldn't tell if her head was
bobbing ever so slightly in agreement or maybe it was just a
small tremor. 'I see,' she said. 'Do you mean you didn't know
anything before you read them? Not even from your mother?'

I nodded. 'That's right. My mother must have talked to you
if you know about the diaries.'

Cricket pressed her lips together as though she wanted to
keep from blurting out something she might regret. Finally she
said, 'You are correct.'

'And?'

'And, what?'

'And they tell one side of their relationship. I figured you'd
know . . . more.'

'And how would you figure that?' She reached over and
picked up her cup and saucer again but this time the tremor
was more evident and the cup clattered against the saucer.

I thought about saying that it was clear she was in love with my grandfather now and that, from what I'd learned, she'd also been in love with him seventy years ago in Paris. Instead he fell for Jackie. But I didn't say anything of the kind because somehow I didn't think she'd forgotten how it had hurt once she realized her affection not only wasn't returned, but instead my grandfather only had eyes for her best friend.

'You were there,' I said. 'You saw them together. Jackie trusted you enough to leave you those paintings. And more importantly, she gave you that half-finished manuscript and a very personal journal. Which is why I assume she probably confided in you, too. Or maybe she didn't need to say anything because you knew exactly what was going on.'

Cricket sipped her tea, her gaze traveling over my head. I knew she was looking at her portrait behind me, the young woman with the teasing, flirtatious smile and the sexy red dress. Her eyes grew soft with memory – and something else. At first I thought it was regret. Then I realized it was pain.

Parker had been right. She'd been in love with my grandfather that year in Paris. I knew it now, too.

'It was all of those things,' she said, shifting her eyes to look directly at me. 'Jackie told me about Luc the very first time they met at the Louvre. And when I finally saw them together I knew they were crazy about each other. When you see two people who look at each other the way they did, that magic, that chemistry, that *fizz* . . . you just *know.*'

Something tightened in my heart and made it hurt. I couldn't swallow or speak because of a sudden lump in my throat.

Cricket was watching my reaction. 'It was a long time ago, Lucie. Times were so different then. The war had ended, people had changed irrevocably. Everyone in France had lost someone, a family member, a friend, maybe more than one person – whether it was on a battlefield or in one of the camps. Anyone who survived was just so glad to be *alive*, they knew how precious a gift life was, something not to be wasted in regret or waiting for second chances. You took what came along, leapt on it. Morals were . . . a bit looser, shall we say?'

She cleared her throat and went on. 'Your grandmother was a beautiful woman, someone I admired – and loved – very much. Luc loved her, too. But we – you, me, your grandfather, any of us – don't get to choose who we fall in love with, because the heart wants what it wants. And sometimes it's the wrong person, the wrong place, the wrong time.'

'What was it for my grandfather and Jackie?' I asked.

'All three,' she said. 'They met because they both loved art and loved going to museums and galleries together. Luc took her everywhere, showed her the beauty and culture she craved, shaped her love of France and all things *français* that left such an indelible stamp on her life – and, ultimately on her time in the White House.'

She fell silent. She had told me many things – which had pained me more than I expected – but not the answer to my original question.

'You didn't say whether Pépé was with Jackie when she bought the paintings that will be exhibited at The Artful Fox.'

'He was. They'd gone out together for the afternoon and it started to rain, just ever so lightly, you know, a mist. They stepped into the shelter of a *bouquiniste's* that happened to have a couple of drawers filled with art – prints, paintings, maps, that sort of thing. Jackie was so excited when the two of them brought those paintings back to her room. She told me all about them afterwards, and of course I had to see them.' Her careful, controlled poise fell away and her voice grew sentimental.

The Paris *bouquinistes* were legendary. Sellers of used and antiquarian books, stamps, trading cards, and old journals, they occupied permanent stalls set up along both sides of the River Seine and had been there since the 1600s. Over the years, everything from the precise amount of space they could occupy, the size of the boxes in their stalls, and even the time of day they could do business – sunrise to sunset – became regulated by Parisian law. Not long ago the three or so kilometers along the banks of the Seine where the *bouquinistes* were located was declared a World Heritage Site.

'Please go on,' I said, but Cricket didn't seem to need prodding.

'Jackie chose the paintings because she was fascinated by the life of Marie Antoinette and, of course, Luc – who taught Jackie so much about French art and history – told her all about

Élisabeth Vigée Le Brun, the most famous and sought-after portrait painter of eighteenth-century France. It was only after her death that she went from being a celebrity to a complete unknown. As for Marie Antoinette, Jackie had always been intrigued by court life in pre-revolutionary France – the elaborate manners, the over-the-top pomp and ritual, the fantastic clothes, powdered wigs and make-up – all of it. And she saw a woman – a young girl, actually – who was sent away from her home to marry someone she didn't know, to a foreign land where she was terribly lonely and misunderstood. God knows Jackie herself was misunderstood after she married Ari. She went from being the beloved, bereaved widow America claimed as its own to being vilified as a socialite who loved nothing more than shopping and partying – it devastated her,' Cricket said. By now she seemed to be speaking more to herself than to me. 'Jackie also understood what it was like to be the wife of a powerful man – actually, two powerful men in Jack Kennedy and Ari Onassis. Marie Antoinette's husband was the king of France. Vigée Le Brun was married, but because of her talent and her powerful clients she was the successful one, a rarity for a woman at that time.'

She stopped speaking. I remained silent, digesting what she'd just told me, and waited. I had a feeling she still wasn't finished.

'Later, as an editor at Doubleday, one of the first books Jackie worked on was a collection of letters between Marie Antoinette and her mother, Empress Maria Theresa of Austria.' Cricket folded her hands together in her lap and gave me a smile full of sadness. 'I read that book. There was so much heartache in those letters. Of course Jackie would want to edit it.'

'I didn't know any of that.'

'Well, you won't know this either, but after we finished university, Jackie wrote an essay that won her an internship at *Vogue* – six months in New York and six months in Paris. She never went. Do you know what she told me?'

'No,' I said. 'I don't.'

'That if she went back to Paris, even for just six months, there was a good chance that she would stay and never come home again.' Cricket gave a graceful shrug. 'Of course that's not what happened, is it? She stayed home, got engaged to a stockbroker in New York, broke it off when she realized he was crashingly boring, and then met Jack Kennedy while she was working in Washington.'

'How did it end?' I asked. 'Jackie and my grandfather?'

Cricket's head reared back in surprise. 'Why, they knew it would end from the beginning.'

'So it was just a fling? Nothing serious?'

'It was plenty serious,' Cricket said. 'But, Lucie, darling, some relationships just aren't meant to be. They both had other obligations – life demanded bigger things of each of them. Your grandfather wanted to serve his country in the French diplomatic corps, just as he'd done in the Resistance. France needed to rebuild after the war and he wanted to be involved, to create its rightful place as a leader in the new post-war world after Germany had been defeated. Jackie needed to go home and finish her studies – she belonged in America and she knew it. Three years later she married John F. Kennedy. A decade later she was First Lady of the United States.'

My tea had grown cold. I set the cup and saucer back on the silver tray.

'Thank you for telling me all of this,' I said. 'I had no idea. In fact, I'm fairly sure my grandfather doesn't know my grandmother knew about him and Jackie. Nor does he know that my mother found out.'

'I'm quite sure you're right,' she said.

'Did Jackie write about her relationship with my grandfather in the journal she left you? The one Harry has now?'

Cricket hesitated and I knew the answer was yes.

'I see,' I said.

'Based on what Harry told me, there's nothing indiscreet or improper in that journal.'

'You haven't read it?'

Her smile was tired. 'It's in longhand. My eyesight isn't what it used to be.'

'So Harry knows about the two of them?'

'There's nothing scandalous there. Don't worry, my dear. Harry doesn't know much.' She paused. 'Nor anything about your grandmother's journals.'

'Good.'

'Lucie, your grandfather loved your grandmother until the day she died. That's *all* that matters any more.'

'He loved Jackie, too. Once,' I said. 'I'm sure that mattered as well.'

'Sometimes love isn't enough.' Cricket gave me a world-weary look. 'Though you might wish it would be. Sometimes there are other, more pragmatic matters that are more important. It's not always about bells ringing and birds singing, you know.'

'I must be an incurable romantic,' I said, 'because I think the only thing that can keep a relationship going through all the hard times, the challenging times, *is* love.'

'Then you must never have had your heart broken,' she said.

She was so wrong. I had, more than once, as a teenager and in college. Wasn't it a rite of passage for anyone who risked falling in love, that end-of-the-world feeling when you wear your heart on the outside of your body where everyone can see it all battered and vulnerable? The last time it happened to me I was living in France, recuperating from my car accident – and this one was different. I'd found out the hard way there was someone new – he didn't even bother to tell me.

Then after I moved back home I met Quinn. It took a while until I realized that all the boys I'd loved before, the angst and heartache of messy break-ups and matter-of-fact 'this isn't working' goodbyes, even that catastrophic *cauchemar* in France – all of those relationships were the reason I knew with absolute certainty that this time it was right.

I stood up to leave and wondered if Cricket had been talking about me or herself when she said love wasn't enough. The day after tomorrow my grandfather would be here. Would we be able to keep all these matters of the heart bottled up with no discussion of the past?

I would find out soon enough.

'I'll bring Pépé by on Wednesday, probably around four thirty or five o'clock unless traffic is bad,' I said. 'I'm sure he'll text or call you. And thank you again for the tea.'

Cricket didn't reply and at first I thought she didn't hear me. Then I realized she was a million miles away.

Lost in memories, in her own world. Paris in 1949.

FOUR

Harriet Delacroix pulled into the circular driveway driving a black convertible BMW and parked behind my Jeep as I stepped outside a few minutes later. She got out of her car and stared at me with a mixture of dismay and confusion. Obviously I'd been to see her mother or my sister – or both of them – when she wasn't around and it didn't seem to sit well with her.

Harry was in her mid-sixties, but she had inherited her mother's striking good looks and her father's lean, athletic figure, so if you met her on the street you'd take her for a woman in her early fifties, maybe even late forties. Harry took care of herself; she looked good. Just now she had on a tennis outfit, a swingy little green-and-white-striped pleated skirt, a white and green sweater, and an expensive-looking pair of Nikes, white with green trim. Long, bare legs with a sun-kissed just-returned-from-a-Caribbean-beach golden tan, highlighted blonde hair pulled into a perky ponytail, age lines and wrinkles airbrushed away by a surgeon's magic wand.

'Hi, Harry.'

Her perplexed expression vanished, but she still looked unhappy, flashing a smile that didn't make it all the way to her eyes.

'Hello, Lucie. What brings you here? Stopping by to check up on our artist-in-residence?' The question was neutral enough, but I could hear an underlying thrumming in her voice.

'No, not really. Your mom wanted to talk about plans for my grandfather stopping by when he gets in from Paris on Wednesday, so I thought I'd come see her so we could chat in person,' I said.

She could check out my story later, but for now it was good enough. And it was mostly true.

Harry was high strung, high maintenance. Cricket and Édouard's only child. Indulged, spoiled, any transgression forgiven and the mess cleaned up. The rumor was that Cricket had had to pay off Husband Number Three, the Count of Monte Cristo or some such bogus title that had totally impressed Harry, who wanted to be a countess. Cricket ended up writing a check for a significantly less substantial but mutually agreed-on final settlement after her private investigator produced embarrassing photos that could cost Three his job and very likely get him in trouble if anyone checked the age(s) of the girl(s) with whom he was keeping overly friendly company. In return for Cricket handing over the photos, she tied the sleazy and impoverished *soi-disant* Count up in enough legal knots to make sure he had no claim on Harry's financial assets and would never ask for alimony.

Harry nodded at me, my presence apparently explained to her satisfaction. 'Mom can't wait for your grandfather to get here. She's looking forward to her birthday and the gala at the gallery, but his visit is what really matters most to her, you know? She's outlived so many of her friends there's hardly anyone left. And no one she's known as long as she's known Uncle Luc.'

She pulled her tennis racquet out of the back seat of the BMW. The logo on the case said Wilson and the racquet inside probably cost a fortune.

'I'm bringing him here from the airport so they'll see each other right away,' I said.

'Great.' Harry brushed something off the racquet cover with the back of her hand. Her mind was on something else. It didn't take her long to let me know what it was.

'Look, Lucie, I'm sure you came by to see the mural, so I'll get to the point. I'm concerned Mia's not going to finish in time. We can't have the solarium half painted, you know? It'll look like hell, a half-assed job. She doesn't seem to be working very quickly?'

Harry had a way of ending some of her sentences so a statement sounded as if it might be a question that required an answer. Mia had just complained about getting an earful from Harry this morning, telling her she wasn't speedy enough. Now Harry was giving *me* grief.

'She told me she's working her butt off to be done by your

deadline, Harry. She even sort of joked about moving in so she could spend more time here,' I said. 'You've asked her to paint something that looks like Alphonse Mucha did it. That's a lot of work.'

'If she couldn't do it, she should have said no.'

'Don't worry, she'll finish in time. Mia takes her work seriously.'

One of Harry's perfectly arched eyebrows went up. 'I guess we'll find out? Still, maybe you could talk to her? Maybe if she spent a little less time with her good-looking boyfriend she'd be further along.'

Whoops, where did *that* come from? She almost sounded jealous, which, to be honest, wouldn't be hard to imagine. Sergio was nearer to Harry's age than he was to Mia's. Good-looking wasn't the half of it. When Sergio walked into a room, female heads turned and eyes stared. Quinn had already teased me about my eyes being out on stalks when he was around.

Mia and I had not parted company on the best of terms on the very subject of Sergio a short while ago, but she was my sister. Family stands up for family.

'They live together, Harry. It's sort of inevitable they'd spend time with each other, don't you think?'

'She's being well paid for this, Lucie. I expect results.'

'And you're getting them. Come on, Harry, she's working full time on it,' I said. 'She's already got Sergio helping her and Willow hang Jackie's paintings in the gallery before the exhibition. Plus apparently there's some extra work now that you've decided to include excerpts from Jackie's journal with the paintings.'

The expression in Harry's eyes changed from surprise to consternation to thoroughly pissed off. *Damn.* Hadn't Mia just told me Harry's decision to use Jackie's journals wasn't known yet? Had I just betrayed a confidence?

Well, so what?

Thanks to what Cricket had just told me I knew Harry was aware of Jackie and Pépé's relationship. Thanks to Mia I knew Harry had promised the excerpts would shock people. And two and two always equaled four. Harry was going to use journal

passages about the two of them buying the paintings together
in the Paris *bouquiniste*.

The one thing I didn't know – and Harry did – was what
Jackie had said about that afternoon. And Harry wasn't about
to tell me, either. *Top secret*, Mia had said, until the exhibit.

'How do you know about the excerpts?' Harry asked me
now.

'Come on, Harry. Your book publicist is going to put out a
press release or something, right? The whole world is going to
know soon. What difference does it make?' I said. 'Tell me
something. Why isn't it enough just to hang the paintings by
themselves? Why do you need passages from Jackie's journal?'

Harry gave me a *duh* look.

'Because,' she said, as if I were a slow-witted child, 'that
kind of wall text – that's what it's called, Lucie – will generate
interest in Jackie's book. The book *I'm* finishing now. A lot
of interest and a lot of media attention. People who wouldn't
have known anything about a little exhibit in a small art
gallery in Middleburg will find out about it because of what
I've done to connect it to Jackie. And they'll eventually want
to read the book.'

'Any book that Jackie Onassis was working on before her
death would generate a lot of interest for a lot of people.
Especially a subject she knew so much about, something she
was passionate about.'

'It depends on the audience you're trying to attract,' Harry
said. 'In my case, it got me a very, *very* sweet book contract
with a substantial advance. Seven figures, no ones in the
numbers. And a choice of more than one offer. It actually went
to a bidding war.'

Her eyes shone.

'My agent and I have spent the last couple of days in talks
in D.C. with multiple editors and publishers,' she went on.
'Everyone came down here from New York so I've been wined
and dined. Plus, of course, the usual hoo-hah with lawyers
going over Jackie's papers to make sure they were legit and
there wouldn't be any, you know, lawsuits?'

Hoo-hah. Lawsuits. Yes, lawyers liked hoo-hah because
lawsuits could be pesky. Presumably the publisher wanted to

be indemnified from liability issues. Harry could hang out to dry, for all they might care. I wondered if Cricket knew about any of this. And how smart and savvy Harry's agent was and whether she read anything in her contract beyond the paragraph with the numbers, none of them ones, in it.

'And they looked over the journal as well, I presume?' I said. 'For *your* book. Not just the papers Jackie left for *her* book, the book *she* intended to write.'

Harry ignored the little jab. She held the winning hand of cards, anyway.

'Look, Lucie, I get it that you might not be happy about this. But my mom is fine with it and as far as I'm concerned I don't need anyone else's permission to use something that is now legally hers.'

'You mean any reference to my grandfather's friendship with Jackie and being with her the day she bought the paintings?'

She folded her arms across her chest and gave me a confrontational look. Gloves off. And now she knew that I knew she was aware of the affair.

'That's right,' she said.

'Harry, he's still alive and he's your mother's dear friend. None of this has been made public before. Why can't you just let it be?'

'Oh, for God's sake, Lucie, stop being such a prude,' she said in disgust. 'A book about Marie Antoinette and the woman who painted her portrait thirty times is only so interesting, you know? I mean art scholars and historians might be interested?'

'If Jackie Onassis wrote it, plenty of people will be interested.'

'And if Jackie's personal diary is part of the story, everybody on the *planet* will be interested. People are still fascinated by anything to do with her life – a romance no one knew about is icing on the cake.'

'Everyone around here who knew her – and that includes you – knew how much she valued her privacy,' I said. 'This is the last thing she would have wanted.'

'She doesn't get a vote and neither do you.' Harry's voice was sharp. 'No one's going to tell me what I can and can't do, do you understand?'

She took a step toward me, the knuckles of the hand holding the tennis racket white as she clenched it. For a moment I thought she was going to raise it at me, but she seemed to catch herself and stopped.

'Have you actually signed the book contract?' I wanted to steer this conversation back to civility.

'I *signed* it this morning. I had breakfast with my agent in Leesburg and he brought it. The press release will be out by the end of the day. Keep it to yourself until that happens.'

'No worries.' I also decided not to ask her when she would receive her thirty pieces of silver.

But I did know this: Cricket might have given Harry carte blanche to use Jackie's private journal – or at least not done anything to stop her from doing what she wanted with it – but when my grandfather found out about it I was almost certain he would not let it go quietly into this good night.

I wondered if I would be around for the explosion.

FIVE

'You're awfully quiet tonight,' Quinn said. 'Is something wrong?'

We were in the kitchen cleaning up after dinner. I hadn't yet blown out the candles, which were flickering like wraiths on the oak trestle table, probably caught in an air current escaping through a bad seal in one of the old windows. Quinn had turned jazz on Sirius; the Rippingtons were playing something that made me think of sundrenched days, pristine white beaches, and turquoise water that you only found in the tropics.

Dinner had been outstanding. After the holidays Persia Fleming, our Jamaican housekeeper, decided it was high time to introduce Quinn and me to her native cuisine. Tonight she'd made curried chicken cooked in ginger-infused coconut milk. Quinn had thirds.

'We eat it for breakfast in Jamaica,' she'd told us in her lilting accent before she left for her apartment above my brother Eli's architectural studio in the carriage house next door. 'But for you two, I made it for dinner.'

Dessert was vanilla ice cream and one of the few remaining jars of the peaches we canned last summer, still tasting of sweet sunshine.

Quinn picked up a clean dishtowel, wrapped it around the back of my neck like a scarf, and pulled me to him for a long, deep kiss. 'Everything OK, baby?' he murmured into my hair.

I slipped my arms around his waist and rested my head on his chest. 'I spent the morning with Parker. We went over the final design and the list of plants we need for the wedding garden. It's going to be beautiful.'

'Good,' he said. 'I'm glad.'

I smiled. Quinn probably wouldn't care if the garden was full of kudzu and pokeweed instead of roses and azaleas, but he knew I did. He knew I wanted the fairy tale, all of it, a white dress and a bouquet of wildflowers he picked for me and family

and friends gathering in our flower-filled garden on a perfect
May day to witness Eli, who had agreed to marry us, ask Quinn
and me if we promised to love each other for the rest of our
lives.

'I didn't hear from you all afternoon,' Quinn said, but it was
a question, not a statement.

'I went over to Mon Repos to see Mia's mural and talk to
Cricket about plans for when Pépé is here.'

'Uh-huh. And?'

I still wasn't ready to tell him about my grandfather's intimate
relationship with Jackie Onassis. Nor Harry Delacroix's decision
to use excerpts from Jackie's journal about the two of them at
The Artful Fox exhibit. Before I said anything to him or Eli or
Mia, I wanted to talk to Pépé first; I *needed* to talk to him first.
It seemed only right.

'And . . . nothing. Just a lot on my mind right now,
that's all. Pépé, the wedding, the dying vines,' I said. 'By the
way, Parker promised me he'd take a look at them – the
vines, that is – in case he had any insights. In case there's
something else growing that we didn't consider, either wild
or cultivated, that might have served as a host for whatever
is killing them.'

'Did you tell him Josie is coming to check out everything?'

'I did. He calls her "Doctor Grapevine" and says she's the
best of the best. But if this has to do with the warm weather
we had last winter, we're dealing with something that happened
because of climate change.'

Quinn let go of the towel and looked down into my eyes.
'I have an idea. How about if we get that bottle of brandy that's
open on the sideboard, go outside and sit on the veranda for a
while to clear our heads?'

Plus he wanted his evening cigar and I had a hard and firm
rule about smoking cigars in the house.

Don't. Or else.

Before I could agree, he added: 'Then maybe you could tell
me the rest of it.'

I tried to muster enough righteous indignation to say, 'The
rest of *what*?' But I couldn't. Because he was right and we both
knew it.

'Clearing our heads might be a good idea,' I said. 'I'll get the brandy. You get the coats.'

We brought a couple of hurricane lamps outside and sat together on the wicker sofa. The flickering candlelight made the veranda look as if it had been gilded and the orange glow from the tip of Quinn's cigar lit up every now and then like a winking summer firefly. The backyard had turned into an ocean of blackness; even the Blue Ridge seemed to be swallowed up by the night sky.

'What made you decide to drop by Mon Repos?' Quinn asked, draping an arm around my shoulder and running a finger down the side of my neck. 'Checking up on your sister?'

'I was *invited*. Mia told me to come by any time I wanted and have a look at her mural. So I did.'

'Oh, yeah? How's it going?'

'Slow. What she's done so far looks terrific and when she finishes it's going to be amazing. I think Mia's even more talented than Mom was. Unfortunately, Harry decided she wants something totally Art Nouveau that looks like Alphonse Mucha painted it,' I said, and because I was fairly certain he had no idea who Mucha was, I added, 'He was a Czech painter mostly known for some theater posters he designed in Paris in the late 1890s.'

'You mean the posters for Sarah Bernhardt's plays?' he said. 'The Art Nouveau movement really didn't last that long. Too contradictory and at odds with itself, but very stylized and intricate. It's going to take Mia quite a while to paint that entire solarium, I'd say.'

I pulled away from the crook of his arm and stared at him. 'How do you know all that?'

He looked smug. 'Art history minor in college.'

He had let me believe he majored in beer and minored in girls, that he'd been quite a California party-boy-surfer and that books and studies had been optional.

'Art history – *really*? How come you never told me? You've been holding out on me all these years.'

'Waiting for the right time,' he said, still grinning, 'which apparently was now. So Mia is painting a mural that looks like a Mucha poster?'

'Yup – the flowers, not the women. She's trying to do some-thing resembling his *Seasons* series – which I'm sure you're intimately familiar with.' I paused and he chuckled. 'But today she told me Harry keeps bugging her about when she's going to be finished and it's driving her nuts.'

'I hope your sister told her to stick a sock in it.' Like Parker, Quinn wasn't a big Harry fan.

'No. As a matter of fact I saw her – Harry, that is – as I was leaving after having tea with Cricket. She started in on me, too.'

'Figures. What did she say?'

'Mia had better finish on time – blah, blah, blah – and maybe she should stop spending so much time with Sergio and more on her work.'

'That's weird.'

'I thought so, too.'

'Do you think Harry has the hots for Sergio?' he asked. 'Wait . . . that's a dumb question. Half the women in Atoka and Middleburg think he's hotter'n hell. Present company included.'

'*Not* true. I only have the hots for you.'

He leaned in and kissed me. 'Is that so? Well, I expect proof tonight, cupcake.'

'Don't worry, my love, you'll have it.'

'Good.' He puffed on his cigar, looking pleased.

'There's more,' I said.

'What?'

'Harry told me she just signed a multi-million-dollar contract this morning to finish Jackie Onassis's book. Apparently she and her literary agent have been spending the last few days being wined and dined by multiple publishers and the book went to auction. She's over the moon about how much money she got for it.'

'Multi-million-dollar, huh?' Quinn shook his head as if he couldn't believe it. 'Maybe she can pay her mother back some of what it cost to get her out of the marriage from hell to the Prince of Darkness, or whoever he was.'

'He was a count,' I said. 'Supposedly. Not a prince.'

'He was a sleazebag. No supposedly about that.'

'Mmm.'

He refilled my brandy glass. 'You sound kind of upset about

Harry and her book deal. You're not jealous of her, are you –
all that money practically falling into her lap?'

I nearly choked on my brandy. 'Me? Don't be silly. Of
course not.'

'Uh-huh.'

'I'm *not*.'

'Then what is it?'

'Nothing.'

He waited me out.

'OK.' I leaned back against the sofa. 'It's the way she's going
about it. Plenty of people around here still remember Jackie
and what a private person she was. Harry using Jackie's
notes and the outline to make money off her is going to
upset a lot of folks.' I paused. 'She also decided to use excerpts
from that diary she found and hang them next to the paintings
at The Artful Fox. Personal stuff.'

Quinn rubbed his chin with his thumb, a thoughtful gesture
I knew meant he was trying to understand the real meaning of
what I had just said. In other words, what I *hadn't* said. 'She
wants to make a buck, sweetheart. Or a couple million bucks.
She may be self-absorbed and selfish, but she's also human.
You can't stop her.'

'I know, but there's going to be a lot of anger and outrage
in town once word gets out about this. Even Parker ranted on
about it when we talked this morning. He's furious.'

'Parker? What dog does he have in this fight?'

'He adored Jackie. I didn't know this until today, but she
edited a book he wrote years ago. Not a gardening book, but
a book called *Porch Wisdom*. He said she wouldn't take any
credit for it, either,' I said. 'So he feels fairly protective toward
her as well.'

'Lucie, let it go. You can't get in the middle of this.' He blew
a perfect smoke ring. 'Besides, from what I hear, Parker has
plenty of problems of his own at the moment without wading
into this one.'

Was he talking about the death threats?

'What do you mean?' I asked.

'I ran into Gabriel Seely leaving the General Store this
morning. He looked like he was ready to commit murder.

Parker's monthly column in the *Trib* comes out tomorrow. He's kicking ass and naming names. According to Gabriel, Parker claims that the research paper Gabriel just released about his success in being able to prolong the life of a dying plant is a lot of BS. Parker said Gabriel made stuff up so his results are bogus. It sounds like he was pretty brutal.'

'Parker told me about that when we talked,' I said. 'I didn't know he wrote about it in the *Tribune.*'

'Neither did Gabriel until this morning.' Quinn puffed on his cigar. 'Parker's really pulling the pin on the grenade with this one. He'd better be absolutely, positively, one hundred percent right because it's going to have an impact on business at the nursery. Some folks will be loyal because they love Gabriel's old man and they've known Gabriel since he was a kid. But I'll bet others will wonder about his honesty and stay away.'

Gabriel's father Noah had played Santa Claus at Christmas in Middleburg every year for the last dozen or so years and his wife played Mrs Claus. The kids loved them. Gabriel had been good-natured enough to go along with the family act by playing a North Pole elf. The kids loved him, too.

So Parker was going after one of Santa's beloved helpers, among other things.

'*Is* Parker right?' Quinn asked me.

'He says he is. And he's not naming his source, either.'

'That's a given. Except then it just turns into a he-said-he-said argument. Gabriel swears Parker has it in for him because Gabriel talked a couple of Parker's clients into changing the plants Parker recommended for their gardens to something he thought would work better. Parker thought Gabriel was undermining him.'

'I didn't know that,' I said.

'Yeah, well, you don't stomp on Superman's cape. Parker does act like he's a bit of a god, don't you think? An ego like his, he doesn't take it well if anyone questions what he says or does.'

'He *is* good at what he does, Quinn. Look at his reputation,' I said.

'Gabriel's no slouch, either. He had that fellowship at Kew

Gardens in England, remember? The seed bank where they're trying to save the plants of the world before they go extinct.'

'Are you taking Gabriel's side?' I asked.

'Just telling you what he said. The things you learn at the General Store. Are you taking Parker's?'

'Same. Just telling you what *he* said.'

I finished my brandy and he smoked while we sat in silence.

With *The Angry Earth* generating so much controversy, and now taking on the next generation owner of a respected and beloved family-owned local nursery, Parker seemed to be spoiling for a fight. *It's an ill wind*, he'd said.

Sure it was, but the rest of that maxim went *that doesn't blow somebody some good.*

What if he wasn't that somebody?

Because for everybody else, an ill wind was just that. Something that blew no good at all.

SIX

The sound of a fox crying in the middle of the night will always make me bolt upright in bed convinced, as my heart slams against my ribs, that a child is being strangled somewhere in the dark. When I was a little girl those agonized screams sent me straight to my parents' bedroom where I would dive into my mother's arms. In my childhood fairytale books, Mr Fox was always the villain, the evil one, intent on eating the sweet bunny, the helpless chickens, or the gingerbread man. In Aesop's Fables, he was cunning, cruel, and devious.

Then the next morning in clear-eyed daylight I would see a magnificent red fox make its way across my backyard, the sunshine glinting like gold on its beautiful coat, or a pair of cubs playing together on the lawn and think how utterly adorable they looked. And I would wonder how such a gorgeous animal could make that haunting, keening noise, a sound to wake the dead.

I sat up the instant the screaming began, dry-mouthed with my pulse pounding. This time it was not my mother, but Quinn who pulled me into his arms and murmured into my ear through the tangle of my hair, 'Go back to sleep, darling. S'just the fox from the den behind the summerhouse. S'OK. Nothing's wrong.'

And though a few moments later his breathing had quieted to the slow, steady rhythm of sleeping, I was still jolted awake. Downstairs the grandfather clock chimed four. I knew I should go back to sleep, but I couldn't. Not until I checked outside because something was not right.

I slipped out of Quinn's arms and slid from between the covers, finding my slippers with only minimal contact between my feet and the floor. I was still naked and so was he after an intense earlier session of lovemaking. My nightgown was on the floor where he had dropped it and my robe was draped over a settee across the bedroom. Both were visible in a strip of light in the velvet darkness where the curtains hadn't quite been pulled together. Through the gap I could see that the moon had risen again and the sky was now filled with filamentous clouds that occasionally passed in front of it, casting long shadows on the ground as if the garden were full of snakes.

I dressed quickly and took the back staircase, avoiding the treads that would creak, and pushed open the door to the kitchen. It was warmer here than any other room in the house and the faint scent of ginger and curry from our dinner still hung in the air. I found a box of peppermint tea in the pantry, stuck the little sachet in a mug of water, and put it in the microwave. When it was ready, I got Quinn's heavy winter jacket, which hung below my knees, zipped it up, and went outside on to the veranda.

The air was so cold I could see my breath, but it felt good. I cupped my hands around the tea mug to warm them, but in this cold the hot liquid would grow tepid in no time. The bushes and trees were dark unsubstantial shapes silhouetted against the rest of the garden, which was as quiet as a graveyard. Later in the summer fireflies would light up the night, a quick flicker of dancing gold before they disappeared. Now, though, there was nothing. No light, no sound. No fox.

What had made it cry?

I finished my tea, went back inside, and waited until the chilly night air no longer clung to me and would give away where I'd been. Upstairs in our bedroom, I spooned my body into the warmth of Quinn's. He stirred, turned over, and pulled me into his arms

I heard the clock chime five and what seemed like only a few minutes later, it chimed six. At seven the alarm woke me. The imprint of Quinn's body on the bed sheets was there but he was gone and the smell of freshly brewing coffee wafted up the back staircase.

He handed me a mug when I walked into the kitchen a few minutes later, kissed me, and said, 'What were you doing outside last night? The door alarm beeped when you went in and out. You were gone a while.'

'Sorry, I thought you were too sound asleep to hear the beep.

I wondered why that fox was crying, so I decided to take a look.'

I sipped my coffee and tried not to grimace. My fiancé liked his coffee so strong you could use it to repair potholes. He thought mine looked and tasted like dirty dishwater. We compromised by drinking the pot of whoever got up first and brewed it, no complaints allowed. Though I'd considered adding 'second coffeemaker' to our wedding registry list.

'I figured that fox was the reason,' he said. 'Did you see him?'

'Nope.' I went over and cut a couple of slices from Persia's homemade sourdough *miche* and stuck them in the toaster. 'Shall I make us some eggs?'

He gave me a hopeful look. 'Persia said in Jamaica they eat that chicken dish for breakfast. It'd be nice to show her we appreciate her cooking by eating it like the natives do.'

I laughed. 'There are leftovers. Heat it up and go for it.'

'Want some?'

The toaster dinged. 'No, it's all yours. I'll have toast and yogurt. I need to fit into my wedding dress.'

I got butter, homemade fig jam, and a carton of Greek yogurt from the refrigerator while he heated up the leftover chicken.

'Ash and Dominique are coming by this morning to finalize everything for the garden,' I said. 'Before they get here I'm going to take another look at those dying Merlot vines before Parker and Josie do. See if there's any change.'

Quinn pulled the casserole dish out of the microwave and helped himself to chicken. He licked a finger that had curried ginger and coconut milk sauce on it.

'When is Parker going to stop by?'

'I guess on Wednesday afternoon. He said he'd text or call me if he could get by last night. Since I didn't hear anything, the next time he said he'd be free was Wednesday when I'm supposed to be at the airport. Maybe you could meet him?' I asked.

Quinn gave me that look men get after you've asked them to go clothes shopping with you. Like a root canal would be a more preferable option. 'He'd rather meet you than me, you know that. And if you can't make it he could just let us know if he finds anything, don't you think? He doesn't need a babysitter.'

We sat down at the trestle table. Quinn and Parker didn't really get along. Nothing overt: they just didn't. I'm pretty sure it had something to do with each of them wanting to be the alpha male and two alphas in the same room or even in the same vineyard was never a good idea.

I changed the subject. 'What are you going to do today?'

'First, finish our report for the Winemakers' Research Group,' he said. 'The meeting isn't until next week, but with Luc coming and all the parties and stuff, I figured I might as well get it out of the way. You did all the charts and graphs. I'll take care of writing up the results.'

The Winemakers' Research Group was just what the name implied – a group of winemakers and vineyard owners who were increasingly concerned about the extreme weather we were experiencing here in Virginia and wanted to tackle the problem by collaboration and research – or try to. Once upon a time a severe drought that lasted all summer or monsoon-like rains that flooded fields and resulted in some vineyards not filling a single lug with grapes during harvest had been an aberration: once-in-a-blue-moon type unusual. Now it happened often enough that it was becoming the new normal.

But here was the scary thing. The new normal was that the weather would be extreme. You just didn't know extreme *what*. Or when it would happen.

We had detractors who thought *we* were extreme and just hadn't learned to roll with the punches. To them we were the Whiners Research Group, ha-ha. But Josie Wilde backed us, which conferred credibility and legitimacy. A friend of hers – a high school chemistry teacher who lived in Charlottesville as Josie did – hosted our bi-monthly meetings, sometimes down in C'ville, sometimes up here in Northern Virginia. If you were a member, you had to commit to experimenting with new and different methods of winemaking and grape growing and report on your findings.

The project Quinn and I had taken on was testing two pesticides on different blocks of the same grape varietal – organic and a 'regular' one – to see how the grapes fared. As expected

– or feared – the organic pesticide hadn't protected the fruit enough to keep away bugs during an unusually rainy summer and a hotter than normal autumn: specifically Japanese beetles and another pest known as the glassy-winged sharpshooter.

We cleaned up the breakfast dishes together and left the house – me in the Jeep, Quinn in the old Superman-blue pickup we'd owned forever. I followed him down Sycamore Lane, the private road that wound through the winery, until I turned off onto a dirt lane that led to the cottages where the winemaker and farm manager usually lived. Sergio's dark-green Fiat was in front of the winemaker's cottage, but Mia's car was gone.

I didn't see Parker's bronze Lexus until I reached the Merlot block because it had been obscured by a stand of trees, nearly invisible in the straw-colored winter grass. What was he doing here now? Why hadn't he called or texted?

I had told him to park by Sergio and Mia's cottage, not to drive right up to the vines, though Parker did as Parker wanted, so that wasn't really a surprise. I walked over to the Lexus. It was wet from the morning dew as though it had been here a while. I touched the hood. Cold.

What time did he get here? Dawn? Before dawn?

I called his name and waited for him to yell back, 'Over here.'

'Parker.' I raised my voice and continued walking toward the failing vines since he hadn't replied. 'Are you all right? Where are you?'

I should have at least seen a flash of color, the bright-red L.L.Bean jacket he'd worn yesterday morning, the color as a don't-shoot beacon for when he found himself working some-where that was potential hunting territory.

I rounded a corner and stopped abruptly. He lay splayed awkwardly on the ground between two rows of vines. I moved toward him with all the speed I could manage, but one of the complications of my accident is that I can no longer run. At times like this mostly I curse under my breath and hope my bad foot doesn't give way under me.

'Parker . . . can you hear me? Answer me. *Please.*'

He didn't stir, didn't move. I already knew I was too late. His body was turned away so I couldn't see his face and his neck was at a weird angle. He lay on one side, bent and crumpled as if he had collapsed in a heap like a rag doll. One leg was twisted underneath him.

I got to him and knelt down, searching for a pulse or any sign that his chest was rising and falling, maybe shallow breathing.

Nothing. I fought back stunned tears.

Parker Lord was dead.

SEVEN

I called 911 and reported a death in my vineyard, trying to explain precisely where to find Parker and me in the middle of a field where there were no road signs or markers. The dispatcher fired off questions one by one in that preternaturally calm just-the-facts tone of voice they have to adopt to get the information they need while also keeping the caller from becoming hysterical and having a total meltdown. I told her everything in my calmest voice, but I had to turn away from Parker while I did it. I couldn't watch him lying there and keep my cool.

After I disconnected with the dispatcher I called Quinn. He said 'I'm coming' in a terse voice and the phone went dead.

Distant sirens sounded far down Atoka Road just as Quinn reached Parker and me. He knelt beside me and slid an arm around my waist.

'You OK?'

'No.'

He let go of me and checked Parker for a pulse or a heartbeat.

I said in a flat voice, 'I already did that. He's dead.'

'I know. Just . . . doing it for myself. Jesus, I can't believe this.'

'Me neither.'

'I saw his car over there.' Quinn gestured to the trees at the edge of the Merlot block before looking down at Parker again. 'The windshield was all misted up like the car had been outside, maybe all night. How long do you think he's been out here? Didn't you tell me he said he might come by the vineyard yesterday at the end of the day?'

'I did, but he was going to call or text me when he did. I don't know why I didn't hear from him.' My voice broke. 'He's been here for a while. My God, Quinn, he could have been here all night. That *fox*. You heard it.'

'I know,' he said again.

'There's a blanket in the pickup. We should cover him. We can't leave him like this.' I didn't say it but I thought it: he looked as exposed and vulnerable as if he were completely naked. He'd also soiled his pants. I'd smelled urine when I had laid my head on his chest.

'It's too late to do anything, sweetheart. We shouldn't move him, either. In case . . .' He stopped and my heart skipped a beat.

'In case what?' My voice felt strangled.

Quinn helped me to my feet and maneuvered me so we were not hovering over Parker's dead body, an arm clamped firmly around me.

'In case it's something other than a heart attack or a stroke or, I don't know . . . a brain aneurysm.'

Or maybe none of the above. Death threats, Parker had said to me only yesterday morning, before trying to pass it off as a bad joke. Although, thank God, I hadn't seen any blood or bruising – no sign of a struggle.

The sirens were louder and closer now as they came down Sycamore Lane and turned off near the cottages.

'They're here,' I said.

'I'll show 'em where we are,' Quinn said. 'You stay with Parker.'

He started to sprint toward the noise and commotion, but before he'd even gone fifty feet, four men and a woman wearing navy jumpsuits appeared in the clearing, running toward us for all they were worth, carrying anything they might need – medical bag, oxygen tank, defibrillator. As if there might still be a chance of reviving Parker and they could pull off a miracle, God bless them.

Three of them – two men and the woman – went to work on Parker right away; another took Quinn and me aside and started asking questions about what had happened and what we knew about Parker's medical history. The fifth moved away from us and got on his phone, probably to report in to someone. It didn't take long before the EMTs who were bent over Parker got up.

They were done.

I heard one of them say, 'The ME is on his way. We'll see what he has to say.'

More car doors slamming, coming from the direction of Mia and Sergio's cottage, and seconds later Sheriff's Office deputies were everywhere, talking to the EMTs and the guys from the fire department who'd shown up with them; tan and brown uniforms moving with quick efficiency among the blue jumpsuits to where Parker still lay in that weird twisted position in the middle of my vineyard. By now Quinn and I had been handed over to a young deputy since the EMTs were finished with what they could do.

The deputy immediately separated us, which I knew was one of the first things they did at any accident or crime investigation: keep each person on the scene away from the others if possible so they wouldn't collaborate on stories, or worse, pollute or distort someone else's memory of what they saw or thought they saw.

Bobby Noland, who was a senior detective with the Loudoun County Sheriff's Office and whom I'd known since I was five and he was seven, had told me this over and over: people see what they want to see, they see what they expect to see. And that was always different from what really had transpired. Once Bobby found out it was Parker Lord lying here at Montgomery Estate Vineyard, with all the subsequent media interest – if not frenzy – his death was going to cause, I would bet good money he would be making an official appearance here, maybe sooner rather than later.

The young deputy, whose name tag said Gonzalez, was in the middle of asking me what Parker was doing at the vineyard when Sergio Ianelli moved into my line of sight across the field. Dressed in faded jeans and a gray sweatshirt, hands jammed in his pockets, a breeze ruffling the curls of his longish salt-and-pepper hair, he leaned against a fence post, crossing one leg over the other and watching me and everyone else as if he were among the audience in a movie theater.

Of course he would have seen and heard everything from the get-go, with emergency vehicles screeching into the little driveway in front of his and Mia's cottage, probably lined up like a row of crooked teeth. Maybe he had been told not to show up here and get in the way, which is why I'd only noticed him now. He would have no idea what was going on, unless one of the EMTs or deputies told him there was an urgent medical situation – and probably left it at that. They wouldn't share a name or release any information.

Besides, Sergio didn't know Parker – or did he? Parker had mentioned that Sergio's name sounded familiar, a memory from years ago, perhaps someone with whom he'd done business at a New York art gallery. And he thought he'd remembered some-*thing* about Sergio as well, although what that was I'd never know now.

It turned out that Deputy Gonzalez, who had the wide-eyed growing-into-the-job look of a rookie along with dark hair gelled so short and sharp it made me think of razor blades, didn't know who Parker was, either. I told him. It made an impression.

I also told him what Parker was doing in my vineyard.

'Any idea when he got here?' Gonzalez asked.

'He said he'd either come by at the end of the day yesterday or else Wednesday afternoon.'

'You're saying he could have been here since late yesterday? Maybe, what, four, five o'clock?'

'I don't know,' I said. 'I hope not. If he had been gone all night, Ashton Carlyle, his husband, would have reported some-thing. So maybe he came by really early this morning. And Ash . . . he doesn't know about Parker. He needs to be told.'

'I think someone's trying to reach out to him already.' But I watched Gonzalez write Ash's name in the reporter's notebook where he'd been taking down everything I said.

'He's supposed to be here at nine o'clock to talk to my cousin and me about a project I hired him for,' I said. 'Planting a vegetable garden.'

Deputy Gonzalez gave me a look as if he wondered why I couldn't throw a bunch of seeds in the dirt and water them myself without hiring someone to do it for me. He glanced at his watch.

'It's eight forty-five.'

'Then he's on his way.'

* * *

Win Turnbull arrived before Ash did.

Dr Winston Churchill Turnbull was Loudoun County's newest medical examiner, a retired octogenarian surgeon who had returned some months ago from a stint doing what he called his 'Peace Corps work', volunteering in a military hospital in Iraq in the days when we were still welcomed there.

He raised a hand in a half-salute to Quinn and me, but then gave his attention to another deputy who led him to the place where Parker lay.

'Are we finished?' I asked Gonzalez.

'Yeah,' he said. Then he added, as if reading my mind, 'Stay out of the ME's way.'

He wasn't asking. He left and Quinn came over to me. The two of us moved so we could see Win, who was on his knees examining Parker. But out of respect – and obeying the deputy's orders – we kept our distance. Win would no doubt come talk to us when he was finished and then we would learn what he suspected was the possible cause of death. Win being Win, the first thing he would say was that he needed to do the autopsy before making any official pronouncements. But after sixty years of taking care of thousands and thousands of patients, he had enough experience to have a gut feeling about what had happened to Parker. Plus he was past the age of caring about covering his ass or hedging his bets in case he might be wrong.

My phone dinged with a text just as I caught sight of Ash running hard toward us and my heart missed a couple of beats. Ash must know about Parker or he wouldn't be here. Someone from the Sheriff's Office had told him. His skin was paler than death, as if it had been stretched taut across the elegant bones and hollowed contours of his handsome face. I could tell by his eyes, red-rimmed, that he had been crying. A deputy intercepted him before he reached Quinn and me, maneuvering himself to shield Ash – from us, I think – so we could not see him, nor hear their conversation.

My phone went off again. Another text. Both were from my cousin. Dominique was probably at the site for the garden where Ash and I were supposed to be meeting her.

I'm here. Are you coming? No Ash yet.

Then: *Still waiting. Lucie?? Where are you??*

I texted her, explained what happened, and where we were. Another ding. *Mon Dieu. I'm coming.*

I looked up to see the deputy taking Ash over to Parker's body, where Win was finishing up his examination.

'Oh, God,' I said to Quinn. 'I can't bear to watch.'

We both heard Ash's anguished cry as he dropped to his knees in front of his husband. It was my land, my vineyard, but just now we were all trespassers on Ash's private, lonely oasis of grief and loss. Win laid a fatherly hand on his shoulder and the deputy who had accompanied him made a pretext of fake coughing so he could walk away, his back turned. I buried my face on Quinn's scratchy jacket.

He stroked my hair and I could feel his heart slamming hard and slow against his ribcage. 'Win and Ash are coming over here,' he said after a minute. 'You OK?'

I wiped my eyes. 'Fine.'

We met them halfway. Ash looked drained and terribly pale. Win – who, I knew, had been Parker's doctor for years before he retired from private practice – was unusually somber. This one was personal for him.

I hugged Ash. 'I'm so, so sorry. If there's anything we can do . . .'

His arms went around me and said in a dull voice, 'Thanks, Lucie. Right now, there's nothing. I'm still trying to take it in . . . I can't believe it. What was he *doing* here?'

I told him and then looked at Win. 'Do you know what happened yet?'

He gave a weary shrug and said what I'd expected. 'I'll have to do the autopsy before I'm certain. I really can't say anything just now.'

'How long has he been here?' Quinn asked. 'There was overnight dew on the car and his clothes were damp.'

Ash's dark eyes flashed, but he was silent.

'At least twelve hours,' Win said. 'The temperature of a body starts dropping by one and a half degrees Fahrenheit after the first two hours postmortem until it becomes even with the ambient temperature. Parker's body is still warmer than the temperature is right now. Plus there's still full rigor, although it's starting to loosen in his face and his jaw. In other words, definitely overnight.'

'So.' Ash fought to keep his voice steady. 'You think maybe it was a heart attack or a stroke?'

'There's no sign of trauma,' Win said. 'It looks as if he just collapsed. The lividity is consistent with that and there's no sign of, say, his body having been moved from another location.'

'He was supposed to call me when he got here,' I said. 'Or text.'

'The Sheriff's Office took his phone. He fell on top of it when he went down. They'll dump it and see if he tried to call or text anyone – maybe nine-one-one, maybe you, Lucie, or maybe Ash. Maybe he realized what happened and tried to get help.'

'You mean,' Ash said, and this time his voice cracked, 'that maybe he suffered. Maybe he didn't die right away.'

I slipped my arm through Ash's and hugged it. 'You can't think about that now,' I said. 'You don't know anything yet.'

'Ashton, I promise I'll take good care of him and get my examination done as soon as possible,' Win said in a gentle voice. 'I should be getting back to the lab now, anyway. The sooner I get started on my work, the sooner we'll all know. After that you can have him back to start . . . making arrangements.' He gave Ash a long, sober look. 'Do you need anything to help you get through this, son? Something temporary, that is, only for a few days. I'm not talking long-term.'

Ash tightened his lips and shook his head. 'I've already got a prescription for sleeping pills. I'll take a couple if I need to knock myself out. Thanks, anyway, Doc . . . I should be going, too. I guess I need to start doing . . . things. Letting our family and friends know.' His sigh was ragged as if what lay ahead – burying Parker – seemed overwhelming.

If he remembered why he'd been on his way here to begin with – our final meeting to discuss the garden – he showed no sign of it. Frankly, he still looked pretty wrecked.

'Ash,' I said to him, 'come back to the villa with Quinn and me. You need coffee or a cup of tea and something to eat. You're in shock. There'll be plenty of time to do all of that later. You look like you're about to pass out. I'll drive you home after you look a little better than you do now. Quinn or Antonio or one of the guys will take your car back to your place so you don't need to drive it.'

He didn't need persuading. 'All right,' he said. 'Thanks.'

The last remaining EMTs had held off removing Parker's body from the vineyard as long as Ash was still here – that small consideration would have been Win's doing – but just now I heard the metallic sound of a gurney being wheeled to Parker's side.

Quinn caught my eye and jerked his head toward the driveway where we'd left our cars.

'We should go,' he said, moving to Ash's other side and taking an arm.

Ash was heavy now, almost dead weight, still numb with grief. We pulled him along and tried to keep him from stumbling.

I caught sight of Dominique, who must have arrived while Quinn and I were talking to Win and Ash. She was waiting with Sergio; I guessed she had hung back to give us some privacy. Next to Sergio's tall, lanky six-foot-something frame, my cousin looked like a waif, all five feet two of her, pixie haircut, black jeans, black turtleneck, paisley scarf knotted around her neck. She also looked devastated. Sergio leaned down and said something to her. She nodded and broke away to join us. He followed.

She reached for Ash's hands. 'Lucie told me, Ash. My heart breaks for you.'

Ash nodded and gave her a vacant stare as if he couldn't figure out what she was doing here.

Then he said, 'Oh, God. The garden. We're supposed to be meeting, aren't we?'

'Forget about the garden,' I told him. 'It doesn't matter right now.'

'We should go,' Quinn said with some urgency and I knew he wanted to get out of here before the gurney arrived with Parker's body strapped to it, zipped into a black body bag. Ash would come completely undone. 'Lucie, you drive Ash back to the villa, OK? I'll meet you there.'

'What can I do?' Dominique asked.

'Food?' I said.

'Yes, yes, of course. I'll have the caterers pack a basket and we'll bring it to your place this afternoon, Ash,' she said, 'so you don't have to worry about meals for a while.'

'I don't think I could . . .'

She cut him off. 'Yes, you can. You have to. You can't stop eating.'

He gave her a weak smile. 'OK.'

'What can I do?' Sergio spoke up for the first time, his Italian accent softening his pronunciation so the words sounded like a caress.

Ash gave Sergio a puzzled look. 'Who are you?'

'Sergio Ianelli,' he said. 'Mia's . . . partner.' He added, 'I also am sorry for your loss.'

I didn't realize Ash hadn't met Sergio before, though he did know Mia had moved back here and was living with him in the winemaker's cottage. We'd talked about it during our discussions of where to locate the vegetable garden.

By now we were standing in front of the cottage. The little semi-circular driveway was still jammed with cars – mine, Quinn's, Dominique's, Ash's, and Sergio's, plus the van that was going to take Parker's body to the morgue.

Ash was frowning at Sergio as if he were trying to work something out. 'Parker would have had to drive by your place for his car to be where he left it, am I right?'

'Yes.'

'So you must have heard his car. Or seen it.'

'Unfortunately, no. I work in the back of the cottage,' Sergio said. 'And because my work is so painstaking, I usually wear noise-canceling headphones to block out any ambient sound. It also allows me to listen to music. I hear nothing, not even my cellphone ringing.'

'That means you wouldn't have heard the car,' Ash said. 'Did you see it?'

'No. I did not.'

'You're sure about that?'

Sergio stared at Ash as if he were trying to figure out what he was really asking. 'Is there some reason you think I wouldn't be sure?'

'I don't know. I just want to be *sure* you're sure.' By now Ash was acting punch-drunk, as if he were spoiling for a fight.

'Come on, Ash,' Quinn said, trying to mollify him, and giving Sergio a *cool it* look. 'Let's get you something to drink and eat.'

He ushered Ash into the passenger seat of the Jeep and shut the door. 'Meet you at the villa, Lucie,' he said and turned to Dominique. 'Are you coming, too?'

She shook her head. 'There's nothing I can do here. I should go back to the inn and help with lunch. I'll talk to the caterers about fixing a hamper full of food for Ash.'

She kissed me quickly, once on each cheek, and got into her car.

After she left, Sergio stood in front of Quinn and me, his arms folded across his chest. 'Before you go, I'm not sure why he acts like he thinks I saw a car when I didn't,' he said with an edge in his voice, jerking his head toward where Ash sat in the Jeep. 'But if his husband came by yesterday to check out your vines, that means he didn't go home last night, right?'

I got where Sergio was going with this. I'd even brought it up with Deputy Gonzalez. If, say, Quinn didn't come home for an entire night and his side of the bed wasn't slept in the next morning, I might notice that tiny aberration. I might even wonder where he was and what had happened – if I hadn't already been tossing and turning with worry all night anyway. Or been trying to call or text him and gotten no reply.

Ash had been overcome with grief when he saw Parker at my vineyard – that was genuine – but if Parker hadn't come home last night, why hadn't Ash mentioned that fact? Parker had a studio in Middleburg where he met clients. It was also a bolt hole where he could lock himself away and write his books. Maybe Ash thought that's where Parker had been, pulling an all-nighter, working on some project. Although if that were the case, surely they would have touched base with each other so Ash knew what was up, right?

Maybe they had quarreled, an argument so full of can't-walk-it-back anger that neither was speaking to the other. Though that didn't sound right, either. They had only been married a few years and I'd always thought that despite the age difference,

they'd been genuinely happy, really crazy about each other.
Parker had mentioned that Ash hadn't been pleased about him
calling out Gabriel Seely over doctoring the results of his
research experiments, plus Ash was one of Gabriel's financial
backers, but Parker hadn't made it out to be anything overly
serious.

Once we got back to the villa and Ash was less distraught I
intended to ask him what had happened last night: what he
was doing and when was the last time he'd seen Parker.

Alive.

Sergio hadn't seen or heard a bronze Lexus drive past his
cottage, which was located on a quiet, normally deserted
cul-de-sac. Ash hadn't mentioned that his husband might have
gone missing last night.

What I wanted to know was why.

EIGHT

On a Tuesday morning in mid-March you might not think you'd find anyone in a winery tasting room having a drink before noon, but you'd be wrong. We're always packed on weekends and most evenings when folks come by to unwind after work – talk, chill, listen to music if someone's here playing or singing – but on weekdays we get a small but predictable crowd that seems to consist mostly of ladies who lunch (early), retirees enjoying their well-earned freedom, and tourists passing through.

I knew we wouldn't have more than one person working the bar because we didn't need anyone else, plus it was technically still the very end of winter, which is the slow season. Usually Francesca Merchant wasn't the one waiting on clients, but when Ash, Quinn and I walked in to the villa's sunny, spacious tasting room a few minutes later, she was slotting clean glasses into the overhead wine racks.

Quinn must have called to give her a head's up so she knew about Parker and that Ash would be with us, still in shock. She'd probably sent whoever was working the bar to help in the kitchen, or maybe told him or her to take a break, and said she'd cover. She also had, no doubt, ordered flatbread sandwiches and a plate of cheese and fruit from the kitchen so everything would be ready when we arrived. Served in the library, where we'd have privacy.

Frankie ran the retail side of the vineyard with military efficiency and did such a good job of anticipating anything I needed there were times I was convinced she could read minds or else she inhabited part of my brain. She took off her glasses when she saw us and used them like a headband to hold back her shoulder-length strawberry blonde hair. Her blue eyes were grave and unsmiling and they went straight to Ash.

The *Washington Tribune* lay open on top of the bar; she must have been reading it before we arrived. Parker's monthly

column was in today's paper, skewering Gabriel Seely for
sloppy research and falsifying results about the potential
game-changing possibility of being able to flip a switch, so
to speak, so a plant would stop telling itself to die. I had
intended to read what he wrote as soon as I got to the winery,
but a detour to the vineyard had derailed that plan. Frankie
seemed to realize I was staring at the *Trib*, because she cas-
ually flipped it over and slid it under the counter out of sight.
Her mouth tightened and I knew she'd read what Parker had
to say. It wasn't good.

She came over, hugged Ash, and asked if there was anything
she could do. As expected, she said there was food, a pot of
coffee, and a pot of hot water for tea waiting in the library.
Plus a couple of bottles of unopened wine, some glasses, and
a corkscrew.

She tapped my arm as Quinn, Ash, and I started to walk
toward the library.

'I need to talk to you,' she said in a low voice. 'Without the
guys.'

This wasn't going to be good, either. Quinn looked over his
shoulder and I mouthed '*Go ahead*'. He and Ash disappeared
around the corner in the direction of the library.

I said to Frankie, 'What is it?'

'I don't know how word got around so fast, but I already
had a call from News Channel Three. Your favorite reporter,
Pippa O'Hara, said she heard that Parker Lord was found dead
at Montgomery Estate Vineyard,' she said. 'Cause of death
unknown, pending an autopsy by the Medical Examiner's office.
Confirm or deny.'

I groaned. 'That woman has a source, some mole, in the
Sheriff's Office. Or else she's bugging someone's phone. She
already *knew*, dammit. She'll be out here in a shot doing her
stand-up in front of our entrance for the six o'clock news. Or,
unless someone stops her, she'll find the spot where he died
and do it there. It was the Merlot block, the place where the
vines are dying. Parker said yesterday that he'd take a look to
see if he had any idea what might have caused them to die
when he . . .'

I stopped, closed my eyes, and rubbed my temples, making

small circles with my fingers. My head throbbed. 'When he collapsed.'

Frankie gave my wrist a sympathetic squeeze. 'I'm so sorry, Lucie. Please let me know what else I can do for Ash, or for you and Quinn. Do you want me to talk to Antonio and get him to have the guys keep an eye on those vines? Shoo away any pesky visitors who show up and decide to check out some place they shouldn't be?'

'That would be great,' I said. 'What did you tell Pippa?'

She gave a small, tight smile. 'What do you think I said?'

'No comment.'

She pointed her thumb and index finger at me like she was shooting a gun. 'Bingo.'

Ash and Quinn had already tucked into the flatbread sandwiches and had done some damage to the cheese and fruit plate when I walked into the library. It was a cozy room: the walls lined with bookshelves filled with books on wine, Virginia tourism, and Virginia history and two of my mother's paintings of the vineyard hanging above a sofa that was surrounded by a couple of upholstered club chairs. We used it when we held small private events – there was space for more chairs if we needed them – because it was like inviting someone into your home.

Quinn had opened a bottle of our Cabernet Sauvignon. I was grateful it wasn't Merlot. At least not today. I wasn't ready for wine before noon, so I had coffee and took one of the sandwiches. Ash ate as if his last meal had been a few days ago.

I sat down in one of the club chairs across from Ash, who had taken the sofa.

'Can I ask you something?' I said to him.

He leaned back against the cushions, holding a glass of wine by the stem, and crossed one leg over the other so it was resting on his knee. He fussed with the cuff of his jeans, pulling it over his work boot. The expression on his face said he knew exactly what I wanted to ask.

'You *can*.'

Wise guy. '*May* I ask you something?'

'You may.'

'Did you see Parker last night?'

Quinn, who had been leaning against the credenza where Frankie had set out our food, shifted uneasily when I spoke, but he kept mum.

Ash possessed striking good looks – slim, raven-haired with sharp, intelligent eyes, and a smile that showed off two dimples, making him look adorably boyish as if he could persuade you to do anything he asked. Just now he wore a few days' growth of a beard – not his usual clean baby-faced look that still got him carded in bars and restaurants. The fuzz suited him, made him look older. Parker told me once that Ash's straight-out-of-college looks caused a lot of his potential clients to underestimate him the first time they saw him. They only did that once.

What they soon found out was that Ash was very, very good at what he did, because he not only understood the art of garden cultivation and management, but also the science behind it. Maybe you didn't know why your tomato plants looked like Jack's beanstalk with not a single tomato on them, but Ash could give you the scientific explanation why that had happened and tell you how to fix it. The big commercial gardens that sold their produce to the chain grocery stores had him on speed dial.

His career really took off after he was invited to be an advisor for Michelle Obama's White House vegetable garden, the youngest horticulturalist on her team. Later he'd helped with the book she'd written about it – *American Grown* – and that had put Cultiveo, his business, on the map. Not just in the Mid-Atlantic, either.

Ash looked me straight in the eye just now and said, 'No, I didn't see Parker last night.'

I had asked the wrong question so I tried again. 'Was he at home and you didn't see him?'

Parker and Ash lived in a big rambling Victorian just outside Middleburg; it had three storeys and several outbuildings, including a cottage that each of them sometimes used as a place to work. So it wasn't impossible that Parker could be home and wouldn't have crossed paths with Ash.

'I don't know.' He played with the stem of his wine glass. 'I took two sleeping pills and passed out. Early. I've been working flat out and I was just shattered. I'd had a couple glasses of wine – maybe a few too many – before I took the pills, which was dumb, I know. So I was out cold until I woke up this morning around six thirty. Parker – obviously – wasn't there then, either.'

'When did you last see him?'

Ash gave me a look that said I was pushing it with the questions, but he answered anyway. 'Yesterday. I stopped by his office in town. He'd just been to see Cricket Delacroix over some problem-or-other in her butterfly garden.'

'What time was that?'

'Late morning. I don't know, maybe eleven or eleven thirty.'

'Was everything all right between you two?'

A long pause filled with enough weight to answer the question before he confirmed it. 'No.'

I kept silent and waited for him to go on. This time he looked into the bowl of his wine glass, which was now nearly empty, as if he might find words or answers there. Quinn got up and refilled it for him.

'I suppose sooner or later this is going to get out.' He gave us a look like a kid who finally decided things are going to work out better if he 'fessed up, rather than continuing to prevaricate. 'We quarreled. Parker went after Gabriel Seely for a paper he just published in the *Journal of Plant Pathology*. He claimed Gabriel falsified the results of his experiments to make it look as if the project was more successful than it was.'

'I heard about that,' I said. 'Yesterday. From Parker.'

'If he was your source, you only heard part of the story.'

'What's the rest of it?' Quinn asked.

Ash drank some wine. 'Gabriel thought it might be possible to stop a plant's death spiral by manipulating a stress marker – the amount of glutathione it produced – before it was too late. He was in the early stages with this, sure, so there is a lot more work, but it's potentially an incredible breakthrough especially in this era of accelerated climate change. Maybe Gabriel took an early victory lap that he shouldn't have done. But the Board of Governors at New Dominion University is already looking into terminating his grant because of what Parker accused him of in his column in today's *Tribune*. Which would be disastrous.'

If I read him right, Ash believed Parker was unjustified in

throwing the baby out with the bath water: that it hadn't been necessary to slam Gabriel for embellishing his research results if it helped bring in more money to continue important, innovative work.

'Just to be clear,' I said, 'was Parker wrong about Gabriel falsifying his research results?'

'Gabriel was doing good work,' Ash said, evading the question. 'Hell, Lucie, Gregor Mendel, the father of freaking genetics, has been accused of falsifying experiment results when he wrote about what happened in his pea experiments. Every kid who ever took high-school biology read about those damn peas. Cross a yellow pea with a green pea – the yellow is dominant, green is recessive – and the end result is that three times out of four you get yellow peas. That's what the math says. That's what logic tells you. Or so Mendel said.'

'I remember studying those peas in biology class,' I said. 'And all the math we had to do for the final exam on genetics.'

'Me, too,' Quinn said. 'Are you saying Mendel was wrong? After how many hundred years?'

'What I'm saying,' Ash said, now sounding weary, 'is that there is new information that Mendel might have massaged his calculations so he got the results he was *expecting*, based on the math and what he thought was common sense. In other words, Mendel didn't allow for aberrations and weird one-off mutations that would then be transmitted to future generations. It still didn't stop him from doing great work, did it?'

Quinn and I exchanged glances. No point getting into a messy ethical discussion about Gregor Mendel, the father of modern genetics, going a bit off the rails and ending up with results that were sort of loosey-goosey and not actually true, but nevertheless using them to prove the point he wanted to prove.

True or false? Right or wrong? Lies, damn lies, or statistics? Um, yes. All of the above.

'So you and Parker argued over Gabriel?' I asked.

'I didn't think he needed to destroy Gabriel's career.' Ash took a long swig of wine and when he spoke his voice broke. 'It doesn't matter now, does it? He's *gone*. I wish I could take it back, wish I'd talked to him last night.'

I reached over and laid my hand on his arm. 'Don't. And nobody needs to know about this, either – the way it ended between you and Parker. Quinn and I won't say anything. Everyone knows how much you two loved each other. That's all that matters. People argue. They quarrel. It's part of life, part of any relationship. Don't beat yourself up over it.'

His eyes were damp. 'Maybe,' he said. 'I don't know.'

'Is there anything we can do now?' Quinn asked. 'What do you need?'

'I need to go home,' he said. 'I need to deal with the fact that he's gone.'

'If we can help . . .' I said.

He nodded and set his glass down, wiping his eyes with his fists. 'Thanks,' he said. 'I just wish I could turn back time.'

Kit Noland, the Loudoun bureau chief for the *Washington Tribune*, and my best and oldest friend since we were five years-old, called my mobile as I was driving back to the vineyard after dropping off Ash. Her name popped up on the Jeep's console and I knew instantly why she was calling. If Pippa O'Hara already knew about Parker, so did Kit. Besides, her husband was Detective Bobby Noland, though she always said that made it harder, not easier, for her to get information from the Loudoun County Sheriff's Office.

'He makes me work my ass off before he'll say a word,' she told me multiple times, 'so it doesn't look like he's cutting me a break. I'd have an easier time getting blood out of a stone than a "no comment" from my own husband.'

I answered and said, 'What's up?'

A moment of silence and then she said, 'Seriously, Luce? Come *on*.'

We can finish each other's sentences. Start each other's sentences. 'What do you want me to say?'

'*Jeez*. What do you think? What *happened*? You found him. What was he doing there, any idea when he showed up? Yadda, yadda, yadda. All of it.'

'Kit, it's Parker. *Was* Parker. I've known him since I was seven, eight . . . almost as long as you and I have known each other. The last time I saw him he came over to the house to go over his design for our wedding garden.' *Yesterday. The last time I saw him was yesterday, the day he died.* 'I don't want my comments to be in block quotes in your story.'

'Whoa. Unfair. You know better. I would never do something like that.' She sounded hurt.

'I'm sorry. I know you wouldn't. I guess I'm still stunned. And I just dropped Ash off at home.'

'Oh, God. How is he?'

'Like you'd think. Devastated. Heartbroken.'

I heard her sigh through the phone. 'I couldn't believe it when I found out. Everyone around here is in shock.'

'I haven't read his column in today's *Trib* yet.'

'I wish we hadn't run it today of all days. Don't read the online comments. We're going to shut them down pretty soon because . . . well, he's dead.'

'They're as bad as that?'

'No. Worse.'

'I could drive into Middleburg and pick up two lattes at the Cuppa Giddyup,' I said. 'We could meet at our old place and talk there. It's turned into a pretty nice day. What I mean is, the weather is nice. The day sucks.'

'I'd like that,' she said. 'I just finished dropping something off at the assisted living home for Mom so I'm close by. I could meet you there in fifteen.'

'See you then.'

Our old place was the Goose Creek Bridge just outside Middleburg on Route 50, otherwise known as Mosby's Highway. Constructed in 1810 just after Thomas Jefferson's presidency, the two-hundred-foot-long four-arched stone bridge was originally a turnpike bridge and the site of a minor Civil War battle. On June 21 1863, Major J.E.B. Stuart tried to provide a screen to keep Union soldiers from discovering that most of Lee's army was resting nearby outside the town of Upperville. Stuart wasn't successful and a few days later both armies met at Gettysburg.

The construction of Route 50 in the 1950s meant the demise of the bridge, which was now cared for by the local garden club and listed on the National Register of Historic Places. And it was almost always deserted. Kit and I had had our heart-tohearts there for years, many of which were facilitated by bottles of wine I filched from the winery so we could drink them while talking over our angst-filled teenage problems with each other. Years later I found out that Jacques, our first winemaker, was wise to me and used to leave bottles that were deliberately watered down for me to 'find'.

Kit's red SUV was already parked at the end of Lemmon Bottom's Road when I pulled in fifteen minutes later. She obviously heard the sound of my tires crunching on the dirt and gravel because she came up the path from the bridge as I was getting our coffees out of the cup holders on my console.

Once upon a time Kit and I ran cross-country together in high school and we were *good*. Then came my accident and I had to give up running. I wasn't sure why Kit gave up, but journalism became her new passion and a more sedentary life-style, often sitting at a computer, resulted in a few more pounds on her once-slim figure, and then a few more and so on. Now she was on a forever-diet, yo-yoing and trying to lose the Frickin' Forty as she called her excess weight. She had been working on getting down to the Dirty Thirty, but Christmas – two and a half months ago – had derailed her.

'I thought I smelled coffee,' she said in a cheerful voice, but I knew she really showed up so I didn't have to navigate the path to the bridge carrying a cardboard cup holder with two coffees in one hand and using a cane with the other. 'I'll take that for you.'

I handed her the cup holder. 'Thanks. I can manage, you know.'

'I know. I just wanted my coffee and didn't want to wait.'

'You're a liar.'

'Tell me about Parker.'

I told her on the way to the parapet where we always sat, our legs dangling over the side with Goose Creek below us. In summer the bed might be completely dry. In the rainy season, it could be a torrent. Just now in March, it was flowing well, gurgling peacefully, on its slow but inevitable way to the Potomac River.

'Parker was checking some vines we're having a problem with as a favor to me,' I said. 'He told me he might have some idea why they were dying and that maybe he could help before Josie Wilde comes by in a few days. I wish I'd never . . .' I fiddled with the lid of my coffee cup and didn't finish my sentence.

'Stop,' she said. 'Don't do that. You know better.'

I had chastised Ash not so long ago about cudda-wudda-shudda. Told him it went nowhere.

'I know.'

'What do you think happened? I heard Win was there. What did he say?'

'You know Win. He won't make a definitive announcement until he knows what he's talking about. But, honest, Kit, it looked like Parker just collapsed. Maybe a heart attack, maybe a stroke . . . Who knows?'

'Apparently,' she said, 'he might have been out there overnight.'

I knew where this was going.

'He told me he might be able to stop by at the end of the day yesterday,' I said. 'But he was going to text or call me and he never did.'

'How come nobody missed him if he was gone all night?' She gave me a pointed look. 'Like, say, maybe his husband.'

Quinn and I told Ash we weren't going to betray his confidence, reveal anything about the quarrel he and Parker had over Gabriel. I loved Kit like my sister, but she always said to me that you don't burn a source.

And I believed you didn't go back on your word.

'I imagine *your* husband is busy finding out the answer to that question,' I said. 'Tell me about the online comments people are making about Parker's column.'

Kit knew I'd ducked the question – like I said, we practically breathe for each other – but she let it go. Then she shook her head in disgust. 'Half the comments say Parker is a tree-hugging lunatic who doesn't know what he's talking about. They just want to rag on him about *The Angry Earth*. Some of it's really sick, threats like "We know where you live".' She shuddered. 'We took anything like that down right away.'

Death threats. Parker hadn't been joking.

'What were the other half of the comments about?'

Her smile was lopsided. 'People who were pissed off at Gabriel for falsifying his results. Writing things like "You can't believe anyone any more." Or "We already know politicians are a bunch of lying criminals, now scientists are just as bad." And my personal favorite: "Trust no one."'

'Did anybody get into whether Parker was right in discrediting Gabriel? People just assumed he was?'

She gave me a slant-eyed look. 'I don't think so. Why? Do you know something?'

This got into Ash and Parker's final argument again. But all I said was, 'Quinn saw Gabriel at the General Store yesterday morning. He said Gabriel doesn't think Parker was right.'

'Well, he wouldn't.'

'He also told Quinn that he changed some of Parker's plant recommendations when clients came to him and Parker was so outraged at being undermined and second guessed that this column is sort of payback.'

'Gabriel is going to get the last word, Luce. Parker is dead now. He's not going to be able to rebut anything Gabriel says. It's going to be a one-sided battle.'

We sat for a while without talking, swinging our legs back and forth like a couple of kids.

What was left of my coffee had gone cold. I stirred and said, 'I probably ought to get back to the vineyard.'

'And I need to get back to the bureau. I'm writing the story on Parker's death – and his life.'

'Can you leave me out of it?'

'Your vineyard? You found him? Are you serious?'

'No block quotes, OK?'

'No block quotes.'

'Do I get to see it before you turn it in to your editor?'

'If you were the President of the United States you wouldn't get to see it before I turn it in to my editor. You know that.'

I did. Didn't hurt to ask, though.

We walked back to our cars together. I backed out first and she followed. I turned right off Mosby's Highway onto Atoka Road and honked my horn. She honked back, hand out the window in a salute.

She didn't have much of a story until Win completed his

autopsy and determined the cause of death. The rest of it would
be an appreciation of Parker's life, his unique contributions to
landscape design, his work on some of America's most beautiful
public gardens as well as many significant private gardens, and
his role as a climate-change activist.

Even before I turned on to Sycamore Lane I could see the
television trucks with their satellite dishes rising in the air like
periscopes and a scrum of cars parked outside the main gate to
the vineyard. The news of Parker's death must have gone around
like wildfire. I wondered how many media organizations were
represented in that little cabal.

Pippa O'Hara, a standout in her electric blue Channel 3 jacket
and Flamin' Hot Cheetos red hair, was standing near the
Montgomery Estate Vineyard sign as I turned off Atoka Road.
I knew she was going to zero in on me right away and she did,
brazenly walking into the middle of the road and standing
there so my choices were to either run her over or stop and be
ambushed. I was angry enough that the former was looking
like the better option, but I stopped the Jeep just as she knew
I would.

She rapped on my window, her cameraman right behind her,
filming our little tableau. I hit the power button and lowered
the window halfway. Pippa and I had tangled before. It had
been all the fun of diving into a full-sized aquarium tank with
a barracuda.

'Lucie Montgomery,' she said. 'How nice to see you again.
It's always such a pleasure.'

'I'm glad it is for you, Pippa,' I said and waited for her to
do her thing, which I knew would take about a nanosecond.

It did. She stuck her microphone in front of me. 'Lucie
Montgomery, do you have any comment on the death of Parker
Lord's body being discovered here at your vineyard this morning
– I believe by you?'

Damn. She really did have someone on the inside at the
Sheriff's Office.

'There's nothing I can tell you that you don't already know,'
I said. 'Honestly. Win Turnbull is the one who is going to be
able to determine the cause of death, so you really ought to
be over at the Medical Examiner's office. It looks as if Parker

collapsed out in the vineyard and wasn't able to call nine-one-one, or anyone for that matter, for help before he died.'

She wasn't going to budge. 'What was he doing here?'

'A favor. Checking some vines we're having problems with.'

'I see. Can you describe your reaction when you found him? Take us through what happened, how you felt.'

I *hate* stupid gotcha questions like that. What did she think I was going to say?

'I felt the way any normal person feels when they discover that someone they know and love is dead.' I nearly said, *Which doesn't include reporters like you who might not be actual human beings capable of real feelings and emotions*, but I didn't.

'That's *all*, Pippa. There's nothing else.'

'Any idea what time it happened?'

'Ask Dr Turnbull.' I powered up my window and shifted the Jeep into drive.

She moved out of the way, though with some reluctance – probably figuring the odds against being run over might not be in her favor any more – and I drove through the main gate. A couple of minutes later I parked in front of the villa and wondered what Bobby Noland's unmarked black SUV was doing here.

I found out as soon as I walked in the door. He was sitting on a barstool, finishing a cup of coffee. Frankie was still behind the bar. Bobby swung around when the door clicked shut and stood up.

'I need to talk to you, Lucie,' he said, 'in private.'

He'd been waiting for me. His expression was bland, but there was an undertone of something gone wrong in his voice.

'Use my office,' Frankie said.

It was down a hallway near the kitchen.

We walked into the small paneled room that had been my office before it became Frankie's – and my mother's before it was mine. Then a few years ago Quinn and I moved to new quarters with a state-of-the-art lab above the barrel room.

'Have a seat,' I said to Bobby before I realized he had already taken the chair facing the desk. I shut the door and took my old seat behind the desk, folding my hands together as if I were praying.

'I'm afraid I've got bad news,' he said.

'Is it about Parker?'

I don't know why I asked – maybe to stall hearing what he wanted to talk about – because of course it was about Parker. Bobby nodded. 'He didn't die of natural causes, Lucie. You and I need to talk. Parker Lord was murdered.'

NINE

'**M**urdered?' I said. 'How?'

'Poisoned. Win found traces of a chemical in his system.'

'What chemical?' My God, at a vineyard we worked with chemicals all the time, many of them highly toxic and potentially fatal, if not used correctly. Pesticides, insecticides, herbicides, fungicides, to name a few – and that was just outdoors in the field.

'Tetrahydrozoline,' Bobby said.

'Pardon?'

'It's something you find in eye drops.'

I knew that, but it didn't make sense. 'Parker was murdered by an overdose of eye drops?'

'Not in his eyes. He ingested the stuff. Ate it with food, drank it in some drink. It's toxic if enough gets into your system. And from what Win told me, it might have caused breathing problems, Parker's blood pressure shooting up or else dropping really low, which would result in mental confusion . . . ultimately a seizure, which is what Win thinks killed him. He probably wasn't feeling great, but Parker being Parker he'd soldier on – and then suddenly, wham. Things just got so much worse,' Bobby said. 'We found his cell phone underneath his body. It looked like he might have been trying to call nine-one-one but for some reason he never managed to push the button. It's probably when he had the seizure.'

It felt as if Bobby had just punched me hard enough to knock the wind out of me. *I* should have been there with Parker. *I* could have saved him, called 911 right away and they would have come in time. He hadn't needed to die.

Bobby read all that in my eyes because he reached over and put a steadying hand on my arm.

'It was a really toxic dose, Lucie. By the time an ambulance

got to him – out there in the middle of that field – it still would
have been too late.'

I shook my head, not wanting to believe him. 'The ambulance
could have come in time if I called the moment he started
showing symptoms of distress. You can't be sure it wouldn't.'

'Don't do that to yourself. Once he got to the vineyard he
must have gone downhill really fast and couldn't help himself
in time. It's awful, but it's what happened. I'm sorry. I know
you two were close.'

He let me sit with that for a minute, my mind racing through
a million different scenarios. The first thing I wanted to ask
Bobby was who would want to kill Parker, but the words died
before I could get them out because Parker had made plenty of
enemies, mostly professionally.

For starters there was Gabriel Seely, though I couldn't
possibly imagine Gabriel – Middleburg's favorite North Pole
elf – committing murder. But what about someone who left a
threatening comment on the *Trib*'s website today? Someone
who said they knew where Parker lived?

'What happens now?' I asked. 'I was just with Kit at the
Goose Creek Bridge. She said a lot of people left horrible,
intimidating messages in the comment section of the *Trib*
after they read Parker's piece today. You're going to check them
out, right?'

'Goose Creek, huh? What were the two of you doing there
in the middle of the day and did it involve alcohol?'

I tried to look indignant, but it had been known to happen,
so he wasn't far off the mark. 'It was *coffee*. Bobby, Kit said
the comments were really menacing.'

'We'll check into it. But these things usually work out that
it's a person the victim knew, not some random stranger.
Especially not someone who left an anonymous message on a
website.'

'Right.' My throat started to constrict. Was he talking about
Gabriel? Ash?

'Win can't say for sure when Parker ingested the tetrahydrozoline. We need to go back and reconstruct his day – all of it:
what he did, where he was, and who he was with yesterday.'
Bobby pulled a spiral notebook and a ballpoint pen out of the

inside pocket of his blazer, opened the notebook and clicked his pen. The sound made me think of a trigger being cocked and I flinched.

He noticed. 'Tell me again about your meeting with Parker yesterday. From the beginning.'

I looked him in the eye. 'Do you suspect me? Really, Bobby?'

'Lucie,' he said, 'you know I'm only doing my job. I gotta ask the questions, OK? And I'm going to need to talk to everyone who worked here yesterday, including anyone who was out in the field.'

Our immigrant workers. Dear Lord. There wasn't a day that passed for many months now, actually probably the last couple of years, that Quinn and I didn't worry about someone going home at night who might not return the next day because they'd been picked up by ICE. Or someone in their family was rounded up and then they went to ground and we would never see them again, never know what happened.

'Bobby . . . our workers. You know they're going to be terrified to talk to a cop. They won't want to do it . . . maybe Quinn or I can ask them your questions instead?'

'Sorry, but no dice. You need to tell your crew that I swear on my mother's grave that no one's going to check their documents. A man was murdered and we want to find the killer. That's *all*. And tell them it will be worse if they don't talk to us voluntarily. Because then we will have to show up where they live,' he said. 'No one's gonna like that. Including me.'

I folded my arms across my chest and glared at him. Bobby was my childhood friend, best friends with Eli growing up; he practically lived at our house. He put a frog in my school backpack when I was seven and I'd been so scared I'd peed my pants when it hopped out. I retaliated by putting a tadpole in his water bottle and he drank it, so we were even. Later I tutored him in math for honor society hours when he was in danger of flunking out of high school and practically had a chair with a well-polished seat and his name on it in the principal's office. Then he went to Afghanistan, two tours, won awards for bravery, and came home deciding he wanted to *be* the law, not on the wrong side of it. He married my best friend and my wedding gift to them was to have their wedding at the vineyard.

None of that mattered one bit right now.

'Right,' I said in a tight voice. 'I'll tell the guys you'll be talking to them.'

'Good. Thanks. Now tell me about your meeting with Parker. When, where, what you talked about . . . anything to eat or drink?'

'He brought two coffees from the Cuppa Giddyup, one for him and one for me. And, no, neither of us was using eye drops.'

Not even the tiniest crack of ironic amusement in that granite cop face of his. 'What time was this?'

'Nine.'

'OK, go on.'

'We talked about his design for our wedding garden and he offered to take a look at some dying vines in the Merlot block in case he had any insight about what might have caused them to become diseased so fast. That's it.'

'He told you he'd stop by yesterday to do that, right?'

'He said he would if he could and it would be at the end of the day. Otherwise not before Wednesday, which was the next time he was free. He said he'd text me or call when he got there so I could join him and we could look at the vines together. He knew I wouldn't be able to meet him on Wednesday since I have to pick up my grandfather at the airport, so maybe that's why he made an effort to come by yesterday.'

I wished he hadn't.

Bobby's eyes flickered when I mentioned Pépé – the two of them got along like a house on fire – but then he was all business again. 'And did he call or text?'

They'd probably checked Parker's phone by now and Bobby already knew the answer to that question.

'No.'

'So you had no idea he might be out there last night?'

'*Was* he out there last night? For sure? Is that what Win says?'

'Yeah. Win says time of death was maybe five, six o'clock – p.m. not a.m. Unfortunately he probably . . . suffered . . . for a while.'

I bit my lip hard and willed the tears not to come. I didn't want to go over this again, didn't want to think about Parker lying in agony in the middle of the vineyard with no one there to help him.

'I told Parker to leave his car in the driveway by the wine-maker's cottage,' I said. 'If he had, Mia and Sergio would have seen it. They would have known he was here and probably called Quinn or me to ask what was going on.'

'Why didn't he do that? Parker, I mean.'

Why, indeed? I gave Bobby a weary shrug. 'You know Parker. He doesn't like to be told what to do. Didn't . . . like to be told.'

'On that subject,' Bobby said, 'did you two talk about anything else besides your wedding garden?'

We'd talked about two things and, Bobby being Bobby, he was going to get around to both of them. I picked the least inflammatory subject first.

'We talked about his new book. *The Angry Earth*. He said he was getting death threats and then he sort of joked about it.'

'Joked about it?' Bobby drummed a staccato beat on his notebook with his pen, frowning as he seemed to ponder why death threats might be a joke. 'Why would he do that?'

'He said that all the negative attention had driven the book to the number one position on *The New York Times* bestseller list, so it was actually sort of a good thing.'

'Did he mention anyone specifically who was threatening him?'

'No.'

'What else did you talk about?' When I hesitated he said, 'Come on, Lucie. This is a murder investigation.'

'I know that.'

'So?'

'When I said we'd buy the plants he recommended from Seely's, Parker said he was persona non grata there because of his column about Gabriel Seely in today's *Trib*,' I said. 'Have you read it?'

'I, uh, heard about it before it was published,' he said. 'But, no, I haven't read it yet.'

Kit had told him.

'That's all, Bobby. He said he was on his way to see Cricket Delacroix because she asked him to stop by and look at something in one of her gardens. Her butterfly garden, I think it was.'

Bobby did some more pen tapping and stared at his notes before he looked up. 'Nothing else?'

'Nothing else.'

He eyed me. 'What?'

'Gabriel isn't a murderer, Bobby. He just isn't, even if he was angry at Parker.'

I knew he wasn't going to take the bait, or offer a reply or a rebuttal. 'What time did Parker leave your place?'

'Maybe around nine forty-five? I don't remember checking my watch. Our meeting was set for nine.'

He nodded and I had the feeling he was doing some calculating. Did Parker mean what he'd said to me about going straight to Mon Repos? Or did he take a detour and stop somewhere else along the way? Ash thought he saw Parker around eleven or a bit later.

Bobby's mouth was set in a firm line and I'd bet money I knew why: there had been some zigging and zagging in Parker's timeline, the difference between where he really went and where he said he was going. Bobby flipped his notebook shut, clicked his pen, and stood up.

'If you think of anything . . .'

'I know. Call you.' I stood too. 'Now, what?'

'Our guys are out in your vineyard walking a grid to see if they get lucky and find a bottle of Visine,' he said. 'And, I'm sorry, but the area is now a crime scene.'

'So we can't go near it.' I gave him a you-can't-do-this look, though we both knew he could. 'Bobby, that place has got to be completely trampled over by now, mostly with footprints from your people, the EMTs, all the rescue folks who showed up. Plus my footprints and Quinn's.'

'I'm well aware of that.'

'And I hope your grid-walking doesn't mean your guys need to do anything that might damage my vines, right?'

'They'll do what they have to do.' He sounded irritated.

'But no one is going to deliberately or willfully damage your grapevines. Besides, the good news for you is that because the place already had more damn people traipsing through than the DC metro at rush hour, it probably won't be off-limits to you for long.'

He opened the door to the office and waited for me to go through first. 'I already talked to Frankie and everyone else who works in the villa before you got here. Next up is your barrel room. I need to talk to Quinn, Antonio, and your other guys.'

'Most of them don't speak English, or at least not very well. You're going to need a translator,' I said. 'Maybe Quinn or Antonio could help you out.'

'Thanks, but we got our own guy. You met him yesterday. Name of Gonzalez.'

Of course he had a translator.

'Right.'

We walked into the tasting room together, but just before we entered the room I said in a quiet voice, 'Do you really think Parker knew the person who killed him?'

'Someone got close enough to pour a bottle of eye drops on something he ate, or more likely, in something he drank without him noticing. Someone he was with yesterday. I'm pretty confident it wasn't a waiter or waitress in some restaurant or coffee shop having a bad day or pissed about lousy tips and deciding to act on their anger.'

He was right. Of course he was. So who had Parker been with yesterday that I knew about?

Just three of us: Ash, Cricket, and me.

'Who are you going to talk to once you finish here?' I asked.

'Anyone who was with Parker,' Bobby said in a laconic tone of voice that told me to knock off fishing for information. 'You got anyone else to add to my shortlist besides Cricket?'

'No. Surely you don't suspect her? She's going to be ninety in a couple days.'

'It doesn't matter if she's going to be a hundred and ninety in a couple days,' he said. 'Right now everyone's on the list. Age doesn't disqualify anyone. Plenty of people had an opportunity, including you. But I'm also looking for means and a motive. For example, you had the opportunity, plus since you were drinking coffee, you also had the means. What you don't have is a motive. That I know about.'

'Thanks.' I gave him a challenging look, which did not go unnoticed.

'You're welcome.'

So who had all three qualifications? Gabriel, maybe. But had Parker seen him yesterday?

My mind kept circling back to Ash.

I wondered if Bobby's did as well.

TEN

I texted Quinn after Bobby left the villa and told him that it was his turn and the crew's to be interviewed. Bobby would be there with a translator in tow and expected to talk to everyone. Quinn sent back a four-letter reply, but he knew as well as I did that Bobby needed statements from all the guys. Parker had been poisoned before he got to the vineyard; that seemed obvious and logical. Had he gone somewhere else instead of taking a look at our dead vines, the Sheriff's Office would most likely be investigating a different crime scene. But Bobby still needed to check all the boxes and that included talking to everyone at Montgomery Estate Vineyard. A moment later I got another text.

He just got here. Where R U?

> *Villa. Crime scene tape around the Merlot block and deputies looking for evidence. Going to check it out, make sure everything is ok.*

Let me know. Bobby is going to scare the crap out of the guys. Text U when it's over.

I drove the short distance from the villa to the winemaker's cottage and parked in the driveway. It was a sweet little house that always reminded me of a very large dollhouse or a house a young child would draw with a chubby set of crayons so that it looked vaguely like a face: windows like eyes, a door as a long nose, and front steps for the mouth. The cottage, like its twin where the farm manager lived, had been built of fieldstone quarried from our land. Two Bentwood rockers sat side by side on the wide front porch. The front door was painted a cheerful shade of turquoise and Mia's homemade wreath of rushes, pinecones, and dried flowers hung on it.

Smoke drifted out of the chimney, scenting the air with a pleasant tang.

The farm manager's cottage where Antonio, his wife, and baby daughter lived was identical, except the door was painted fire-engine red, Valeria Ramirez's favorite color and the exact color of the dress she wore at her wedding seven months ago. That house sat placidly at the other end of the cul-de-sac, mostly screened by a stand of oaks, tulip poplars, pine trees, and hollies. Antonio or Valeria would have had to have been leaning out over the railing at the far end of their porch in order to have seen Parker's car when he drove through here yesterday. If Antonio had seen anyone driving toward the vineyard, or Valeria had told him about it, I know with absolute certainty he would have gone out there to see what was going on. He would have found Parker.

If only.

I got out of the Jeep. Sergio's Fiat was parked in front of his and Mia's place as it had been this morning; my sister's car was still gone. She was probably at Mon Repos working on Harry and Cricket's mural. I half-expected to find a couple of Sheriff's Office cruisers here, but they were gone, too. Bobby's deputies must have finished their search, at least for today. I'd bet good money they'd turned up nothing, not a single clue as to who might have poisoned Parker. Especially because he'd been poisoned somewhere else.

Except for that languid curl of smoke, the winemaker's cottage was quiet. Perhaps Sergio was once again in the back bedroom wearing his noise-canceling headphones and listening to music as he worked on his current project. Parker told me yesterday he thought he knew Sergio from when he lived in New York, possibly through a connection at an art gallery or somewhere in the art world. But Sergio hadn't even been aware that Parker drove by the cottage yesterday afternoon and left his Lexus on the edge of the vineyard, so whether they knew each other or not, that had eliminated Sergio from Bobby's suspect list.

Unless, of course, Sergio was lying. What was it he and Mia were covering up about why they left New York? And why did my sister insist she didn't need to know anything about her enigmatic boyfriend's past?

I started walking toward the Merlot block. It was going on five o'clock and, even though the days were longer, the sun had already faded so there were no shadows. Birds twittered in the grove of trees where Parker had left his car. The Lexus was gone, as I knew it would be. Yellow crime-scene tape, looking out of place in a serene landscape of pale spring greens and dusty winter browns, had been strung from tree to tree like a Christmas garland.

At the vineyard itself more yellow tape fluttered in the breeze surrounding a couple of rows of vines. It was forbidden to cross the taped-off area so I didn't, but from what I could see, it looked as if no damage had been done to the vines. Fortunately this wasn't a few weeks later when they would have budded out. Knock off any of those tender, delicate buds if you were, say, pushing aside a vine to see if anything had fallen on the ground and it was all over but the crying. No buds meant no bud break, no grapes, no harvest, and no wine – at least not this year.

But it was too early for that to happen and today I'd take good news any way I could get it – even if it was something that *didn't* happen.

I was about to turn around to walk back to my car when I got the distinct feeling I was being watched. The hairs on the back of my neck prickled.

I turned around.

He had come up behind me on quiet cat's feet and now he was so close I could reach out and touch him. Why hadn't he called out, said my name? Warned me he was *right here* so I hadn't nearly jumped out of my skin?

I said, with a calm I didn't feel, 'You scared the life out of me. What are you doing here, Sergio?'

'I came to check on you,' he said in that soft, sexy voice. 'I wanted to make sure you were all right, that nothing had happened to you out here by yourself. Are you OK, Lucie?'

He had sneaked up behind me only a few yards from the spot where Parker had died. As Bobby said, it was an intimate crime, not some random killing by a stranger. Whoever poisoned Parker was almost certainly someone he knew, maybe standing as close to him as Sergio was to me right now.

Sergio knew he'd unnerved me. All right, he'd scared me. What I didn't understand was *why*.

The crime-scene tape swirled and twisted like party streamers in a stray gust of wind. The landscape had begun to fade to dusky grays and browns, except for the yellow tape that seemed to glow against the dark silhouette of the vines and the darker distant Blue Ridge.

'I'm *fine*,' I said to Sergio. 'Why didn't you say something instead of creeping up on me like that?' I sounded like a cross parent scolding a kid. Plus I'd let him see just how much he'd rattled me.

His smile was melt-your-heart contrite. 'I'm sorry. I didn't mean to frighten you. I know you lost a good friend this morning and I thought maybe you had come to pay your respects, say a prayer for him. I didn't want to intrude.'

I wasn't expecting that.

'How is it that you knew I was here now, but yesterday you didn't know about Parker?'

'Simple. I saw your Jeep through the window when I walked into the kitchen to get myself a drink. Parker left his car over there in the bushes.' He pointed at the grove of trees. 'I never saw it. Anyway, I was certain you'd be out here, so I came to find you, make sure you were . . . well . . . OK.'

'I see.' I believed him, but he still had surprised me. 'Um, thank you.'

'Have you finished what you came to do?'

'I think so. I just wanted to check on . . . everything . . . now that the Sheriff's Office deputies are done with their investigation for the day.'

He gestured toward the cottage. 'In that case, perhaps you would join me for a drink? I was about to open a bottle of wine – a good bottle of Barolo. Mia isn't home . . . I doubt she'll be here for a while. She's putting in a lot of hours on that commission at Mon Repos. It would be nice to have company instead of drinking alone. Besides, you and I don't really know each other very well.'

If he was propositioning me – and I wouldn't put it past him – he'd dressed it up nicely and tied it with a respectable bow. Mia not being home much, him tired of being alone, and the two of us getting to know each other. An innocent invitation to be taken at face value.

Or maybe not.

Before I could reply, my phone dinged with a text. I pulled it out of my pocket. Quinn.

Didn't take long. Bobby's done. Meet you at home for a drink? Everything ok?

When I looked up, Sergio gave me a knowing look. 'You can't stay,' he said. I couldn't tell if he sounded disappointed or matter-of-fact.

'I really can't,' I said. 'I need to get home. Bobby Noland, who's in charge of the investigation into Parker's death, questioned our workers just now. Some of the guys were pretty freaked out because of their immigrant status. That text was from Quinn; he's going to fill me in on how it went. I'm worried that not everyone will come back tomorrow.'

I texted back. *Talking to Sergio. Leaving soon.*

'That wouldn't be good,' he said.

'No. They have families, kids. They're scared. I don't blame them, but Bobby promised he wouldn't check their status and he keeps his word.'

Sergio held out both hands palms up and shrugged *whatever*, as if he doubted the veracity of Bobby keeping his word. 'Maybe he won't say anything this time, but you don't know what it's like to be scared of cops, to try to be invisible to anyone who can send you home, even a neighbor who makes a phone call.'

'And you do?'

'There was a time I wasn't exactly here legally, you might say.'

Not exactly legal. Was that like sort of being a virgin?

Either way, it *was* news. I wondered if Mia knew. Or why he'd admitted that fact to me. 'Really? How did you fix your dilemma?'

He gave me a cryptic look. 'Someone did me a favor.'

I'd bet my life the 'someone' was a woman and I'd bet she married him. The gleam in his eye was a dead giveaway.

Before I could ask him to explain, he said, 'I'll walk you to your car. And I guess I'll have to drink that Barolo by myself.'

'Rain check?' I said. 'You're right. We really should get to know each other.'

He gave me a sly smile that was part dare, part challenge. He'd put out the hook; I'd taken the bait.

Mia had kept her time in New York a well-guarded secret. Eli and I knew almost nothing except the carefully curated people and events she chose to share.

My sister's parting words to us on her way out the door had been blunt to the point of rudeness. She wanted to make it on her own as an artist, she wanted to start her life over again, and she wanted to go some place where no one knew who she was. In other words: *butt out.*

From what we could gather, the new plan hadn't worked out so well and she'd usually call when she was crashing on the couch of some semi-stranger or housesitting for people who were out of town. Otherwise she had no fixed address, just a PO box. I sent her money because I didn't want her sleeping in her car – or someone else's. I think Eli did, too.

Finally, she straightened out, went to art school, got a job in a New York gallery and started getting her life in order again. One day about a month ago she turned up on the doorstep with Sergio and said, 'Hi, Lucie, I'm home. And I've brought a friend.'

As if she'd been out for the afternoon and came back with a dinner guest. No further explanation had been forthcoming. It hadn't taken long for her to get a job at The Artful Fox, followed soon after by Harry offering her the well-paid commission at Mon Repos.

'Harry Delacroix is putting a lot of pressure on Mia to finish that mural in the next few weeks,' I said to Sergio. 'I'm sure once she's done you'll see her more often.'

'I hope so,' he said. 'As for Harry . . . do you know her well?'

'I've known her all my life. Why?'

'No reason. She's a woman who knows exactly what she wants and does whatever she needs to do to get it, don't you think?'

Harry had seemed more than a little interested in the devastatingly good-looking Sergio when we spoke yesterday. Did he mean that she had made a play for him? Third divorce in the rear-view, free as a bird once again. That would be just like

Harry. The fact that Sergio was living with Mia would only make it a more interesting challenge.

'I do. But I'm sure you met a lot of Harrys in New York,' I said. 'Especially in the business you're in.'

He gave me a surprised sideways glance. 'You're right,' he said. 'She's not my first Harry.'

I said, as if I'd just thought of it, 'Parker mentioned that he thought he knew you, and that you two had met when he was living in New York. A connection with an art gallery, perhaps?'

Sergio's forehead creased in a frown. Then he shook his head. 'If we did meet, I'm surprised he would remember me. I'm sure I would remember meeting Parker Lord.'

'You don't know him?'

'No. Since Mia and I moved here, I heard about him, of course. But we never crossed paths,' he said. 'I'm really sorry he's dead, Lucie. Mia told me he was very close to you and your family.'

'He was. Someone poisoned him, Sergio. Bobby Noland is certain it's someone Parker knew.'

Sergio shoved his hands in his jeans pockets and shrugged as if that were no surprise. 'Since I have been here, I have learned what a small town this is. Everyone knows everything about each other. Especially that woman who owns the General Store.'

He didn't sound as if he'd warmed to Thelma Johnson's unique charm and her talent for ferreting out information from any handsome stranger who wandered into her store as if it were her God-given duty.

'You mean Thelma.'

'I do,' he said.

'She takes some getting used to, but she's got a good heart.'

He smiled, but there wasn't much warmth in it. 'So what you told me is that the killer is one of you – a friend or a neighbor.'

Had I?

'Bobby said it was someone *Parker* knew. And Parker knew a lot of people. It doesn't necessarily mean whoever killed him is someone who lives in Atoka or Middleburg.' I gave him a challenging look. 'It could be someone from his past, when he lived in New York, for example.'

'Do you really believe that?' A dangerous little current crackled through his words. He stopped walking abruptly and faced me. I nearly stumbled into him and he put both hands on my shoulders to steady me, gripping me hard. 'No, Lucie, I did not kill him. I already told you I never met him. He was mistaken if he thought he knew me.'

'Pardon?' I had just poked a hornet's nest. He was mad.

'You did everything but ask outright if I killed Parker Lord,' he went on. 'I thought I'd save you some trouble.'

He had given me as good an opening as I'd ever get. Mia wasn't around; it was just the two of us.

'No one knows anything about you, Sergio, about your past. Who you are, where you've been, what you've done. Including my sister. Why did you two leave New York? Any artist in his or her right mind wants to be there. Or London or Paris. Not here, fifty miles outside Washington, D.C.'

He gave me an enigmatic smile and I knew what came next would be a smoke-and-mirrors version of the truth. 'Mia wanted to come home. She said she missed everyone, missed Atoka.'

Not too likely. When Mia left she made it clear she wanted to shed herself of Atoka the way a snake sheds a dead skin. She was done. Finished.

A car, driving too fast, turned down the cul-de-sac leading to the two cottages. A moment later it screeched to an abrupt stop on the dirt-and-gravel driveway and a car door slammed.

'That's Mia's car,' Sergio said. 'Something's wrong.'

He took off running. I followed as fast as I could but I couldn't keep up with him. Once, he glanced back over his shoulder, aware he was leaving me behind, but he didn't slow down or wait for me.

By the time I reached the two of them, his arms were wrapped around Mia and she was shaking. When she saw me, she broke away and ran to me, flinging herself into my arms and burying her head on my shoulder.

'What is it, baby?' I held her tight, stroking her long blonde hair with one hand. 'What happened?'

'I didn't do it,' she said.

'What are you talking about?'

'I didn't kill him.'

'Kill who?' A panicked feeling bloomed in my chest and started to rise into my throat. She didn't mean . . . '*Parker?* Mia, are you talking about Parker?'

She nodded and choked back a sob.

Dear God, Bobby thought my sister had murdered Parker. My mind reeled.

Sergio sounded incredulous. 'Of course you didn't kill him, *cara mia.*'

'Bobby thinks I did. Or at least he suspects me.' Her words were muffled through tears. 'He took me down to the Sheriff's Office and questioned me. He said I could have a lawyer if I wanted one, but I told him I didn't do anything so I didn't need a lawyer.'

Jesus Lord. Bobby told her she ought to get a lawyer and Mia said thanks-but-no-thanks. The right answer would have been 'let me make a call'.

Sergio's eyes met mine above Mia's head. He looked furious. I felt numb.

'Why does Bobby think you did it?' I asked. This wasn't good if he'd questioned her officially and brought up the subject of needing counsel.

Mia lifted her head from my shoulder. Her face was tear-stained, her eyes were red, and her mascara had left two black streaks on her cheeks. 'He found a bottle of eye drops next to my paint brushes when he came by Mon Repos this afternoon. He confiscated it and said I needed to talk to him at the station in Leesburg. He didn't handcuff me or anything, but I had to go with a deputy in one of the patrol cars.'

Sergio's eyes were black as coal, a quiet fury brewing in them. 'You should have called me, *mi amore.* You should not have gone there alone.'

'I didn't *do* anything,' she said. 'It's some huge misunder-standing. I figured Bobby would realize it was a mistake and it would be over. I could leave. I mean, Jesus, Lucie, it's *Bobby.* He *knows* me. He's known me since I was a baby.'

'If the only reason he suspects you is because he found a bottle of eye drops, that's crazy. You're not the only one who uses them,' I said. 'Besides, he has to realize you do a lot of close work, painting in light that isn't always great. It's understandable why you'd need something for your eyes, for eye strain. Anyway, you didn't even see Parker yesterday, did you?'

I was trying to rationalize this whole thing. Mia was right. It was a mistake.

Instead she nodded, looking miserable. 'I did see him. He came by to take a look at the mural when he was visiting Cricket. We talked for a few minutes and he told me he liked what I was doing, told me he was a big Alphonse Mucha fan. Then he left.' She shrugged. 'He was fine, by the way. Perfectly fine.'

Well, that was a game-changer. Mia's name on the list of people who had spent time with Parker yesterday. OK, so she had means – the eye drops – and opportunity, because he stopped by to see her. Didn't it matter to Bobby that Parker had sought Mia out, not the other way around? And what could he possibly believe her motive was?

'Did Bobby say why he thought you might have poisoned Parker?'

'No,' she said.

'He couldn't say because you don't have a reason,' Sergio said. 'So case closed.'

My sister turned her enormous blue eyes on her boyfriend. 'He's going to look for one, *amore*. He's going to check me out.'

'When he does,' I said, 'he'll reach the logical conclusion. He's not going to find anything and it's over.'

Mia flashed a panicked look at Sergio whose face was as impassive and expressionless as a sphinx.

The penny dropped.

'Wait a minute,' I said, my glance flicking between the two of them. 'Is something going on? Bobby's *not* going to find anything. Right?'

'No.' Mia sounded breathless. 'I mean, right.'

'Mia didn't kill Parker,' Sergio said, in a flat monotone that gave me the shivers. 'So you're right, Lucie. Bobby won't find anything incriminating. Nothing.'

My sister nodded, like a marionette whose head was being

pulled up and down by a puppeteer's strings. Sergio's strings. She was letting him run the show.

When Bobby started digging into my sister's time in New York, he wasn't going to turn up anything that pointed to her as Parker Lord's killer. I was one hundred percent certain of that.

But he was going to find something. If the look Sergio and Mia had just exchanged was any indication of how worried, how *frightened* she was about what he would discover, then it was something big.

She might not be guilty of murder, but she and Sergio had another secret that they didn't want anyone to uncover. Now she was under a microscope in a murder investigation.

And she was terrified.

So was I.

ELEVEN

Mia finally calmed down from her hysterics, but that was probably because shock was setting in. Sergio swept her up in his arms like she was a child and started walking toward the cottage. I watched them leave, aware they had forgotten about me entirely.

'Hey,' I said.

Sergio stopped and half-turned around.

'I'll take care of her. Go home, Lucie,' he said. 'Quinn is waiting for you and you have enough on your mind as it is. I can handle this.'

My sister said nothing, her head lolling on his shoulder, as limp as a ragdoll's.

I wondered what *this* was. Because I didn't think he was talking about whether or not Mia was guilty of murder. She wasn't. I knew it, Sergio knew it, and I was pretty damn sure Bobby knew it, too. What Bobby might uncover when he started to check out her story was another matter entirely.

Sergio sounded calm and composed, but he was giving an alarm-bells-going-off vibe and his eyes didn't quite meet mine.

'Sure,' I said. 'I'll be going.'

At least he would have someone to drink that Barolo with after all. My sister looked like she was badly in need of a drink or three.

For that matter, so was I.

Dinner was sort of a mess. Persia had left everything ready for us to put together a *salade Niçoise*, but I didn't feel like eating and a liquid meal would have been fine with me after everything that had happened today. Finding Parker dead in the vineyard; EMTs and Sheriff's Office deputies swarming all over the place; whatever 'thing' was going on between Mia and Sergio; our guys freaked out because Bobby needed to know where they'd been and if they'd seen anything yesterday. And the overarching question, the key to everything: Who murdered Parker Lord?

I had been letting the calls on my mobile go to voicemail all afternoon unless I knew who it was – although I was ducking most of them as well. When I had walked in the front door of Highland House, the answering machine on our landline – yes, we were still conventional enough to have one – beeped at me from the small demi-lune table in the foyer. One look at the display and I saw ten missed calls and seven messages.

Quinn met me with a whiskey and a kiss, so I knew it was going to be one of those nights. 'They're all from media people,' he said, nodding at the phone as it emitted another beep. 'I listened to two of the messages and scrolled through the rest of the numbers. What do you want to do about them?'

I took the glass he handed me and said, 'Right now, nothing.'

'The six o'clock news will be on in a couple of minutes,' he said. 'Want to watch?'

'Sure,' I said. 'Might as well get it over with. I haven't seen Pippa O'Hara since the Sheriff's Office came out with the statement that Parker was murdered. She's like those reporters on the Weather Channel. Nothing spins them up like a good natural disaster – a Category Five hurricane, a derecho, snowmageddon . . . whatever. Pippa's going to be all over this like it's the Second Coming or the Rapture.'

Quinn put an arm around my shoulder and pulled me to him. 'We could go straight to dinner, skip the news.'

'No, then I'll wonder what she said about Parker. About him being found here.' I made a face like I'd eaten something bad and needed to spit. 'And about me, as vain as that sounds.'

'It doesn't sound vain, it sounds like self-preservation,' he said. 'Go turn on the TV. I'm going to get rid of the beeps.'

Pippa had the lead story on the local news at six. Hyped as I'd expected, including a cut of me telling her to go camp out at the Medical Examiner's office if she wanted to know time and cause of death and saying 'no comment' to her other questions. In light of the subsequent news that someone had killed Parker, I looked and sounded like an idiot.

I buried my head on Quinn's shoulder and groaned. 'I hate her. She spoke to me before Win said Parker had been murdered. She's making it sound as if I had something to hide.'

Sure enough.

Pippa was standing at the entrance to the vineyard where I'd seen her this morning, our sign clearly visible in the background. She brushed a windblown strand of flaming-red hair off her face and looked directly into the camera, as though she were about to report breaking news concerning two items Moses had brought with him when he came down from that mountain.

'Tonight there are more questions than answers about what happened to Parker Lord out there . . .' She paused to turn and point dramatically behind her. 'Among the vines of Montgomery Estate Vineyard in the tiny hamlet of Atoka. And why no one reported him missing for an entire night. Here in the heart of Virginia's wealthy horse and hunt country, among the gated old-money estates, exclusive thoroughbred farms, and expensive vineyards where a bottle of last year's Cabernet Sauvignon can set you back forty dollars or more, someone is harboring a secret. Someone knows the *truth* about what happened to Parker Lord. How long will it take until the Loudoun County Sheriff's Office finds that person? Because people are *scared*. They want answers. Keep it here for the latest. Back to you in the studio.'

'My God, that woman would throw her own mother off a cliff if she were standing in the way of a story.' Quinn pointed the remote at the television and clicked it off. 'I thought hamlets *were* tiny. That's why they're hamlets. Smaller than a village, bigger than a campsite. Am I right?'

'You are. Clearly she needs an editor. And some do-over time at J-school, less time in drama class.'

'Why does she get away with crap like that?'

It was a rhetorical question, but I answered anyway. 'Because sensationalizing the news attracts viewers, which means better ratings, which means they get to brag about being the most watched local news station in D.C., Maryland, and Virginia – the DMV, as people like her call it now – which means more advertising revenue, which makes their bosses and shareholders happy.' I finished my whiskey and set the empty glass on the coffee table. 'We go over this every time we torment ourselves and watch her.'

'There oughta be a law.'

'Against what?'

'I don't know. Whatever it is she does. Plus that dig about forty-dollar Cab.' He stood up and held out his hand, pulling me to my feet. 'Let's go put that salad together. I'm starved and you need to eat, too.'

Over dinner we talked about Bobby questioning our crew. Quinn said everyone cooperated, but no one liked it. Not to mention none of them had seen anything or anyone. Even having a Spanish-speaking deputy translating hadn't helped.

'Do you think they'll all be back tomorrow?' I asked, though I knew the answer.

He recited like a mantra, 'Sure, as long as ICE isn't there with a pair of matching bracelets when they get home.'

'I wish we could do something.'

'We employ them, we do what we can, baby. We can't save them all, even though I know you want to try. At least thanks to you they get free medical care here off the grid when the doc stops by.'

It had happened more or less spontaneously a few months ago after one of the Hispanic workers at a neighboring vineyard was wrongly accused of murder. Antonio told me I needed to do something about it – right an egregious wrong – or no one would work for me any more. Gun to the head. Then he told me that Miguel's newborn baby was sick and both parents were too scared to see a doctor after the whole terrifying false accusation nightmare. So I asked Sasha, Eli's fiancée, who was a physical therapist, if she knew someone who could help.

She sent a doctor friend who got the baby antibiotics and then began stopping by one evening a month after her hospital job to check up on our day laborers and their families. Before long, they were bringing friends who were sick. That's when I learned a lot more about the poverty and appalling conditions among the immigrant community – especially the ones who didn't have jobs or steady work. What really broke my heart: one pair of shoes shared among the children, so the kids took turns going to school. Then there was sleeping in their cars – a whole family – and hoping no one found out. Sasha's doctor friend wouldn't let us pay her for her extracurricular visits, but she did let us cover the cost of the medicine and supplies she used. And Quinn and I bought shoes for every child we learned about who needed them.

We cleaned up in silence after dinner.

'I have an idea,' he said when we were finished. 'Let's go outside for a while. I'm wound up after today. We could do some stargazing. It's a really clear night.'

'I don't know if I'm up for it. Maybe another time.'

'Aw, come on,' he said. 'You'll feel better. We can take the rest of the bottle of dinner wine and finish it. Besides, Betelgeuse is still dim and no one can figure out what's going on, whether it's getting ready to go supernova or not.' He frowned, clearly fretting over Betelgeuse as if this were a problem he could do something about.

I smiled and relented. 'Well, since it's Betelgeuse, I guess I could go out with you for a bit. But I'm leaving my phone in the house. I can't take another phone call or text or email tonight.'

Quinn pulled his phone out of his pocket and set it on the kitchen counter. I placed mine next to his.

'Sounds like a good idea,' he said. 'You get our coats. I'll get the wine and two glasses.'

One of the many things that fascinated me about my fiancé was his interest – actually, his passion – for anything to do with the night sky. Years ago when my father hired him to be our winemaker, Quinn brought a telescope from California and asked Leland if he could set it up by our summerhouse, where there was a panoramic view of our land and the Piedmont valley all the way to the lovely, layered Blue Ridge.

Quinn told me once that he'd been called in to see a guidance counselor when he was in middle school because there was some concern about his behavior, maybe problems at home, apparently not getting enough sleep. One of the first questions she asked him was 'What's keeping you up at night?'

Quinn answered her literally. 'The stars,' he'd said, and that was the end of the meeting.

Even before he moved in with me, we had developed a habit of going out to the summerhouse after dinner where we'd left

two Adirondack chairs that faced the valley with its wide open
second-star-to-the-right-and-straight-on-til-morning view of the
sky. There was light pollution, but at least we were facing west,
not east toward the bazillion lights that lit up D.C. and the
northern Virginia suburbs, turning the entire area into one giant
blob of incandescent orange if you happened to look down from
the window of an airplane or maybe from the International
Space Station. But here, overlooking the valley, it was dark
enough for good stargazing.

Each time we came out here he always taught me something
new and I discovered that he had endless patience and a way
of explaining complex subjects so they were easy for a neophyte
like me to understand. If we could have had children – an
impossibility because of my accident – he would have made a
wonderful father. And that broke my heart if I let myself think
about it.

So instead I focused on learning to identify the constellations,
the planets, their moons, comets, and the seasonal astronomical
phenomena like the Pleiades in summer or the Geminids in
January. When there was an eclipse, he always insisted that we
drive out to the middle of nowhere – usually a field – for a
better view. And on nights with a special full moon – a super-
moon, a blue moon, a blood moon – he wanted to watch it rise
so we went early. It was worth it to see the moon so *huge*, so
enormous, just hanging there on the horizon close enough that
I could almost reach out and touch it. Then the next time I
looked as we were on the way home it would be up in the sky
where it belonged, back to normal moon-size again.

Betelgeuse, the reason for tonight's stargazing session, was
a ruddy red star in the constellation of Orion the hunter, located
where the hunter's shoulder would be. It was also one of the
brightest stars in the night sky, so when Quinn told me a few
weeks ago that it had dimmed enough to change the hunter's
appearance I knew it was a big deal. Since then he had been
reading about it on the geeky astronomy blogs he followed to
learn about any developments: specifically whether this time
the reason the star had gone dim was a harbinger that it was
about to die.

While Quinn set up the telescope, I got two quilts from the

summerhouse, wrapping myself in one of them like a swaddling blanket. When I came outside, he was looking through the eyepiece.

'Damn. It's dim. *Really* dim,' he said. 'I just read that it might have something to do with Betelgeuse starting out life as a cannibal.'

'A *what*?'

He straightened up. 'A cannibal star. Maybe the reason Betelgeuse is so big and has so much energy is because it ate another star. A long time ago when it was first forming, of course. They just floated that theory at the last meeting of the American Astronomical Society.'

He really did follow everything and anything that happened in the astronomy world. 'Does this mean it's going to explode?'

He shrugged. 'Hard to say. It's also a variable star, which means it brightens and dims in cycles. This time just seems different. It's bloated and definitely at the end of its life. The sky won't be the same without it. Come over here and take a look.'

I reached for the end of my quilt so I wouldn't trip and joined him. 'You can hardly see it,' I said after a moment.

'Exactly. That's what's got everyone wondering what's next.'

'What happens if it does explode? Will we know about it?'

'You bet we will. Anyone in the northern hemisphere will get a front-row seat.' He picked up his wine glass from the arm of the Adirondack chair and drank. 'Betelgeuse is so huge that if it exchanged places with the sun it would swallow Mercury, Venus, Earth, Mars, the asteroid belt, a couple of spacecraft, and maybe Jupiter. Saturn would suddenly be a tropical destination. You would definitely not miss the explosion, though it would take about six million years before any splattered star guts would reach us. And even then, the sun would probably protect us from that happening.'

Splattered star guts.

'I find that oddly reassuring and I hope it's not just because I know I won't be around.' Some good news, sort of, on an otherwise awful day.

He grinned and pulled a Cohiba out of the pocket of his flannel shirt, a gift from a client who loved our wine and had brought a box back from a recent trip to Cuba. He had presented a couple to Quinn during a wine-tasting session a few weeks ago.

We sat in our chairs, me with my quilt twined around me; Quinn, who is part polar bear, with his draped across his lap. He lit his cigar and puffed until the tip glowed and the sweet, woody scent drifted into the night air, curling around us.

'Here,' he said, picking up the wine bottle, 'you finish the wine. There's not much left.'

I held out my glass and he filled it. I drank in silence as he smoked.

Finally I said – because it had been driving me nuts all evening – 'Who do you think did it?'

We weren't talking about Betelgeuse any more.

'I don't know. If it's someone Parker knew who spent time with him yesterday, I don't like any of the possibilities, because it's someone we know.'

'Including me.'

'*Ex*cluding you. You didn't do it.'

'Bobby's not ready to cross me off his list.'

'That's what he says. But he knows you didn't do it, either.'

'So who does that leave?' I ticked the names off on my fingers. 'Cricket. Mia. Ash.'

'There could be somebody else we don't know about.'

'There could.'

I needed to rationalize this because that's what I was hoping had happened. Maybe a stranger showed up, someone who really *was* angry about what Parker wrote in his book or said during some television interview, angry about those horrible end-of-the-world Armageddon predictions that were scaring the crap out of everyone. Or maybe someone who worked for a company whose stock was taking a nose dive because what they did or produced was part of the reason scientists had just moved the Doomsday Clock one minute closer to midnight. And Parker had pointed the bony finger of indignation at that company or industry.

Quinn eyed me over his cigar. 'We both know if there is another person, he or she won't turn out to be some random, unknown stranger. I'm afraid it'll still be someone we know.'

'Then we're back to who did it, aren't we?'

'Did Parker see Gabriel yesterday?'

'I don't know,' I said. 'He certainly has a motive.'

Quinn blew a smoke ring. 'The best. But if Parker didn't see him, then he's not on the list.'

'What about Sergio?' I said.

'You think Sergio killed Parker? Based on what?'

'Parker told me Sergio's name sounded familiar and that he thought maybe he knew him from when he was living in New York. But Sergio claimed he never met Parker. He told me he would have remembered meeting Parker Lord because he was, well . . . Parker Lord.'

'And?'

'What if he's lying? What if he did see Parker when he drove past the cottage yesterday and they reconnected? Say Sergio invited him in for a drink – just like he invited me today – and then he dumped the eye drops in Parker's drink when he wasn't looking or when he went to the bathroom,' I said.

Quinn's cigar glowed while he considered what I'd just said. Then he shook his head. 'You don't have proof one way or the other. Not to mention no evidence. And what's his motive? Just because the guy might have a sketchy past doesn't make him a killer.'

'I know that.' I drained my wine glass, irrationally irritated at Quinn for poking more holes in what was already a Swiss-cheese theory. 'But we've already established that Mia uses eye drops when her eyes bother her from painting so there's bound to be a bottle of Visine or Murine or whatever in the cottage somewhere.'

'Even if it's true, Sergio says he was by himself, working in his studio and listening to music with headphones on so he didn't hear or see anything.'

I said with stubborn insistence, 'I still think it's possible he could have done it. He could be lying.'

'Your sister's boyfriend is a cold-blooded murderer and a liar. Based on no proof and no evidence. That's what you're saying.'

I didn't like it when he put it like that.

But, yes, I suppose that was exactly what I was saying.

TWELVE

For a second night I didn't sleep well, tossing and turning, dreaming of enormous bottles of eye drops floating in the air, zooming around like mini rockets, and Parker somehow able to talk to me before he lost consciousness and died. He'd managed to tell me that he knew who poisoned him and was on the verge of whispering a name in my ear when he gasped and collapsed. I'd tried to revive him, but it was too late.

'Lucie, wake up.'

Someone was shaking me and the image of Parker lying dead on the ground dissolved to blackness. I opened my eyes. Quinn was leaning over me.

'Are you all right, baby? You were thrashing around, talking in your sleep.'

I half sat up on my elbows. My heart was pounding and my mouth tasted like an army had marched through it. I ran a hand through my hair, which felt wild and disheveled. 'I'm sorry. I think it was a bad dream.'

'It's OK.' He sat up and pulled me to him.

'What was I saying?'

'I don't know. You weren't very coherent. I think some of it was in French,' he said, 'but you were talking about Parker.'

Parker. 'He was going to tell me who killed him, but he died before he could give me the name.'

Quinn had been rubbing my hair with his thumb, smoothing it down, a comforting, calming gesture. He stopped and said, 'Try not to think about that, sweetheart. Why don't you try to go back to sleep?'

'I can't. I'm going to go downstairs and make myself a cup of tea.'

He twisted around so he could look at the lighted dial of the clock on the nightstand. 'It's three fifteen.'

'I won't be long.' I threw off the covers and found my robe and slippers.

'You're coming back to bed?'

'Of course,' I said. 'Go to sleep, darling. I'll be back soon.'
Downstairs in the kitchen I made a cup of chamomile tea,
found Quinn's heavy coat, and went outside on the veranda as
I'd done the night before. This time there was no fox being
strangled and no clouds strafing the sky, which, instead, was
clear and star-studded. The garden was full of dark unsubstantial
shapes, except for a few bushes and treetops that were silver-
tipped by starlight. Silent and peaceful.

Someone had murdered Parker Lord and he had died here,
on my land, at my vineyard. Until his killer was found, I didn't
feel peaceful, *wouldn't* be at peace, until that person was
brought to justice.

But I also knew that justice for Parker could come at a painful
price; in fact, it probably would. Because Bobby was right that
the murderer was someone Parker knew.

And although I'd told Sergio that didn't necessarily mean
the killer lived in Atoka or Middleburg, I knew the odds were
good it did.

The murderer was one of us.

I threw the rest of my tea in an azalea bush next to the
veranda and went inside and back to bed with Quinn.

Josie Wilde called my mobile on Wednesday morning while
Quinn and I were sitting at the kitchen table finishing breakfast. Yogurt, fruit, and granola for me and a homemade
breakfast burrito for him. I'd gotten up first so I made the
coffee. I heard some under-the-breath muttering about dirty
dishwater earlier when Quinn poured himself a cup, so I gave
up, logged into our wedding registry, and added 'coffeemaker'
to the list.

Life really is too short.

I put my phone on speaker so both of us could hear
Josie. The first thing she said was, 'The managing editor from
the *Progress* just called and asked if I'd write an appreciation
of Parker that would run this weekend. I can't believe I'm doing
this, y'all, and that he's dead – I'm in complete shock.'

The Daily Progress was Charlottesville's newspaper; Parker
had taught landscape design years ago at the University of

Virginia before he became famous and they still claimed him as one of their own.

'I know,' I said. 'It still seems surreal.'

'You found him,' she said. 'Jesus, Lord, Lucie. That must have been horrible.'

'It was.'

'The *Progress* ran the story on the front page, including a photo of your vineyard and one of Parker standing in front of a hillside of blooming azaleas at the Arboretum in D.C.,' she said. 'What was he doing at your place, anyway? The article didn't say.'

'Looking at the dying vines in the Merlot block as a favor to me when he collapsed – the ones you're coming to help us with.'

'I was gonna come up and take a look at them tomorrow,' she said. 'Maybe I ought to hold off.'

'Part of the area is a crime scene,' Quinn said, 'although it probably won't be for long. Parker was poisoned somewhere else, not where Lucie found him. It took time for the tetrahydrozoline to do enough damage to kill him. He just happened to be here when it happened.'

Josie made a noise like air leaving a tire. 'I can't even imagine . . .'

'Josie,' I said, 'the workers don't want to go out to that part of the vineyard any more. They say it's *mala suerte* – bad luck – because someone died there. Eventually we need to have a ceremony where he died – a blessing of some sort so Parker's spirit will find peace. But I also don't want the guys to be so completely spooked right now that they won't go near the place.'

'What are you saying?' she asked.

'I'd appreciate it if you'd still come tomorrow. Whatever is killing those vines could very well infect others if it hasn't done so already. The sooner we can figure out what it is and how to stop it, the better. And we're going to need our crew out there helping.'

'All right,' she said. 'In that case I'll see you tomorrow. The Sheriff's Office didn't put all your dying vines off limits, did they?'

'No,' Quinn said. 'Just a couple of rows.'

'Parker wondered whether whatever was attacking them might be coming from a nearby plant or tree that was the host for a vector or a fungus,' I said.

Her sigh sounded heavy and sad. 'I'm really going to miss him,' she said. 'He had such a good mind for figuring out any problem you brought him – grapevines, plants, bushes, trees, flowers. And he was a brilliant landscape designer. All that talent gone now. He was responsible for so many beautiful gardens.'

'The last time I saw him he came over to drop off plans for our wedding garden,' I told her and then realized what I'd just said. 'I meant, the last time I saw him *alive.*'

'Any idea who might have done it?' she asked.

'No good ones,' Quinn said. 'Lucie, Cricket Delacroix, Ash, and Mia all saw him the day he died, so in Bobby Noland's book that makes all of them suspects. Which, of course, is ridiculous.'

'Who's Mia?'

'My sister. You haven't met her yet,' I said and decided not to bring up the eye drops and Bobby questioning her down at the station in Leesburg.

Mia didn't kill Parker. *She didn't.*

'What about Gabriel Seely?' Josie was asking.

'What about him?' Quinn said.

'Well, they had a huge fight.'

'Gabriel and Parker?' I said. 'Parker saw Gabriel on Monday as well? How do you know?'

'Gabriel told me. I called him after he left a message on my phone asking about boxwood blight. That stuff spreads like wildfire. He was still furious with Parker.'

Quinn and I exchanged looks. 'When did this happen?' he asked.

'That they saw each other? It happened at the Delacroixes' home. Gabriel came by Mon Repos to drop off some plants Cricket had purchased – he likes to take care of her, give her that extra attention. I guess she also asked Parker to stop by and the two of them ran into each other,' Josie said. 'It didn't go so great.'

Well, well. Add another name to Bobby's list, a potent possibility. Except I didn't want it to be Gabriel Seely, either.

'And then,' Josie went on, 'there's Ash.'

'What about him?' I asked.

'He was an investor in Gabriel's research project,' she said. 'I heard about it from friends at New Dominion U. Apparently he was trying to keep it on the down-low because of potential conflict of interest issues, but he shelled out a big chunk of change when Gabriel told him about the possible return on investment.'

'Parker knew Ash was involved with Gabriel's project,' I said. 'He mentioned it to me the other day. Although he didn't bring up the fact that Ash had invested a lot of money.'

'Interesting,' she said. 'In spite of Parker knowing about Ash investing in Gabriel's project it still didn't stop Parker from writing that piece in the *Trib* calling out Gabriel. From what my friends told me you could hear doors slamming at NDU and the sucking sound of money drying up as soon as that article came out on Monday.'

'Ash is going to lose what he invested,' Quinn said.

'Well, yeah. Especially if NDU shuts down Gabriel's project,' Josie said. 'Not to mention the fact that Gabriel may face disciplinary action down the road.'

'*Why?*' I said. 'Why would he do something so stupid? Gabriel's brilliant. He had a research fellowship at that seed bank in England, the place that's affiliated with Kew Gardens. They're trying to capture samples of every seed on the planet and store them in underground freezers before the species becomes extinct. I think he got the idea for the NDU project from work he was doing in England. Gabriel didn't need to do something dumb like faking his results.'

'You'd be surprised,' Josie said. 'There's a lot of pressure on researchers to come up with new developments that will get published in a big journal and get a scientist's name – and the lab's – out there. Gabriel's only human. Plus he probably needed a big win, something sexy, to attract more money to keep going.'

'And then Parker called him out,' Quinn said. 'Do you really think Ash would have been angry enough over what he did to Gabriel to kill his own husband?'

'I don't know,' Josie said. 'You never know what someone will do, what triggers a person to do something in a moment of extreme anger or outrage, something you wouldn't believe they're capable of. I love Ash – and I know he loved Parker. You've got to wonder what Parker's motives were for writing that column. But Ash has a temper, too, so who knows? Except I don't want it to be him.'

'I don't want it to be him, either,' I said.

'Same,' Quinn said.

We fell silent for a moment. Then Josie said, 'On that happy note I'll see you two tomorrow, say around ten? I'll leave C'ville after the rush hour traffic clears out.'

After she hung up I poured another cup of coffee and offered one to Quinn who said in the sweetest possible way that he was totally caffeinated. I almost told him about adding a second coffeepot to our registry.

Josie had given us another name – Gabriel's – that would most definitely be on Bobby's list. She had also given Ash an even stronger motive for murder: a substantial investment in Gabriel's research project. If I were Bobby, I'd be looking closely at the two of them. Which might make him shift his focus away from Mia, who *didn't* have a motive.

Bobby always said that there but for the grace of God go any of us: the nicest, sanest, most normal people in the world can – under extreme circumstances – be provoked to do something they swear on their mother's grave they would never do. A flash of anger in an unguarded moment that turns violent although you never meant it to go too far, never wanted to cross the line, because, honestly, you're a good person, a law-abiding person, OK maybe a speeding ticket or two, but nothing more egregious than that.

It wasn't supposed to end with someone dead.

It was an *accident*.

If that's what happened – if Parker's death was a tragic, unintended, irrational accident – then maybe it was second-degree murder or 'only' manslaughter, and not first-degree murder.

Either way someone would do jail time for this. And lives would be destroyed.

THIRTEEN

After breakfast I drove into Middleburg to get cash to pay the day laborers while Quinn went over to the barrel room to talk to the guys about pruning the north vineyard. My business at Blue Ridge Federal didn't take long; the bank was a block from The Artful Fox.

I already knew I was going to drop by to say hi to Willow Harper. The bank errand had been an excuse to come into town and, to be honest, what I really wanted to do was check up on my sister, who would *not* like knowing she was being checked up on. But it would give me a chance to see how she was doing after Bobby's Q&A session at the Sheriff's Office that had so unraveled her last night. And maybe try again to ask her about the elusive Sergio when he was certain not to be around.

The Artful Fox was located at the beginning of the commercial part of East Washington Street, which was Middleburg's main street and became West Washington after the lone traffic light a block and a half away. Outside of town Washington Street, named for George who had been a friend of Middleburg's founder, became Route 50 again, or Mosby's Highway, as everyone around here called it. That name had been bestowed upon it in honor of Colonel John Singleton Mosby, the legendary Civil War commander better and more famously known as the Gray Ghost. Middleburg may have begun its existence during America's colonial days and our streets named after the Founding Fathers, but it was the Ghost and his daring raids a century later that put this region on the map. Mosby was a Confederate outlier who, along with his band of Partisan Rangers, strafed, terrorized, and generally made life miserable for Union troops by stealing their supplies and horses, as well as keeping them away from Lee's armies in hopes of allowing the Confederates to outmaneuver the boys in blue. To this day people swore they saw the Ghost on moonless nights riding across fields and meadows still looking for Union soldiers.

The Artful Fox was a small two-storey brick building situated in a tiny park – more like a recessed alcove – where a badly tarnished bronze fox watched passersby from a pedestal surrounded by a boxwood hedge and enclosed by a wrought-iron fence. Once upon a time the building had been a bookstore called Books & Crannies; later it became a shoe store, an antique gallery, and a health-juice store.

Sleigh bells hanging on the front door jingled when I pushed it open. The gallery was empty and Sunday-quiet, but immediately footsteps sounded above me as someone clomped down the narrow staircase. The clomping stopped after a moment and Willow Harper appeared.

Parker had said he thought Willow was a bit New Agey and bohemian in her dress and manner, as though she had been stuck in a time warp from the 1970s. Her beauty was startling – she couldn't have been over forty but her hair was silver white, cut in a sleek, glossy pageboy style that brushed her shoulders and a neat fringe of bangs. Her make-up looked as if Morticia Addams' stylist had applied it – blood-red lips, pale skin with not a trace of color on her cheeks, jet-black eyebrows, and dark, smoky eye shadow highlighting long-lashed beautiful violet eyes. Today she wore a couple of small feathers with turquoise beads attached to them that she'd braided into her hair, a pink, yellow, and green tie-dyed tunic over skinny white jeans and Birkenstocks. The look suited her. I'd watched the fiftieth anniversary documentaries about Woodstock, which was my parents' generation, and knew Willow would have fit right in – peace, love, music, maybe a little grass or another drug of choice, and all about experimenting, pushing boundaries, especially as an artist. Her gallery was edgy and a bit outré for Middleburg, which was why it was a surprise to me that she was hosting the Jackie Onassis–Élisabeth Vigée Le Brun exhibit.

At the moment the walls were hung with paintings that were the work of artists I wasn't familiar with: modern oils and graphic collaged canvases of sculpted, textured paint with scraps of newspaper, photographs, string, wire, and other objects I couldn't identify. Some of the art was arresting and intriguing, and I really liked it. Others I couldn't wrap my head around. When Willow found me, I was staring at a large canvas filled with random splatters and blotches.

'That's one of my current favorites,' she said, smiling. 'Do you like it?'

I didn't want to hurt her feelings after she'd said she loved it, but it was one of the ones that didn't do anything for me.

'It's . . . unusual.'

'In other words you hate it.' She grinned when she saw my uncomfortable expression. 'No worries. Art is very personal. One person's masterpiece is another person's where-can-I-recycle-this-thing. If you don't, you don't.'

'OK, I don't. The colors are too muddy for me. It's too sad.' I leaned forward to read what the artist had titled it. '*The Tangled Mind.*'

Willow came over and stood next to me, elbow resting in the palm of her hand, tapping her cheek with a glittery silver fingernail as she took another look at *The Tangled Mind.*

'That's a fair judgment. I can see why you'd say that. But at least you had a strong opinion about it, which is what good art should do. Make you react, make you think.' She eyed me. 'So, since you probably didn't come by to make a purchase, what can I do for you? By the way I heard from Mia this morning. I hope she's feeling better?'

Meaning my sister wasn't here and Willow seemed to think I knew what was going on.

'I, uh, haven't had a chance to talk to her, so I'm not sure.'

'Well, hopefully it's just a twenty-four-hour bug and she'll be fine tomorrow.'

If Mia had called in sick she was probably still flipped out from what had happened yesterday. She wasn't ill; she was playing hooky. Plus it sounded as if Willow knew nothing about Mia being questioned by Bobby in connection with Parker's murder.

'I'm sure it's just a temporary thing.'

'Great. So . . .?' She gave me a bright smile, still waiting for my reply to her original question.

'I was just at the bank and I thought I'd stop by to say hi and see how you're doing getting everything ready for the gala and the exhibit.'

I left out that I'd been hoping to see my sister.

Willow's eyebrows went up. 'Are you kidding me? It's quiet right now but otherwise my phone hasn't stopped ringing. This place is going to be standing-room-only once we open the exhibit to the public.'

'Which is a good thing, right? I mean you're happy you're getting all this publicity and attention when you've practically just opened your doors,' I said. 'Aren't you?'

'Don't get me wrong, it's amazing. But ever since Harry found Jackie's journal and decided she wanted to blow up excerpts and turn them into wall text it's been, like . . . I don't know, open season for paparazzi and journalists. Photographers with cameras that have lenses that could get close-ups of the craters on Mars and reporters wanting to know where Jackie used to live, where did she go fox hunting, where did she buy groceries, did she go to the Catholic church, what patch of ground she walked on like it's a holy, sacred place. Stuff like that. It's insane.'

I thought about Pippa O'Hara ambushing me the other day and her story on the evening news and how I'd come off sounding dumb and uninformed.

'That can go either way,' I said. 'Good or bad.'

'I know. Although however it goes, this exhibit is going to put The Artful Fox on the D.C. art scene radar, that's for sure.'

'Well, then . . . I guess it's good.'

'I'm not complaining. But I'm still the new kid in town, you know. I don't know the local lore, what it was like when Jackie lived here.'

She didn't want to sound dumb, either.

'You could be here for a couple of generations and still be the new kid in town,' I said. 'There are families that have been around since George Washington's cousin sold the town to Leven Powell in 1763.'

'Somehow I guessed that. Plus even though I can claim I grew up in the south, it's South *Brooklyn*. Brooklyn Heights. I already figured out that being a Southerner is more than a sexy drawl, liking sweet tea, and saying "ma'am" or "sir" to your elders. It feels like something you have to be born with – or *to* – not something you can acquire.' She made a mournful face, but grinned to take the sting out of her words. 'Or else it's like being part of a cult.'

I smiled. I wanted to tell her being a non-Southerner around here wasn't as bad as she made it out to be, but she'd landed a couple of zingers – smart, astute observations – that hit home.

'Northern Virginia isn't really the South if you ask some people,' I said. 'Actually, if you ask most people, or everyone who lives any place in the Commonwealth of Virginia *except* here. If those folks had their way, northern Virginia would be annexed by D.C., which is where they think we belong. This region is more like *South-Lite*.'

She laughed. 'OK, but I'm still worried I might have gotten off on the wrong foot with the locals by deciding to host this exhibit. Middleburg doesn't seem to be a town that likes being the epicenter of journalists reporting for *Entertainment Weekly*.'

'We're not,' I said. 'But that's on Harry, not you, when she decided to use Jackie's personal journal as part of the exhibit. Jackie has near-to-sainthood status around here – people still feel really protective toward her.'

'I'm finding that out, too,' Willow said. 'My God, you just have to say "Jackie" and everyone knows who you mean. One name, just like Oprah or Elvis or Madonna.'

'It was like that when she lived here and it's still like that today,' I said. 'A couple of years ago some guy in Richmond found the packing list of clothes Jackie wanted to take on the trip to Dallas – a little piece of paper where she'd written out everything for her personal assistant. The pink Chanel suit was on it, along with clothes she never got to wear. People went crazy when word got out about it – it was so poignant and no one even knew it existed after all these decades. It's in the Kennedy Library in Boston now, tucked away, but there was a fierce debate over whether it should be on display or not. If, after more than fifty years, it was still too raw, too emotional, for people who remember that day.'

Willow looked pained. 'That's why I wish I knew what journal excerpts Harry plans to use for the exhibit. Right now she's keeping it a bigger secret than Donald Trump's tax returns. Though she is publicizing the hell out of the fact she's doing it, the "big reveal" when the exhibit opens.'

Right. Including Jackie's relationship with my grandfather.

'There are a lot of people in town who knew Jackie and remember how much she valued her privacy – including Cricket. Harry knew her, too. I'm surprised you didn't get pushback from anyone else about doing this.'

Willow gave me an are-you-out-of-your-mind look.

'Oh, but I did,' she said, sounding ominous. 'Just one person, but one was enough.'

'Who?'

'Parker Lord. He came by several times and did his best to talk me into reconsidering and not holding the exhibit.'

The last time Parker and I spoke he told me he was upset about Harry pre-empting the premier of Jackie's paintings by displaying them here instead of at the National Museum of Women in the Arts. He knew about the journal, but he hadn't known about Harry's latest idea to use excerpts as wall text. If he had, he would have had a coronary.

'Parker came by to talk to you about that?' I asked. 'I would have thought he'd take it up with Harry. Or Cricket.'

Willow walked over and stood behind the counter, fiddling with a collection of postcards and fliers of upcoming artists who would have exhibitions at the gallery, straightening edges that didn't need straightening, tidying them into a neat row even though they were already lined up.

She looked up. 'I'm sure he did, but there was more to it. He had a personal stake in all of this as well.'

'What do you mean?'

'Before Harry moved home, Parker had persuaded Cricket to donate Jackie's paintings to the National Museum of Women in the Arts. If there was going to be a gala – a big splashy party – it was going to be there.'

I nodded. I knew this already.

She twirled one of the beaded feathers in her hair around her finger. 'Parker's good friend is Marilyn Gilbert Bernard – *was* Marilyn Gilbert Bernard – the museum's senior curator. He designed the gardens at her home in Great Falls. Anyway, when Harry came home at loose ends, she got involved in the project and decided the paintings should be displayed here first – here in Middleburg, that is. So she came to me and, being the new kid and not knowing the whole back story, I said yes. In a heartbeat. I mean, who wouldn't?'

I nodded. Really. Who wouldn't?

Parker hadn't breathed a word to me that he'd been responsible for Cricket donating Jackie's paintings to NMWA. No wonder he'd been so upset about Harry jumping in with both feet and co-opting his plan to suit her own purposes.

'If you want my honest opinion' – Willow stopped fiddling with the feather – 'twenty-twenty hindsight and all that, I think this is about Harry wanting advance publicity for the book she's writing.'

'And you're in the middle?'

'Not any more. Parker's dead. Harry's going to get her way, isn't she?'

'I suppose she is,' I said. 'When was the last time Parker was in here?'

She looked pained. 'Monday. The day he died.'

So Willow had seen him that last day as well. Another name for Bobby's list.

'Was anybody else in the gallery when he stopped by?'

'Do you mean, do I have someone who can alibi me for when he was here that I didn't poison him? Come on, Lucie, give me some credit.' Her face darkened. 'Bobby Noland has already been by questioning me six ways from Sunday, asking just how mad I was at Parker for trying to sabotage this exhibit. I don't need you cross-examining me, too. Or are you asking for a friend?'

Her sarcasm and the prickliness caught me off-guard. Which was interesting because she had at least two of the three factors necessary for committing a crime in Bobby's book: opportunity and the all-important motive. How hard would it be to have offered Parker a glass of water that she'd spiked with a heavy dose of eye drops? In other words, she could have had the means as well.

'Look, get in line,' I said. 'I got the third degree from Bobby since I not only saw Parker Monday morning, I found him the next day. You're not the only one Bobby talked to. There are a lot of us.'

Willow backed down. 'OK, I'm sorry. I shouldn't have

unloaded on you like that. Mia told me you two were close and that he was a good friend of your mother's when she was alive. This must be hard for you.'

'It is,' I said. 'I didn't realize Parker had been so adamant about asking you not to exhibit Jackie's paintings.'

She nodded. 'Oh, we had a huge argument over it, all right. But not for the reason you're probably thinking – not because it was going to help promote my brand-new art gallery. Or even help publicize Harry's book.'

'Then why?'

'Do you have any idea how long it has taken for paintings by these women, artists like Élisabeth Vigée Le Brun – one of the Old Mistresses – to get *any* recognition *anywhere* in the world in modern times? I'm thrilled – it's beyond my wildest dream – to have an opportunity to showcase paintings Jacqueline Bouvier bought in Paris seventy years ago for a couple of francs. The paintings of an artist whose name and work had completely fallen out of public consciousness, someone whose talent and brilliance Jackie Onassis was astute enough to recognize when she picked those paintings out of a bin in a bookstall along the Seine River. Back when no one believed that a female artist whose name is now spoken in the same breath as Rembrandt, Velasquez, Rubens – the *men*, the Old *Masters* – even *belonged* in one of the great museums in the world, regardless of her talent? Art museums throughout the world have been the "Men Only" club for centuries.'

She must have said something just like this to Parker. I wondered what his reply had been.

'I get it,' I said. 'I understand. Obviously Parker didn't share your passion.'

'Well,' she said, 'that's because there's one more thing.'

'What thing would that be?'

'Parker was donating art from his own collection to NMWA – paintings by artists who are also considered Old Mistresses.'

'Are you serious? I had no idea Parker's art collection was . . . I don't know . . . museum-worthy, I guess.'

'I'm not surprised. According to Marilyn, he didn't talk about it much. In fact, he was incredibly private about what he owned.'

'Marilyn, as in the curator of the National Museum of Women in the Arts?'

'Yes. I gather you don't know her.' When I shook my head she said, 'She's pretty fierce. I'm in awe of her.'

'Why?'

'I knew her in New York,' she said. 'She was an art appraiser primarily for MOMA, but also for several of the other New York art museums and major galleries. She had a real talent for finding hidden gems; sleeper art it's called. Paintings other people thought were knock-offs or painted by some unknown artist so barely worth more than the cost of the paint and canvas – except they weren't. Plus I'm fairly sure she was one of the original Guerrilla Girls. From the beginning, long before NMWA opened, Marilyn was always championing female artists.'

'What is a "guerrilla girl"?'

Willow smiled. 'A rebel. Guerrilla Girls are a group of female artists who were so fed up with how few women had their paintings exhibited in art galleries, they banded together in New York in 1985 and started showing up outside male-artist-only exhibitions to protest the absence of female artists. To protect their identity, they wore gorilla masks. The masks were what got them noticed – but now the Guerrilla Girls are pretty famous. Although anyone who is a Guerrilla Girl still remains unknown.'

'No one knows who they are?'

'Nope. They don't even know among themselves. No one ever admits if they are or were a Guerrilla Girl. It's part of the unwritten code, but it's also for protection. Some have been members for years. Others just join for a brief period.'

I wondered if Willow was speaking from experience. And what about Mia? Anonymous protesting, pro-feminist, supporting women artists. *Wearing a gorilla mask.* Something she would absolutely do; it was right up her alley.

'How did Marilyn Gilbert Bernard feel about you exhibiting the paintings before they're donated to the NMWA?' I asked.

'You'll have to ask her. Marilyn's the consummate diplomat. She wasn't going to get involved in anything between Parker and Cricket. Or Harry, for that matter. When all is said and done, the museum still gets the paintings after the exhibit is finished here. And Parker's Old Mistresses as well.'

'Parker owns some of my mother's paintings and I knew he liked botanical art and paintings that had to do with gardens, but I didn't realize it was the kind of collection that you'd donate to a museum,' I said. 'Especially a place like NMWA.'

'Which was how he wanted it, according to Marilyn. Apparently most of his collection has been on temporary loan to small art museums that don't have big budgets or historical sites that have gardens or botanical exhibits,' she said. 'Marilyn talked Parker into thinking about making some of those donations permanent – and considering NMWA for the Old Mistress paintings he owned. It was sort of inevitable that he went to Cricket as well; though if you ask me, Marilyn probably put a bug in his ear and suggested it.'

'She must be quite an amazing person.'

'You have no idea. You don't mess around with her, either,' Willow said. 'She keeps a Venus flytrap on her desk in her office. It's pretty intimidating when you meet her, especially if you have to tell her something she's not thrilled about.'

'A Venus flytrap? Really?'

'Yup. You know what she says if she knows you're going to be the bearer of bad news or tell her something she doesn't want to hear?'

The possibilities were endless. 'I couldn't even begin to guess.'

'She eyes the plant and says, "You know, my plant hasn't eaten in two weeks. Is there something you wanted to tell me?"'

The sleigh bells on the door jingled, startling us both. I whirled around. A beautifully groomed woman walked in. Maybe late fifties, no nonsense and intense.

'Hello, Willow. I was just on my way to a meeting with Cricket,' she said. 'I'm early so I thought I'd drop by and see how everything is coming along here.'

Willow didn't have to introduce me. This woman was Marilyn Gilbert Bernard.

And by the look on her face, her Venus flytrap hadn't eaten in two weeks.

FOURTEEN

Though I knew who she was, it was clear Marilyn Gilbert Bernard wanted to know who *I* was. She raised an eyebrow and gave Willow an expectant glance.

On cue, Willow said, 'Marilyn, let me introduce you to Lucie Montgomery, the owner of Montgomery Estate Vineyard. Lucie, this is Marilyn Gilbert Bernard, the Chief Curator of the National Museum of Women in the Arts, who I was just telling you about.'

Marilyn held out her hand and I shook it. She had a firm, confident grip. 'Let me guess,' she said. 'She told you about Aphrodite.'

It took a moment before I got it. 'Your plant?' I said. 'What a perfect name.'

'I thought so, too,' she said, with the ghost of a smile. Then she turned serious. 'You're the one who found Parker.'

'I am.'

'I still can't believe he's gone.'

'Neither can I.'

She looked at Willow. 'You're going to go ahead with it? The party is still taking place on Friday?'

Willow averted her eyes and I could tell it was a Venus flytrap moment. 'I . . . yes. Honestly, there are too many wheels in motion to postpone now.'

'Of course Harry would want the show to go on,' Marilyn said in a dry voice, casting a glance around the gallery. 'How are you going to keep the paintings and the wall text under wraps until the party, since Harry wants the Big Reveal to take place then?'

'We're putting a large screen in the window so no one can see inside,' Willow said. 'And Mia, Sergio, and I will hang everything Thursday night after we're closed. Harry's paying for extra security for the night, just someone sitting here and making sure everything is quiet. We're more concerned about paparazzi taking photos than someone taking one of the paintings, to be honest.'

Marilyn's eyes met mine for a fleeting second. She knew very well that this was all being staged for the benefit of Harry's book.

'Of course,' she said.

'Willow told me that Parker was the one who persuaded Cricket to donate the Vigée Le Brun paintings to your museum,' I said. 'And that you and Parker knew each other because he designed the gardens at your home.'

'That's right,' she said, 'but that's not the only reason – or even the real reason – Parker spoke to Cricket about donating those paintings.'

'What do you mean?' I asked.

Marilyn pursed her lips together for a moment as if she were conducting some kind of internal debate about whether to answer my question or not.

'I suppose it's OK to tell you,' she said. 'I don't think he'd mind. Not any more.'

Willow's mobile rang and she took a quick look at the display. 'Will you two excuse me? I've got to take this call in private. I'll go upstairs for a moment.'

'Don't bother,' Marilyn said. 'Lucie and I can wait outside. It will give us a chance to chat.'

Marilyn gave me a look that said she had a couple of things on her mind that we needed to talk about. I'd known her for all of about five minutes.

I started to get the front door and hold it for Marilyn, but she was quicker. 'After you.' Her eyes had strayed to my cane.

'A car accident ten years ago,' I said. 'I wasn't supposed to walk ever again.'

'You've come a long way.' It sounded like a compliment.

We stepped outside. The day had turned spring-like warm and sunny, and the light splintered off the tarnished bronze fox, so he looked dazzling. The traffic on Washington Street was light – only a few cars and a horse trailer passing by. A couple of pedestrians stopped in front of the gallery where a sign advertising the Jackie Onassis–Élisabeth Vigée Le Brun exhibit occupied most of the picture window.

'Shall we sit?' Marilyn indicated a white wrought-iron bench that overlooked the fox, the cars and horse trailer, and the sidewalk traffic.

We sat and I said, 'You were about to say something about Parker talking Cricket into donating Jackie Onassis's paintings to the museum.'

She settled back against the bench. 'That's right,' she said. 'Parker owned quite an important collection of botanical paintings – oils, watercolors, engravings – that he acquired over the years. All thanks to Bunny Mellon, who suggested the idea when he was working for her.'

'I didn't know that.'

She smiled. 'Of course you didn't. He didn't talk about it. During his time at Oak Spring Farm and the Mellons' other homes – D.C., New York, Nantucket, the Cape, Paris, Antigua, and a couple I'm probably forgetting – Parker saw their fabulous art collection and how generous the Mellons were in gifting so many of their paintings to museums so that everyone could enjoy them. Good Lord, the National Gallery of Art – America's art museum – got its start thanks to Paul Mellon's art collection, just like the Library of Congress got its start from Thomas Jefferson's personal library. That kind of generosity had a huge impact on Parker, plus he adored both Bunny and Paul. And, as you probably know, Jackie and Bunny were great friends.'

I had seen Paul Mellon's portrait over the fireplace in the Founder's Room at the National Gallery in D.C. so I knew the story behind him donating his personal collection to give the gallery its start. I also knew he believed that America needed to have a national art museum on a par with the National Gallery in London, the Louvre in Paris, or the Prado in Madrid. And though tourists sometimes mistook it for being part of the Smithsonian because it was located on the National Mall along with the Smithsonian museums, and it was also free to enter like the Smithsonian was, it was a totally separate museum.

Marilyn went on. 'Parker was strongly influenced and moved by how the Mellons conducted their philanthropy. So when he decided he wanted to start acquiring art on his own, Bunny's advice – which was worth its weight in gold – was that his money would go further if he could find a niche in the art world that hadn't caught anyone else's interest or attention. That way he could pick up good-quality art at a more modest price.'

'So he chose botanical art?'

'Exactly. Perfectly logical for a landscape designer, don't you think? Flowers, plants, herbs, trees, gardens – all of it,' she said. 'But as it happened, Parker had the same discerning eye in choosing art he loved that he did in the gardens he designed. Many of the paintings he picked up for a pittance decades ago are now worth quite a bit of money.'

'Including paintings by the Old Mistresses?'

Marilyn smiled. 'I gather Willow has been educating you,' she said. 'Yes, including paintings by several of the Old Mistresses. Judith Leyster, a Dutch artist from the 1600s who was well known for her paintings of tulips, and Maria Sibylla Merian, a German artist who was nearly a contemporary of Leyster's, and is considered to be the pre-eminent artist – even today – of scientific drawings of plants and insects. She wasn't well-known for centuries, but now her work is extremely valuable and sought after.'

'Parker is donating paintings by those women to NMWA?' I asked.

Marilyn stared at the traffic on Washington Street as if she hadn't heard my question. I nearly repeated it when she said, 'He was. When he was alive. I need to talk to Ash Carlyle to find out about the provisions of Parker's will. I suspect they're Ash's paintings now unless Parker specifically left them to us. He also planned to bequeath paintings by Mary Cassatt and Georgia O'Keeffe to the museum, in addition to works by a couple of artists who were less well known. It was going to be quite a significant donation.'

Although she had kept her voice carefully neutral I could see that Parker's death had not only been a personal blow, but after what she just told me, it had also been a body blow to the museum. If Ash decided he wanted to keep the paintings or maybe even sell them because he wanted or needed the money it would be quite a loss.

'You're saying it's Ash's decision now whether you still get these paintings?'

'We had just drawn up the final paperwork for the paintings Parker planned to donate. All the vetting to make sure they were authentic and the provenance tracing their ownership had been done in advance, of course. Parker was going to give us his assessment of their value for us to issue a tax letter, so we were nearly finished.' She flapped a dismissive hand. 'The lawyers took care of it. That sort of thing is beyond my ken. Unfortunately Parker never signed the final donation paper.'

It took a moment before I realized the impact of what she was saying.

'So it's possible you have nothing because he didn't officially sign anything?' I said and she nodded. 'Does that mean Ash doesn't have to honor Parker's promise to donate the paintings if he doesn't want to?'

'Aphrodite was not happy when I told her the news,' Marilyn said with a rueful smile. 'But, yes, that's right.'

'I presume you're going to talk to him,' I said. 'I'm sure he'll go through with anything Parker committed to, even if Parker didn't actually sign the final document. Ash knows he intended you to have the paintings.'

'From your lips to God's ear,' she said. 'Unlike you, I'm not so sure. I heard Ash was angry with Parker over something and that they argued about it just before he died.'

She certainly was well informed. I told her about Parker's article in the *Washington Tribune* and why Ash had been so upset.

'I read that piece online. The comments were brutal, especially in light of the backlash against *The Angry Earth*. Some people were downright threatening and I was worried for Parker,' she said. 'But I wasn't aware that Ash had contributed money to Gabriel Seely's research project. Money he presumably will lose if the university shuts down the lab because of improprieties.'

It wasn't hard to do the math: Ash could sell the paintings instead of fulfilling Parker's wishes, and make back the money he lost because of Parker's *Trib* article. A twisted sort of logic and justice.

'I'm sure Ash will want to do the right thing,' I said again, hoping that was helpful though, honestly, I wasn't sure myself any more.

Marilyn glanced over at the gallery's large picture window. 'It looks as if Willow is finished with her phone call. I guess I'd better say goodbye. I'm off to meet with Cricket to see if I can salvage at least part of this donation.' She stood up.

I reached for my cane and got up, too. 'What do you mean?'

'Cricket's decision to bequeath Jackie Onassis's paintings to NMWA had a lot to do with Parker's persuasiveness and his own donation. He promised Cricket her tax write-off would be considerable, not to mention she would know what her generosity had done while she was still alive to see it – not some posthumous accolade and her name on a plaque – along with the legacy she would leave,' she said. 'Unfortunately Harry is not exactly in favor of giving away something that could be sold, so it's possible she might try to persuade her mother to reconsider her decision. And if Ash doesn't want to go through with Parker's donation, I think the scales might tip in favor of Harry getting her way.'

'And the museum gets nothing. From either of them.'

There was another of Marilyn's pregnant silences while she seemed to be evaluating what she was going to say next. I waited.

'I've heard rumors that Cricket has spent quite a bit of her late husband's fortune,' she said and it seemed she was choosing her words carefully. 'Mon Repos is not inexpensive to maintain and Cricket is used to a certain lifestyle. So is her now-unmarried daughter who is living at home on her mother's largesse. Or what's left of it.'

The Delacroixes were nearly broke?

'I wasn't aware of money problems,' I said. 'The birthday party Harry is throwing for her mother is a spare-no-expense event, tied in, of course, with the gala here on Friday. My cousin, who owns the Goose Creek Inn, is catering both events and that's what I've heard from her.'

'Ah. I see.'

I could tell Marilyn had been hoping I might be able to corroborate her story, but if Cricket and Harry had money woes, it was news to me. And it was a remarkably well-kept secret in a town where secrets were hard to keep. Especially if you ever set foot in the General Store.

'So if you're correct, they need the money,' I said.

'If I'm correct, they do.'

'I'm sure if anyone can persuade Ash and Cricket – or Harry – to do the right thing, it's you,' I said. 'Willow said you were quite formidable.'

Marilyn's eyes lit up and she laughed. 'Dear Willow,' she said. 'I was hoping to enlist her on my team as well, which is part of the reason I stopped by.'

'Just tell them all that Aphrodite hasn't eaten in two weeks. I'm sure they'll come round.'

Marilyn threw back her head and roared. 'I might just do that,' she said. 'I'll see you Friday at the gala, Lucie.'

'Absolutely.'

Marilyn reached out her hand and shook mine. That same firm grip.

'I'm leaving for the airport in a little while to pick up my grandfather who's flying in from Paris for the gala and Cricket's birthday party,' I said. 'He's known Cricket and Jackie since their junior year abroad in Paris in 1949 – he met Jackie by accident at the Louvre and after that, he showed her around the art galleries and museums of Paris since it was something they both loved. There are stories in my family that when Jackie was negotiating to bring the *Mona Lisa* to America in 1963, my grandfather, who was the Deputy Head of Mission at the French Embassy in Washington, helped her behind the scenes – of course he never admitted anything to this day. Anyway, I'm fairly certain he would urge Cricket to donate Jackie's paintings to NMWA – he would know that's exactly the kind of thing Jackie would want her to do. I could bring up the subject with him and see if he'd talk to Cricket. Especially since Cricket listens to him and trusts him.'

Marilyn's eyes had widened as I recounted the story of Jackie, Pépé, and the *Mona Lisa*. Now she looked at me with new respect.

'That would be *wonderful* if you'd consider doing that. I'd appreciate having another ally in our court, especially one as impressive as your grandfather seems to be. You absolutely must introduce me to him.' She reached in the pocket of her jacket and pulled out a business card. It looked a bit worse for wear, but she handed it to me. 'Contact me if you need anything.'

'I will. And I know he'd like to meet you.'

'Excellent. Maybe under the circumstances I'll just give Aphrodite her usual diet of freeze-dried worms, crickets, and beetles. It's what she'd rather eat, anyway.'

I laughed and Marilyn went inside The Artful Fox. Through the picture window I watched her chatting and gesturing animatedly with Willow, who was nodding. I left them and walked back to my car, parsing the list of things I had just learned and trying to make sense of all of it.

First, Willow Harper had seen Parker the morning he died so she was now on Bobby Noland's suspect list along with the rest of us – and she had a motive. Second, Parker never signed the contract making it official that he would donate his paintings to the National Museum of Women in the Arts and they probably now belonged to Ash. Third, Harry didn't want Cricket donating Jackie's paintings when she could sell them and raise money because – apparently – they were cash-strapped, even though she was spending like there was no tomorrow for the gala and the ninetieth birthday party.

It was only eleven o'clock in the morning.

But it had already been a hell of a day.

FIFTEEN

The Atoka General Store was on my way home. I nearly drove past it, but in a fit of last-minute recklessness that I knew I might regret, I put on my turn signal and made a tire-screeching right into the tiny parking lot out front. The car behind me honked, a yelp of surprise, justifiably irked since he had to slam on his brakes to keep from rear-ending me. I stuck my hand out the window and gave him an apologetic wave, which earned me another *you-idiot* blast of his horn as he drove by.

The Jeep was the only car in the four-car parking lot, meaning I'd have the opportunity to talk to Thelma privately and find out what she knew about the bombshell that Marilyn Gilbert Bernard had just dropped: Cricket had gone through most of the money Édouard Delacroix had left her and she and Harry might be down to pennies in the bottom of the piggy bank and spare change behind the sofa cushions.

That is, I'd get to question her *after* Thelma finished giving me the third degree. No doubt she wanted to know every detail about what had happened when I'd discovered Parker in the vineyard the other day and my ideas about who, among us, was a murderer. Unless her Ouija board hadn't already spelled out an answer.

Thelma was supremely confident in her ability to communicate with spirits from the Great Beyond who would tell her things they wanted her to pass on, thanks to what she called her 'extra-terrestrial psychotic perception'. Her Ouija board was the conduit for these sessions, which, over the years, had even included conversations with my mother and father. It always freaked me out when she told me one of them had 'stopped by to chat' because it seemed I heard enough of their true voices in what she reported to make me wonder whether my parents genuinely could be communicating with her. Were they really walking her fingers across that board to land on different letters and make words that spelled out some message for me, or was Thelma just very clever at evoking their memories? Maybe she *thought* they were talking to her because she wanted it to be so.

Then there was the rest of her unique world, which was richly populated with made-up people – the characters from an eclectic universe of soap operas, whose destinies, dramas, troubles, and triumphs she was invested in as assiduously as if they were neighbors right here in Atoka. Her newest deep dive was Hispanic soaps, or *telenovelas*, which she watched on cable even though she didn't speak a word of Spanish. As a result she invented her own storyline to suit whatever she thought was happening. The women were so seductive and sexy, she said, and as for the men, well, *ay, yi, yi*. José Antonio, Ricardo, Juan Carlos and the rest of them could leave *migas de pan* – breadcrumbs – in her bed any time they wanted to and she wouldn't complain one bit. No, *señor*.

Like Willow, Thelma had sleigh bells hanging on her front door to let her know someone had arrived. As soon as I walked in I heard the usual voices from the back room – Spanish, by the sound of it – where she was probably absorbed in yet another episode of *Pasión y Amor Prohibido*, one of her current favorites. Someone shouted and it cued soaring music, meaning I had arrived at a good time: the show was ending.

'Coming,' Thelma called in her reedy voice. 'I'll be right there.'

To see Thelma for the first time was always a surprise. Even though her age was somewhere north of eighty, she dressed with the saucy, flirty, over-the-top verve of a rebellious teenager who intended to sneak out of the house before her parents caught her and sent her back upstairs to change right now, young lady, or you're not going anywhere. Short, tight, low-cut dresses or skirts and knit tops and always an eye-popping color, usually with matching stiletto heels. Today she was dressed head-to-toe in cotton-candy pink. Her lipstick was the color of bubblegum and she wore two little pink bows in her orange-lacquered hair to complete the look. Her mascara, however, was the worse for wear and I suspected something had happened just a few moments ago involving either *pasión* or *amor prohibido* that had made her teary-eyed.

She was holding a telltale damp tissue in her hand, but her face lit up when she saw me. 'Why, Lucille,' she said, 'I've been thinking about you these last few days, child. And don't you know I *knew* you'd be in today?'

Of course she did. Her extra-terrestrial psychotic perception had told her.

'Are you all right, Thelma? Is something wrong?'

She flapped the tissue at me. 'Oh, don't mind me. It's just that María, who's been having carnival relations with Diego for the last few months, doesn't want to have Diego's love child because now she's in love with Roberto. Except Roberto is married to Isabella and that boy believes you should be monotonous when you marry someone. But María – who's called "La Guapa" which means "the beautiful" *en español*, except she's also meaner than a snake – is planning to come between them because she wants Roberto for herself. At least I think that's what's happening.'

'It sounds complicated.'

'You have no idea.' She blew her nose. 'Sorry, I just needed a moment, but I'm OK now. Tell me, what can I get for you?'

'A quart of milk,' I said. 'And a loaf of wholewheat sourdough bread, if there's any left from the bakery.'

'There is. But before you do your shopping, why don't you sit with me a spell and have a nice cup of coffee? We could have a little chat. There's one jelly donut left that the Romeos didn't scarf down this morning. I think it's raspberry. And today's fancy is Java the Hutt – a real full-bodied blend. Peps you right up.'

Thelma always had three coffee pots going – plain, decaf, and fancy – on a table next to a large glass cabinet that held donuts, croissants, bagels, and muffins that were delivered fresh every morning from a bakery in Leesburg. It was an easy-going partnership between the two businesses. If Thelma wasn't there in time to open up when the delivery guy arrived, he let himself in through the back window and got the spare key. By noon there was usually nothing left of what he'd brought.

A cup of coffee with Thelma meant you were about to enter the lion's den and she was going to grill you until you were ready to cry uncle and tell her anything she wanted to know,

even if you had no clue what she was talking about. But this
time there were things *I* wanted to find out as well, so I jumped
in with both feet.

'I'd love to have a cup of coffee,' I said. 'I'll fix yours –
decaf, right, since it's almost noon?' She nodded and I said,
'Go have a seat and I'll bring it to you. Plus I can get the jelly
donut.'

A group of rocking chairs was pulled up in a semi-circle
around a pot-bellied stove that sat in a corner of the store and
warmed up the place in winter. The rest of the year that corner
was still Thelma's favorite spot to hold court. She always took
the Lincoln rocker, presiding over the conversation like a queen-
bee-cum-benevolent-dictator, so she could steer the topic to the
latest gossip, or else she would inform her audience – generally
one or more of the Romeos – of the most recent visitors from
Ouija-land.

I got her decaf, fixed a cup of Java the Hutt, and then got
the jelly donut before sitting in my favorite Bentwood rocking
chair.

Thelma sipped her coffee and got right to it. 'I heard you
found Parker the other day, God rest his soul. It must have
been such a turrible shock, just turrible – him expiring right
there in the middle of your vineyard with no one around to
help him.'

It was still hard to think of how his life had ended. I nodded
because I wasn't sure I could speak without my voice breaking.

Thelma took one look at my face and was immediately
contrite. 'I'm so sorry, child. That was thoughtless. I didn't
mean to upset you,' she said. 'I wish it hadn't turned out the
way it did like I know you do, but you know what I always
say – sometimes you've just got to leave someone lay where
Jesus flang 'em. Parker . . . well, maybe God wanted to bring
him home and have him leave this earth surrounded by nature.
In a garden, somewhere he loved. There's something kind of
right about him dying in such a peaceful place, don't you think?'

I hadn't really thought of it that way, but Thelma, for all her
love of two-dimensional TV people and her belief that other-
worldly spirits truly existed, could be remarkably astute and on
point about real people and real life.

'I do,' I said. 'You might be right. I just wish he hadn't been alone.'

'So do I. Then there's the question of who did it. I've heard about all the people who saw him on that last day, but I just don't believe any of 'em could have killed that man. Tell me, Lucille, who do *you* think is the guilty one?'

Here it was. Objection, Your Honor. Calls for speculation. First of all, she hadn't mentioned any names, meaning there was a very good chance she was fishing to see if I'd slip and accidentally bring up someone she hadn't known about who was on Bobby's list. Plus after I left here anything about which I had opined would be broadcast far and wide across two counties within twenty-four hours. Maybe less. Thelma could spread news faster than the Internet.

'I'm one of the people who saw him,' I said, avoiding her question and concentrating on raspberry jelly not ending up on my lap. 'And, no, I don't want to believe that anyone on Bobby's list could be guilty, either.'

Thelma sipped her coffee and watched me. The look on her face told me she'd heard precisely what I'd just said and that in her book there was a seismic difference between not *wanting* to believe anyone was guilty and just plain not *believing* it.

'Then who did kill Parker Lord?' She repeated the question, tugging on one of her pink bows as if it might unlock the answer. 'Someone is guilty of pre-marinated murder, that's for sure.'

I had to digest that comment before I answered.

'I don't know. Maybe it's someone no one knows about yet,' I said. 'Or maybe I just want it to be someone we don't know. Some stranger.'

Though Bobby had already said – and not for the first time – the odds of that being the case were between slim and none. Whoever killed Parker had known him.

'Well, speaking of strangers,' Thelma said, 'there was a woman in here a little while ago, not long before you stopped in. Middle-aged, kind of pretty. Gray hair, no-nonsense, a real serious type. I asked her what brought her to our little corner of paradise and all she said was, "I'm visiting friends".'

'Navy two-piece suit? Wearing an antique diamond and sapphire ring on her right hand?'

Thelma's eyes lit up. 'That's her. Who was she?'

'The Chief Curator of the National Museum of Women in the Arts,' I said. 'Her name is Marilyn Gilbert Bernard. She drove out here from Washington. Willow Harper introduced me to her when she stopped by The Artful Fox.'

Thelma set her coffee mug on a table that was stacked precariously with soap-opera magazines.

'That's the museum that's getting Jackie's French paintings,' she said. 'The ones she left to Cricket.'

There was no way I was going to share what Marilyn had confided in me about the possible change of plans for the Vigée Le Brun paintings if Harry persuaded her mother to back out of donating them or that Parker had intended to bequeath some of his collection to NMWA as well. Thelma liked to pride herself on being the first to know the latest news, but like the children's game of telephone, the more she repeated a story – say, to the Romeos, who would pass it on to their friends who, in turn, would pass it on to their friends, and friends-of-friends, and so on – it would eventually be transformed into a new, totally altered account of what had really happened. The truth could be sort of fuzzy and malleable for Thelma and the Romeos, especially if it got in the way of a better, more exciting story.

Instead I merely said, 'Yes, that's right.'

Thelma nodded. 'I know Jackie left those paintings to Cricket because she was such a good friend, but I think she'd be mighty pleased to know they're going to be some place where folks can appreciate them more than if they're hanging in Cricket's dining room. I'll have to have another chat with her soon.'

'With Cricket?'

'With Jackie.'

'Wait a minute. You talk to Jackie? On your Ouija board?'

'Not very often, but she does pop by from time to time.'

'Right.' I tried to sound like I believed her. 'You knew Jackie, of course? When she was *alive*, I mean.'

Thelma looked indignant, not having missed the slight and my skepticism about her communicating with Jackie from the Great Beyond.

'A-course I did. She used to stop in here all the time for a good old chat. Plus she always bought hoof wax for her horses.'

'What kinds of things did you chat about?'

'Why, books – what else? She was a big-time editor in New York working at Doublemint. They're one of the big publishers. You must have heard of them.'

'Yes. Of course. You and Jackie talked about . . . books?'

'You don't need to look so surprised, missy.' Thelma stood up and smoothed out the wrinkles in her pink knit dress. 'You may not realize it, but I got more going on inside here' – she tapped her forehead again – 'than most folks realize. I may not be what you'd call a regular Steinway in the brains department, but I do just fine.'

She clacked across the floor, her stilettos tapping out an angry staccato as she disappeared into the back room. For a moment I sat in my rocking chair and wondered if I should go after her and apologize. I must have offended her beyond measure for her to walk out on me like that.

At least I could clean up. Then apologize.

I picked up our coffee cups and my plate, which had a smear of jelly and some powdered sugar on it, and set them on a table behind the glass cabinet. As I was doing that, Thelma re-emerged carrying a sturdy-looking stack of books and set them on the counter next to the cash register.

'I brought these out here so you can look at them, Lucille. All gifts from Jackie,' she said. '*Her* books. Books she edited. She'd come by the store and we'd have a good long talk about her latest project and the problems she was having with this author or that publicist or whatever artist was designing the book cover and I'd give her advice. The next time she'd come to Middleburg after the book was published, she'd bring a copy for me from New York. And she always signed it to me, always something special.'

I stared at her, dumbfounded. Thelma had kept this secret tucked away for years, never breathing a word about her relationship with Jackie Onassis and the obviously numerous – if that pile was anything to go by – discussions they'd had about the books Jackie had edited.

Thelma put her hands on her hips and gave me the once-over.

'They're not going to bite you, so come on over here and have a look. I don't show Jackie's books to just anyone, you know. They're probably my most treasured possessions. Jackie was an amazing lady, such a good, kind person. The Good Lord took her too soon. I miss her every day.'

The tissue came out of her pocket again and she wiped her eyes. I crossed the room and put my arms around her. 'I'm so sorry, Thelma. I knew her, too, but I was only a little girl. She and my mother were friends. They used to go riding together.'

Thelma nodded and dabbed her eyes.

'I remember.' She gestured to the books. 'Go on, Lucille. Take a look.'

It was an eclectic, erudite collection. *Atget's Gardens: A Selection of Eugène Atget's Garden Photographs* by William Howard Adams, Introduction by Jacqueline Onassis. *Secrets of Marie Antoinette* by Olivier Bernier. *Empire of the Czar: A Journey through Eternal Russia* by the Marquis de Custine. *Moonwalk* by Michael Jackson. *Paris After the Liberation, 1944–1949* by Antony Beever and Artemis Cooper. *The French Woman's Bedroom* by Mary-Sargent Ladd.

It wasn't difficult to discern Jackie's interests from the books she chose to edit. France. History. Gardens. Beautiful places. People with fascinating stories to tell.

'My favorite is *Atget's Gardens*,' Thelma said, pushing it over to me and pronouncing the name so it rhymed with 'hatchet' instead of 'Aht-JAY' as the French would say. 'Jackie loved the black and white photographs he took of gardens that belonged to palaces and royal parks, places that got all rundown and full of weeds because no one was caring for 'em any more.'

I opened the book and began looking at sharp-shadowed photographs of moss- and lichen-covered statues, empty fountains, broken steps on marble staircases, and parks filled with stark bare-branched trees.

'Jackie told me how she persuaded Mr Adams, who was a friend and famous historian who loved gardens, to do the book for her,' Thelma went on. 'He was a mentor of Parker's as well, thanks to Jackie. I remember him years ago when he was at Monticello working on a project about Thomas Jefferson for the National Gallery of Art.

'Anyway, after Jackie got Mr Adams to agree to do the book, they went to Paris together and she helped him find all the pictures he wanted to use.' Thelma tapped the page I was looking at with a finger, a photo of a solitary statue in front of an *allée* of bare trees bent toward each other like the vault of a cathedral. 'My Lord, how she loved that trip – Paris, her favorite city in the world – and doing that kind of research. You can see, Lucille, how these gardens and the statues are in a right state, all falling apart and going to seed, but that's what Jackie loved about 'em. She said you could tell how much history had happened in those places.'

'You two really did talk a lot about her books, didn't you?'

Thelma arched a heavily penciled eyebrow and gave me a look of utter disdain. 'Jackie wrote the introduction to *Atget's Gardens*. It's not very long. Why don't you read it and see for yourself what a wonderful writer she was?'

She took the book from me, opened it to the beginning, and slid it back over. I started to read.

Jackie loved Paris, all right. It was evident in the way she described 'the noble sweep of the vistas of Versailles', and 'the heroic balustrades framing the emptiness' of Saint-Cloud. The gardens of the Château de Sceaux a few miles outside Paris reminded her of a 'wild Greek island' or 'a sorcerer's wood', a place where 'the malicious smile of Voltaire' might have quivered. As for Eugène Atget himself, she wrote, 'he photographs with tenderness and melancholy.'

I looked up at Thelma when I was finished. In her wildest dreams, Harry wasn't going to come even close to writing something this enchanting and poetic. Jackie's letters to my grandfather must have been sprinkled with this same erudition and graceful way with words. No wonder he had been captivated by her.

Thelma read my mind.

'She was a wonderful writer, not just her books but the letters she sent folks. She had wit and sparkle and she was smart,' Thelma said. 'And she fought hard for each of her books and authors. Though I can tell you she didn't suffer fools or people who thought they were the cat's pajamas and cozied up to her because of who she was. She'd call 'em right out.'

I picked up the book on Marie Antoinette. 'What do you remember about this one?'

Thelma propped an elbow on the counter and rested her chin in her hand, a faraway look in her eyes. 'Jackie was fascinated by Marie Antoinette. Always had been. She lived this kind of crazy rich life when everyone in France was starving to death. Jackie wanted to publish a book so folks would know what her life was *really* like, surrounded by rich, royal people who did ridiculous things and wore fancy clothes and powdered wigs that looked like the insides of a stuffed animal, their complicated, silly manners – folks who had no clue what awful things were happening outside the palace walls.

'Marie Antoinette was fourteen when she was sent from Austria to get married and her husband – the King of France – was fifteen,' she went on. 'So here she was, a little girl far from home, far away from her mother who was the Empress of Austria and pretty busy and important herself. Jackie had done a couple of books with Olivier Bernier, who wrote this book, and they were friends, so when he came to her with the letters between Marie Antoinette and her mother where you could see how homesick and lonely she was, Jackie jumped on it.'

I looked through the other books Thelma had brought out: Michael Jackson's memoir, the book on Paris after the Liberation about a time that Jackie knew first-hand, the wonderfully written account of the French Marquis de Custine traveling through Russia in 1826, and the beautiful and sensual decorator's book on how French women furnished their bedrooms. Then I picked up *Secrets of Marie Antoinette* once again.

What had Jackie written in her journal about Marie Antoinette and Élisabeth Vigée Le Brun – and herself? In a few days at the gala when Harry unveiled the paintings, I guess I'd find out.

'What do you think about Harry finishing Jackie's book on Marie Antoinette and Élisabeth Vigée Le Brun and using her journal as part of the story?' I asked Thelma.

'I mean to ask Jackie that very question the next time we talk,' Thelma said in a stern voice. 'But let me tell you, Lucille, I don't think she'd be happy one little bit. In fact, I know she wouldn't.'

'Why?'

'I asked her once if she thought about writing an autobiography. You know, about her own life.'

'Right. What did she say?'

'She gave me ever such a sad look and said that for years folks had talked to her about doing just that, but she always said no. Even her own mother thought she ought to write about herself. Jackie could have made a whole pile of money if she'd ever decided to tell her story – her side, not someone else writing about her who didn't know the real Jackie because she was such a private person. And you already saw what a wonderful way she had with words.'

'Did she tell you why she said no?' Somehow I didn't think it was because of money.

Thelma nodded. 'She said there were parts of her life that were just too painful to remember. And writing about them would be like going through the hard times, the rough times, all over again. Besides, she got to relive some of her life through her books.' She picked up *Paris After the Liberation, 1944–1949* and stroked the cover. 'She was there – Paris – as an exchange student after the war. She *knew* Paris in those days.'

I thought of my grandfather, who I would be seeing in a few hours. 'She did.'

'I found out later that she was working on this book, helping the authors figure out an ending even though she was so sick. It was only a few weeks before she died. Of course she didn't say a word to them about how ill she was.' Thelma set the book down gently on the counter. 'She was like that.'

I hadn't known Jackie like Thelma or my mother or Pépé had, but just now I felt an ineffable sense of sadness and loss, that somehow she *could* have or *should* have been here for Cricket's ninetieth birthday party at the grand old age of ninety herself, waiting to meet my grandfather, who had first shown her Paris during the happiest year of her life.

'Jackie was finally at peace those last years,' Thelma said. 'She was happy, she loved her job, loved coming to Middleburg to ride, and when she was here she loved the privacy that everyone gave her. She adored her grandchildren, had fallen in love with a good man who loved her back. She was in a really good place, Lucille. Why would she want to go through that heartache all over again, telling the world about things she had put behind her?'

'She wouldn't.'

'Harry had better mind herself with this book she's planning to write,' Thelma said, her tone suddenly harsh and her words sounding like a warning. Or a threat. 'Have you ever heard of the Kennedy curse – all the accidents and deaths and terrible things that happened to so many of the Kennedys over the years?'

'I have.'

'It's a *real* thing, Lucille.' She gave me an ominous look. 'And it doesn't just happen to the family, you know. It also curses their relatives and friends. And people they know. Cricket is one of them.' She paused before delivering her final indictment. 'So is Harry.'

SIXTEEN

I did not expect my grandfather to look so frail and fragile when I caught sight of him as the double doors separating customs and passport control from the rest of the airport opened and an attendant pushed his wheelchair into the international arrivals terminal at Dulles Airport. In the two years since I'd seen him, Pépé had become a little more diminished, his translucent skin more taut against his bones, but – thank God – his eyes were still sharp and bright as he scanned the terminal searching for me.

My throat tightened. I couldn't let this much time pass again before I saw him. He had just turned ninety-three. I hadn't gone back to France since I took over running the vineyard six years ago because there was always so much to do. Instead he had been the faithful one, coming to America regularly to see his grandchildren and the friends he'd made over the years in Middleburg and Atoka.

But what if I did go back to France for a few weeks? Was I really so worried the place would fall apart without me? In truth, Quinn and Frankie could run it with one hand tied behind their backs. Next time, it was my turn to go to Paris to visit my grandfather. Because you never know, do you, how much time is left before you lose someone you love and then it's too late?

I moved out of the cordoned-off area toward the exit, waving at Pépé, whose face broke into a broad grin as he raised his hand in a small salute. For a moment I lost sight of his wheelchair in the crowd of joyous reunions hemmed in by a perimeter of chauffeurs holding up iPads with names typed in huge text or clipboards with a Sharpie scrawl.

When I reached him, he was attempting to stand so he could greet me, while his attendant, a slight, balding man with kind eyes, was equally determined to keep him seated. I knew who would win this tussle.

Pépé slipped the man a folded bill, and said in English, 'My granddaughter will take care of me from here. Thank you for your assistance, sir, you've been very kind.'

The wheelchair attendant, who had been telegraphing warnings in my direction that he was afraid Pépé was going to keel over if the slightest breeze wafted through the airport, finally relented and gave me a he's-all-yours look as he noticed the denomination of the bill he'd just been given.

My grandfather stood up and pulled me into a hug of surprising vigor, kissing me on both cheeks. He smelled of the woodsy, musky cologne he always wore – Givenchy Gentleman – and the lingering odor of Gauloises, his smokes of choice ever since his beloved unfiltered Boyards Caporal Maïs had gone out of production years ago. He'd told me during one of our last phone conversations that his doctor had recently told him to quit smoking or it would kill him. Pépé had raised an eyebrow and said in an amused voice, 'Doctor, I'm over ninety. I'm going to die soon anyway, and I'd prefer to do it enjoying the few vices I have left. Leave me my cognac, my wine, my occasional cigar, and my cigarettes.'

'Are you sure you don't want to keep the wheelchair?' I asked as the attendant said a hearty thank you and started to leave. 'I can bring my car to the door and pick you up while you wait with this gentleman.'

'*Ma belle,*' my grandfather said with fraying patience, 'I may be an old man, but I don't have one foot in the grave just yet. If I hadn't said yes when this gentleman stopped and asked me if I'd like some assistance, I'd still be in line at passport control with most of Europe and half of Asia. The handicapped line was at least an hour shorter.'

'That's the only reason you took the wheelchair?'

He gave me a cheeky grin. 'He offered. Why would I say no?'

I took his suitcase and satchel from the attendant, who handed Pépé his cane. He could still walk, but he moved more slowly now – though I didn't dare mention it since I wasn't exactly the Roadrunner myself – so it took a while before we made it to the parking lot where I'd left the Jeep. I'd asked one more time but he refused to wait while I brought the car to the front door.

'You are so stubborn,' I said.

'Old age, *ma chérie*, is not for sissies. One must be stubborn.'

I paid the parking fee at the toll booth and pulled on to the Dulles Toll Road, taking an immediate right to Route 28 north. At this time of day the trip home could be anywhere from an hour to ninety minutes. The highways of the Dulles tech corridor would be crowded with folks leaving work at the end of the day, although once we reached Mosby's Highway it would probably be smoother sailing unless there was a breakdown or an accident and then all bets were off.

'I heard you've been texting with Cricket,' I said. 'And that she planned for you to stop by Mon Repos on our way home from the airport.'

'I texted her when we landed and after I left passport control, so she knows we're on our way.' He glanced over at me. 'Why are you looking at me like that? I hope it's not a problem to visit Cricket now?'

I shook my head. 'It's fine. You. Texting. I had no idea.'

'Ah,' he said. 'I see. Well, smoke signals are not good for the ozone. Texting seemed like a better idea because it doesn't contribute to global warming.'

I laughed. 'I deserved that.'

'Some day you'll be my age,' he said, 'and you won't want people treating you like an old fossil that can't learn anything new or keep up with what's going on in the world, either.'

'You're right.' I put on my signal to turn off Route 28 onto Old Ox Road. 'Though I do worry about you.'

'And I worry about you,' he said. 'For example, you found Parker Lord the other day and they still haven't caught the person who murdered him.'

'Did Cricket tell you that?'

'She didn't need to,' he said. 'We have this thing in France called the Internet. Also Google News.'

Ouch. 'Sorry.'

'*Chérie*, the story was all over the French news. Parker was an international celebrity, especially after *La Terre en Colère* came out. *The Angry Earth*. It had just been published in France – he was supposed to come over for a book tour in a few weeks.'

'That's right, I think he mentioned it to me. Or Ash did.'

'What I did hear from Cricket is that Bobby Noland is in charge of the investigation, which is good,' he said. 'He'll find who did it.'

'I hope so.'

'Cricket also said that Bobby questioned both her and Harriet because they saw Parker the day he died. When we spoke she was terribly upset about being considered a suspect.' He clicked his tongue against his teeth, a tsk-tsk sound of disapproval.

'Bobby talked to anyone who saw Parker that last day. Including me. And Mia. She was there, in the solarium working on a mural Harry hired her to paint since Mon Repos is on the Garden Week tour,' I said. 'You just said "Bobby will find out who did it." He *has* to question everyone.'

'I understand, but Cricket took it badly, as if Bobby could even imagine she might be guilty. She adored Parker, you know that. She's absolutely *foudroyé* that he's dead.'

Hit by lightning. That was a good way to describe how I felt about his death as well.

'Did you say Bobby also questioned Harry?' I asked. 'She was there, too, when Parker came by to see Cricket?'

How had Harry's name not come up before right now on the list of Bobby's potential suspects? At least, the list I'd known about?

'Yes, she had just returned from a meeting. She saw Parker when he was having tea with Cricket and spent some time with him.'

That must have been when Mia said Harry stopped by to chew her out about the possibility of not finishing the mural on time. After she signed her book contract, the one with the stratospheric numbers, over breakfast in Leesburg, and before she went off to play tennis. I'd seen her after the tennis game when I'd finished having tea with Cricket.

How likely a suspect was Harry? Parker had been upset about her deciding to display Jackie's paintings at The Artful Fox before they were donated to the National Museum of Women in the Arts, and *really* upset about her finishing Jackie's book. He hadn't said anything to me that morning in the garden to indicate he knew Harry planned to use the personal journal excerpts as wall text in the exhibit, but if he'd found out about that when he ran into Harry later on, he probably would have gone nuclear. Still, were any or all of these enough of a reason for Harry to commit murder? Because Parker was mad at her? It seemed pretty low on the spectrum of possibilities compared to, say, Gabriel's motive or Ash's.

'I didn't realize Harry was there,' I said. 'When I spoke to her on Monday she said the only thing Cricket talks about these days is you and your visit. You can calm her down about Parker and the murder investigation, Pépé. She listens to you.'

Plus you're the only person who could talk to her about Harry – and she'd pay attention to what you have to say.

'I will try,' my grandfather said, his eyes on the road as I moved to a right-hand lane to let the Indy 500 driver who was riding my bumper zoom past me.

Pépé didn't say anything as I pulled over, but I saw his mouth twitch and I knew if he'd been behind the wheel, he wouldn't have acquiesced and let the other car muscle him out of the way. Fortunately all of us – his grandchildren – had insisted he stop driving when he turned ninety. He'd grumbled, but finally agreed after being involved in a minor fender-bender that was his fault. But before that he drove like a madman, as if every Parisian street was on the route of the Grand Prix de Monaco, as he slalomed around cars and caromed into busy intersections and roundabouts with abandon while his passengers – speaking from experience – clung to the Jesus strap, one eye closed in terror, the other watching the road, breathless and fervently praying.

'Speaking of Cricket,' I went on as though it were a logical continuation of our conversation, 'I'm sure she told you that Harry is going to finish Jackie Onassis's book about Marie Antoinette and Élisabeth Vigée Le Brun?'

'She did.'

'And?'

'And what?' He shrugged. 'Harry is a journalist. Cricket said the notes Jackie left were very detailed and there was an extensive outline. She's quite confident Harry will be able to finish the book and do a good job.'

'What about Jackie's journal?'

I could hear him quietly exhale. 'What are you talking about? What journal?'

Ah. For all their texting, Cricket hadn't mentioned the journal.

I told him. 'Harry's keeping the contents a secret.' I signaled and moved back into the left lane, overtaking a slower car. 'You didn't know about it?'

'No,' he said. 'I did not.'

I told him about the wall text excerpts, but I left out the part about them including Pépé being with Jackie the day she bought the paintings. 'They'll be a tease to generate interest in the book,' I said. 'She'll keep the good stuff for the book itself.'

My grandfather was silent for a long while. Finally he said in a pained voice, 'Cricket is in agreement with *that*?'

'Apparently. I wonder why she didn't tell you?' I said, giving him a sideways glance. 'Unless she wanted to wait until she saw you.'

Because she knew you wouldn't be happy about it.

'How did you find out about this?' he asked.

'From Mia, who heard from Harry while she was at Mon Repos working on the mural. Harry confirmed it to me later. She said the public relations people from her new publisher are handling the media stuff – it's supposed to generate a lot of pre-sale buzz for the book.'

'Has Cricket read this journal?' he asked.

'No. It's in longhand and her eyesight isn't what it used to be.'

Another nod.

'There's something else,' I said.

We had reached Route 50 west, Mosby's Highway. Red tail lights as far as the eye could see lay ahead of us. I groaned and turned to my grandfather.

'It's going to be a while before we get to Mon Repos.'

'It seems as if we might need the time. You said there was something else?'

'There's a possibility Harry might persuade Cricket not to donate Jackie's paintings to the National Museum of Women in the Arts after all. They might need the money, so they'd be better off selling them. Now with the journal and Jackie's book on Marie Antoinette and Élisabeth Vigée Le Brun in the wings, the paintings will probably sell for even more money than they would have before.'

'You seem to be very well informed, *chérie*. Who told you about this?'

'Marilyn Gilbert Bernard, the Chief Curator of the museum. I met her this morning at The Artful Fox. Apparently Parker was the one who persuaded Cricket to donate the paintings because he was making a significant donation from his own art collection – a series of botanical paintings, quite valuable, all done by women,' I said. 'However, now that Parker is dead, his art collection probably belongs to Ash.'

Pépé looked as if he were putting together a puzzle and discovering the result wasn't going to look like the picture on the box. 'Are you saying Ash might not want to go through with Parker's donation either?'

'I don't know, but that's part of the reason Marilyn drove out to Middleburg today – to see what she could salvage of both donations.'

We had pulled into a conga line of stop-and-go traffic. It would break up in a couple of miles once we left behind the commercial and industrial strip malls of Centreville and Aldie and the scenery became more rural. For now, though, I was riding the brakes.

'Why are you telling me this, Lucie?'

He dropped the question into our conversation like a stone into a still pond. I could feel the ripples reverberating. Here it was. I'm such an awful liar.

'Because Jackie was a friend of Mom's and yours and Grandmama's. I remember her a little from when she used to come over and have tea or a drink with Mom after they went riding.'

'You were very young.'

'I know. But I also hate to see someone exploiting another person for their own purposes. I talked to Harry the day she signed her book contract. She was positively gloating about the money her publisher is going to pay her – mostly because of Jackie's journal and how obsessed people still are with her.'

His mouth twisted into a small smile that was either regret or memory. Or both. 'Someone once said Jackie could charm a building into falling down and it was true. People are still fascinated by her. She was that kind of woman.'

Something in his voice tore at my heart and I knew now that he had never stopped being a little bit in love with her.

'So you don't think what Harry's doing is right?' I asked.

'It doesn't matter what I think.'

'Cricket will listen to you.'

'Cricket,' he said, 'is weary. And she is letting Harry run the show, as you say here. So she will listen to Harry.'

'Even allowing Harry to do something that might be against Cricket's wishes, or her better judgment? Going against something she *knows* Jackie wouldn't have wanted?'

Something you're not going to want either, once you find out what's in that journal.

'It wouldn't be the first time an adult child forced an aging parent to do something that was in the child's best interest, not the parent's,' he said, giving me an equable stare.

'Giving up driving was in *your* best interest,' I said, snapping at him. 'Your grandchildren love you, Pépé. It wasn't about us, it was about you.'

'I didn't mention driving.'

'You didn't need to.'

What was wrong?

This conversation wasn't going at all the way I'd been expecting. Pépé's replies to what I'd been telling him were solemn and measured, but he wasn't angry and worked up the way I was. I had thought he might be concerned or maybe even anxious about the contents of Jackie's journal being made so very public – and whether their affair might be something she'd written about.

Instead he didn't seem to be worried. Maybe it happened so long ago he felt it didn't matter any more, that the subsequent, more important, events of their lives had overshadowed a brief fling seventy years ago.

Whatever it was, he—

'Lucie?'

'What?'

'Why is this so important to you – Jackie's journal, the paintings she left Cricket, her book?'

'I told you why.'

'I'm not sure you did.'

He was already beginning to suspect something. And knowing my sharp-minded grandfather, he was probably beginning to realize there was something in the journal that was about him.

So what was I going to tell him now? That I knew about the affair between him and Jackie – the third generation of women in his life after his wife and daughter to find out behind his back? And that I wanted to protect him?

Or maybe this: that as long as he was still alive, I thought *he* should be entitled to decide whether to reveal what had happened between him and Jackie that year in France and afterwards during a tumultuous, enduring, but mostly discreet friendship – and not Harry Delacroix? That I was worried Harry would sensationalize what she knew – and she would – possibly corroborated by information from her aging mother, turning it into a potboiler about Jackie's love life and my grandfather, rather than the book Jackie had wanted to write – a non-fiction scholarly account of two strong, fascinating women living on the eve of the French Revolution whose lives were inextricably bound together.

And then what? What tabloid journalist, gossip columnist, or entertainment TV host in their right mind wouldn't want Pépé's story, wouldn't hunt him down until they found him? Or, after he politely declined all requests – it wasn't about the money because he didn't have a price, that was for damn sure – what about all the gossip-mongers who wouldn't stop digging until someone found an aging Smith classmate or someone who knew Pépé and would be willing to share a memory, a tidbit, a *soupçon* of information . . . for a small fee? A photo of Pépé and Jackie at the White House or perhaps something that might resurface that had been forgotten about for so many decades? I could see the headlines:

The Resistance Hero Who Seduced Jacqueline Bouvier: HIS Story Told for the First Time.

Jackie's Secret French Romance: The Man Who Captivated Her REVEALED!

Star-crossed Lovers: The Story of Jacqueline Bouvier and Luc Delaunay.

The car in front of us stopped abruptly and I slammed on the brakes. In spite of his seat belt, my grandfather flew forward and put both hands on the dashboard to stop the momentum. The seat belt restrained him hard and I heard him say a quiet 'ouf'.

'I'm so sorry,' I said. 'I didn't mean to do that. And I'd probably better pay attention to my driving so it doesn't happen again.'

'I didn't mean to distract you,' he said.

And for the rest of the drive to Mon Repos, we were both silent and lost in our thoughts.

SEVENTEEN

It was Harry, not the maid, who met us at the front door when we finally arrived at Mon Repos shortly before five o'clock. She was dressed in a pair of expensive-looking fitted black slacks, a white silk blouse unbuttoned just below the point of discretion to give more than a hint of the lacy nude push-up bra underneath. Around her neck, a stunning gold collar embedded with a large diamond looked powerful and vaguely Egyptian. Her three-inch heels – I caught the flash of red on the soles – were Louboutins. If she and Cricket were having money problems, you'd never know it to look at Harry, whose clothes probably cost as much as a monthly mortgage payment. She looked fabulous.

'Uncle Luc.' She threw her arms around my grandfather the moment he stepped into the foyer. I caught the scent of her perfume, something beguiling and oriental, as well as a whiff of alcohol. A nearly empty drink glass sat on a table inlaid with designs in lapis, malachite, and tiger's eye where she'd set it down. 'Do come in, do come in.'

Harry was at least a couple of drinks in – her slightly unfocused glassy-eyed stare was a dead giveaway. She had noticed me noticing the glass and said in a giddy, high-pitched voice, 'It's too late for tea, Lucie. We're having cocktails instead. Mom thought Uncle Luc would need a drink after that long flight? Maybe a couple of drinks – it's way past five o'clock in Paris.' Then she giggled at her little joke.

Definitely tipsy. Still speaking with that funny inflection that made it seem as if everything she said was a question.

My grandfather caught my eye as Harry slipped her arm through his and walked him down the hall toward the drawing room where Cricket was waiting. I followed behind.

'We're meeting the rest of the family at the Goose Creek Inn for dinner in a little while,' I said to Harry. 'We can't stay too long.'

'Nonsense,' she said. 'You have time for one drink? *At least* one drink.'

'Is Mia still here?' I asked. 'Maybe she could join us.'

Harry looked over her shoulder at me and made a pouty face. ''Fraid not. Your sister's at The Artful Fox. Willow needed help with something so she left about an hour ago.'

'Too bad.'

Or maybe just convenient. Mia and Sergio had already begged off dinner at the Goose Creek Inn because she'd claimed she had too much work and that Sergio had a deadline for a client's project. But the real reason, if you asked me, was her ongoing strained relationship with Pépé over her explanation of what had happened the day my mother – his daughter – died. He'd managed to put his life mostly back together after my grandmother passed away and he lost his wife of nearly fifty years, but I didn't believe he would ever stop grieving over the death of my mother.

Pépé, Harry and I walked into the drawing room; I was still behind the two of them so I did not see the look on my grandfather's face when he caught sight of Cricket. But my heart tightened as I watched her face light up with pure joy and unmistakable longing when she saw him. Cricket loved him. She'd loved him in Paris seventy years ago and she loved him now.

Pépé disengaged himself from Harry's arm and went straight to where she was seated on the tufted blue sofa, exactly as she'd been the other day, regal as an empress, her eyes never leaving his face. He took her hands in his, bent over and kissed them, murmuring something tender and low that I couldn't hear. Nor did I hear her reply.

I glanced over at Harry, wondering if we shouldn't adjourn to another room to leave the two of them to this very intimate reunion, but she swept in oblivious to what was taking place between her mother and my grandfather and said in a cheery voice, 'What can I get you to drink, Uncle Luc? Wine? Sherry? Port? A glass of champagne? We should celebrate.'

Pépé straightened up and turned around, their private moment over. He looked nonplussed; Cricket looked dismayed.

'What are you drinking, Geneva?' he asked Cricket.

She smiled. 'You're the only one who still calls me that. I'm having a sherry. Do sit down with me, Luc.'

'Then I'll have the same,' Pépé said to Harry, taking a seat on the sofa next to Cricket.

Harry poured his sherry and handed it to him. 'What about you, Lucie?'

'Sparkling water, please.'

'Oh, come on.' She looked like she wanted to add *spoilsport.* 'Have a drink.'

'Really, Harry. Just water. I'm driving.'

She gave me my water, poured herself another Scotch, and sat down on a burnt-orange wing chair, crossing one leg over the other and swinging it back and forth. I took my familiar spot on the love seat across from Cricket and my grandfather.

'So,' Harry said, 'how was your flight, Uncle Luc?'

We made awkward small talk for a few painful minutes, but neither Harry nor I should have been in that room: we should have left Pépé and Cricket to themselves. Harry wasn't exactly drunk, but she was well on her way, so she rambled on. If I could have found her off-switch, I would have leaned over and flipped it.

I tried catching Pépé's eye, hoping he'd say something about being a bit fatigued and that maybe he and Cricket could meet up tomorrow, but Harry wasn't having it. Instead she had an agenda and she was angling the conversation around to it. The topic of Jackie's book and probably the journal were going to come up.

Soon.

She didn't even bother with subtlety. 'Uncle Luc,' she said, 'Mom says she told you about the notes and outline Jackie Onassis left behind for a book about Marie Antoinette and the artist who painted her portraits. She also said you know that I'm finishing it? Or more like re-writing it?'

'Élisabeth Louise Vigée Le Brun is the name of the artist,' Pépé said in a pointed voice. It sounded like a rebuke. Cricket sat up straighter, suddenly on alert.

'Yes, of course. I know that.' Harry leaned forward, uncrossing her legs, elbows on her knees, directing all her energy and attention at my grandfather. 'I signed a contract with a publisher the other day. They're very, *very* interested in this project.'

Harry wanted something; that was clear. But being a little drunk made her reckless and cocky. I knew she had underestimated my grandfather, a world-class diplomat with decades of experience. He wasn't going to make this easy for her.

She seemed to be waiting for him to say something, but when he remained silent, she went on. 'So I was hoping you might be able to help me.'

'And how would I do that?' he asked in a polite voice.

At least he hadn't said *why.* Though I would bet money he was thinking it.

Harry shot a look of frustration at Cricket, whose face had turned impassive, while Pépé continued to act as if he had no idea what she was talking about. I hoped I didn't look like a deer caught in the headlights, which was how I felt. Harry plunged ahead.

'You were with Jackie the day she bought those paintings,' she said. 'She wrote about it in her journal. It sounds like you two were . . . very close, if I read between the lines correctly?' She glanced at Cricket again. 'Plus, Mom says you were seeing each other that year in Paris?' She put finger quotes around 'seeing each other'.

Pépé glanced at Cricket. 'Is that true, Geneva?'

'Luc.' She sounded apologetic. 'Jackie wrote about it. What could I say?'

My grandfather set his untouched sherry glass on the coffee table, his mouth set in a hard, thin line.

'There's nothing I can tell you that would contribute to what you apparently already know, Harriet. It sounds as if you have all the information you need for your project,' he said in a clipped voice.

'Oh, come on. You were *there.* You *know* what happened? The two of you were walking along the Seine and it started to rain so you stepped into a *bouquiniste's* and shared a kiss. Jackie spotted the paintings and you told her about them, about Vigée Le Brun. Jackie was enchanted with her story. That's what she wrote.' Harry sounded like an insistent little kid who couldn't believe she wasn't going to get her way. 'I just want you to tell me about it – you're the only one in the world who can. It's a lovely story, so romantic and sweet – especially the two of you kissing. What's the harm about it coming out now?'

Pépé looked over at Cricket, whose hand had moved to her throat as if she couldn't catch her breath. For a moment I thought she might pass out. As for my grandfather, I had never, ever seen him so angry.

'The *harm* is that you want me to betray the confidence of a dear friend I loved very much. She may be dead, but Jackie is still a woman with whom the world remains fascinated. I have no interest in discussing my relationship with her.' He turned to Cricket. 'Were you aware Jackie's journal had been so detailed and specific, Geneva?'

Cricket fiddled with the stem of her sherry glass, visibly upset. 'No,' she said in such a quiet voice I nearly didn't catch her denial.

She lifted her head and looked at her daughter. 'Harry, darling, I don't want Luc to be upset over you revealing something so deeply personal between him and Jackie and he clearly is. I've changed my mind. I don't think you should use those excerpts from Jackie's journal in your book. They were never meant to be made public. I'm sorry, but I made a mistake agreeing that it was all right.'

Harry gave her mother an incredulous stare. 'Come *on*, Mom. It's too late. My publisher's lawyers have already looked over the journal to make sure it was the real deal? You can't stuff the genie back in the bottle now. They *want* this romance to be in the book. That's why they bought it, paid so much money for it. Plus I signed a contract and agreed to it. You *know* that?'

'Jackie wouldn't want it. She would have hated it,' my grandfather said to Cricket. '*You* know that.'

'It doesn't matter any more,' Harry said, dismissing him. Now she was angry. 'She's a public figure – what she would or wouldn't have wanted isn't the issue. Besides, you can't go back on your word, Mom?'

'Harry . . .' Cricket began.

Harry stood up. 'And, Uncle Luc, if you don't want to help me, I can write the book without you. There's plenty of information in that journal and a few things that I can infer? Plus there are bound to be people who knew about you and Jackie. Obviously I'd prefer to do this with your cooperation, but . . .'

She shrugged and took a slug of Scotch.

'Harry.' Cricket's voice cracked like a whip. 'How dare you talk to Luc like that?'

'Like what? I don't understand either of you,' she said to Cricket and Pépé, slamming her glass down on the coffee table. 'You're acting like I'm committing a crime or revealing some sacred must-be-kept-at-all-costs secret. What's the problem?'

Pépé glanced at me and our eyes locked. He knew now why I'd urged him to talk Cricket into telling Harry not to use the journal. He also knew I was completely in the picture about him and Jackie. And I had let him walk into this situation blindsided.

'The problem is that it's not your story to tell, Harry,' I said. 'Jackie was one of the most private women in the world – as everyone in Middleburg knew – which is why she loved to come here. You knew her, too. Of course you sold your book for a huge advance – because it's *Jackie*. You know very well people will buy anything – dog food, tissues, hand sanitizer – if her picture is on it and it will sell out. Come on, the journal was private. It was almost certainly an accident that it ended up in that box with the other documents – Jackie was working on the project when she got sick. My grandfather and your mother were part of this story – it's *personal*. You don't have to do this to them.'

Harry swung around on me. 'Oh, Jesus, Lucie. Cry me a river,' she said. 'Jackie gave Mom all her papers and book research information when she gave her the paintings. Including the journal. I don't get you people. Any journalist in the world would do what I'm doing.'

'No they wouldn't. Not every journalist would choose to exploit the intimate details of someone's private life, especially when it's one of the most famous women of the twentieth century. Some people would have a conscience,' I said. 'You don't need to turn my grandfather's life into a public spectacle, either. Not everything ought to be for sale, Harry.'

'*You have no right—*'

'That's *enough*,' Cricket said with force. 'Both of you.'

'I agree.' Pépé stood up as well. He turned to me. 'We need to leave. Now.'

'Luc.' Cricket looked like she was about to cry. 'You and I need to talk. Please.'

'Tomorrow,' he said. 'Just the two of us.'

He walked out of the room without saying goodbye to her or acknowledging Harry. There was nothing else for me to do but follow him.

And wait for the explosion that I knew was going to come once we were in the car. When he wanted to know, quite justifiably, what the hell had just happened.

I started the Jeep. So far he hadn't said a word. I waited. He was still angry – incandescent, actually – but I also thought he was hurt. Because of all three of us: Harry for planning to write a titillating, vaguely salacious account of his relationship with Jackie; Cricket for not stopping her daughter from doing it; and me for not warning him . . . enough.

I turned on to Mosby's Highway toward Middleburg. The rest of the family would be gathering at the Goose Creek Inn. My grandfather and I needed to straighten things out between us before we got there.

'How long have you known?' he said at last.

'A little over a month.'

'I thought you hadn't seen the journal.'

He meant Jackie's journal.

I sucked in my breath. It now fell to me to tell him that there was more than one journal. Six weeks ago I wouldn't have known it existed. Then over Valentine's Day weekend I had to finally change the damn light bulb that had been burned out for ages in the attic and discover the cache of my grandmother's journals. Talk about irony.

'There's another journal – actually, journals,' I said. 'Grandmama's. I found them in the attic in a Galeries Lafayette box a few weeks ago. Mom must have taken them after she died.'

He flinched as if the news were a physical blow. 'I did not know that.'

'I figured you didn't. Pépé, I'm so sorry.'

'For what?' He sounded surprised. 'None of this is anything for you to be sorry about.'

'I should have told you about . . . everything . . . before we got to Mon Repos. But I wasn't sure what was in Jackie's journal and I didn't want you to know I . . . knew.'

'You mean you didn't want me to know you knew about Jackie and me. And that you found out by reading your grandmother's journals.' Statements, not questions.

'Yes.'

'Why didn't you want me to know?'

'Because what happened seemed like something private and intimate between you and Jackie. Sacred, almost.'

More silence from him. I felt as if I were watching him pick at the scab of a very old wound. Except it still hurt like something that was fresh and raw.

'It was.' He shrugged, but his shoulders sagged and he looked so defeated my heart went out to him. 'I always suspected your grandmother found out. She never said anything and we never discussed it, *bien sûr*. But something changed between us – *she* changed – and I guessed that's what it was.'

'You didn't ask her the reason?'

'No.'

'I don't understand,' I said. 'You and Grandmama weren't married when this happened. Neither was Jackie. Why was it so . . . wrong . . . for you to fall in love with her?'

He seemed to need time to figure out how to answer me. Surely he'd thought of it himself over the last seventy years?

'Because your grandmother and I had an understanding,' he said and it sounded like a painful admission, a guilty secret. 'We knew that we would marry each other, even though I hadn't actually proposed to her. And Jackie and I knew from the beginning, from the day we met, that our . . . relationship . . . was impossible. It wouldn't last . . . couldn't last.'

'That must have been sad.'

He shook his head and smiled, but the smile was full of melancholy and nostalgia. 'It wasn't. It was wonderful. We enjoyed every moment, every second we were together.'

I had never heard him like this. He'd never spoken about my

grandmother with such love and longing . . . and a heart that still ached.

'But you loved Grandmama, right?' I wanted him to reassure me. *Needed* him to reassure me.

'Of course I did.'

'You loved Jackie, too?'

'Yes.'

'Did she love you?'

He didn't answer right away and I couldn't tell if he didn't want to answer or wasn't sure what the right answer was.

'I . . . yes. I believe she did. But she was a pragmatist. Her family would never have approved of me. She was supposed to marry someone – an American – who came from wealth and a prominent family. I didn't fulfill any of those requirements.'

I wanted to ask him if my grandmother had become a second choice, someone he 'settled for' because he'd made a promise to her and he kept his word. And he couldn't have Jackie.

'You stayed in touch with Jackie after she returned to America.'

'Yes. We wrote each other and then I saw her when I was the Deputy Head of Mission at the embassy and she was First Lady.'

'Is it true you helped her when she wanted to bring the *Mona Lisa* to America? That's always been a rumor in the family.'

He gave me a sideways glance.

'Oh, come on. Tell me the truth, Pépé . . . after all this time.'

'If I do, I don't expect to read about it in Harry's book.'

'How could you even . . .?' I began, before I caught the ghost of a smile. 'Wait, you're teasing, right?'

'Of course, *ma belle.*'

We had turned on to Foxcroft Road. The inn was just up the street and we were running out of time. Already Dominique had texted me.

Où êtes-vous?

'Since you're such a texting wizard and Dominique just asked where we are, can you let her know that we'll be there in five minutes?' I passed him my phone. 'And you didn't answer my question about the *Mona Lisa*.'

'I may be a texting wizard,' he said, 'but I refuse to multi-task as you Americans do. It's very bad for your brain, you know. So let me reply to Domi.'

I heard the whoosh of a sent text and twenty seconds later the chirp of my cousin's reply.

'Ah,' he said, 'she says we are dining in the private dining room and to come directly there when we arrive. We can park around the back and enter through the side door.'

'Excellent. So what about the *Mona Lisa*?'

'It's a story for another time,' he said. 'If you want me to tell you about it, you need to hear all of it.'

'So that would be a yes?'

'Lucie,' he said, 'life is not always black or white, yes or no, true or false. Sometimes it's complex and complicated.'

The inn was just around the corner. We weren't going to have time to finish this conversation.

'I see,' I said, but I didn't.

Because I wasn't sure whether we were talking about the *Mona Lisa* any more – or my grandfather's love affair with Jacqueline Kennedy Onassis.

EIGHTEEN

The Goose Creek Inn sits on the edge of the woods in a bend of a curve on Foxcroft Road surrounded by flowering cherry trees, dogwoods, magnolias, and a magnificent weeping willow. It was nearly twilight when Pépé and I arrived so the fairy lights in the trees and the tiny white lights outlining the ivy-covered half-timbered building were on, glowing softly in the dusky light. The dogwood had just begun blooming and the hundreds of emerging white blossoms made the place look as if it were floating in the clouds, an enchanted scene from a child's book of fairy tales.

My late godfather had bought the nineteenth-century Tudor mansion more than forty years ago and relied on my mother's good taste and eclectic artistic style to help him furnish and decorate it, turning it into something resembling a comfortable French *auberge*. She scavenged antique stores for vintage furniture and searched for oil paintings and old prints to give the place a homey feel. When she was done, the inn looked as if it might have been plucked from a village somewhere in the middle of *la France profonde* – the heart of France. Over the years Fitz, my godfather, and Dominique, my cousin, had received numerous accolades for their creative menus and excellent cuisine, but the Goose Creek Inn was best known for its reputation as the most romantic place to dine in the Mid-Atlantic.

Dominique had reserved a table for our family in the green dining room, a small jewel of a room with a fireplace, an Impressionist-style painting of a square in Montmartre hanging above it, views of Goose Creek through three large leaded-glass windows, and dark, glossy hunter-green walls that gave the room its name. Half a dozen tables set a discreet distance apart were, surprisingly, not occupied tonight, though Dominique would have seen to that. We had the room to ourselves.

Usually special guests who required a certain amount of privacy were seated here – a President and a First Lady out on a date night, a senator or cabinet secretary who needed a quiet place to bring a 'niece' or a young nubile secretary, or someone who wanted an off-the-grid meeting and had a Secret Service detail waiting outside. The extra advantage of this room was a door in the adjacent hallway through which guests could enter and leave without anyone else in the restaurant being aware they had dined here. Pépé and I used the private entrance.

Dominique, Quinn, Eli, and Sasha were waiting for us seated at a table in a corner of the room. My brother had his arm around Sasha, his head bent close to hers as she fiddled with a strand of long golden-brown hair and nodded at something he'd just said. The two of them had met eighteen months ago at their children's daycare center – her son Zach and his daughter, who was my beloved niece, Hope. Eli is two years older than I am, typical anointed eldest child, occasionally bossy in the lord-it-over-me big-brother way, Type A organized and annoyingly precise, a stickler for details, an incredibly talented architect, and a brilliant pianist who could have gone to Julliard if he'd wanted to. Sasha was laid back, calm, serenely patient, and totally cool; she owned her own physical therapy practice and worked with children with severe neurological disorders so her priorities about what really mattered in life were grounded in the struggles her young patients dealt with every day. She was also the best thing to happen to my brother and I adored her.

When Eli's first marriage had fallen apart and he was drowning in debt from his ex-wife's profligate ways, I asked him and Hope to move in with me rent-free in return for his pro-bono services to repair anything that needed it (I already had a long list) as well as designing and supervising an overdue renovation of the winery. He'd also renovated the old carriage house next door to Highland House, turning the spacious place that had once housed my family's horse-drawn carriages and, later, our cars into an architecture studio for himself. He also updated the second floor living space, turning it into a cozy apartment for Persia. There had been moments when he and I nearly killed each other, but we'd also grown closer. Then when Quinn and I got engaged and Eli and Sasha had decided to get married, he had designed and built a house for his new family on our land; now they lived a two-minute walk from Quinn and me.

Dominique saw Pépé and me first and got up, throwing her arms around my grandfather. Eli was next, introducing him to Sasha, followed by Quinn who had finally acquiesced to the French custom of what's called *faire la bise* – kissing on both cheeks, even between men – instead of the more macho greeting of a firm handshake. After we all sat down, Dominique passed Pépé the wine menu and told him he was in charge once everyone chose what they wanted for dinner.

'My grandfather belongs to the *Confrérie des Chevaliers du Tastevin*,' Eli said to Sasha. 'It means the "Brotherhood of the Knights of Wine Tasters". It also means he knows everything there is to know about wine. So we *always* let him choose what we drink – and, of course, it's going to be French. Especially because he swears by the French paradox.'

'The what?' she asked.

Pépé grinned and said, 'Eli gives me too much credit. And I think he should be the one to tell you about the French paradox because we are the reason you Americans now drink so much red wine.'

Sasha turned to her fiancé, propped her elbow on the table, and leaned her chin on her hand. 'I need to know about this.'

'It goes back a few years,' he said. 'I think it was the nineties.'

'Eighties,' I corrected him.

He made a face at me and said, 'OK, the nineteen eighties, when a report came out explaining that in spite of the French eating a diet high in saturated fat, they have a really low incidence of coronary heart disease – which is the opposite of what's supposed to happen.'

'A paradox,' Sasha said.

'Exactly,' he said. 'So how could this be?'

'Because the French drink so much wine?' she said.

'Right. But specifically red wine,' Eli said. 'And more specifically an antioxidant called resveratrol that's in red wine and is supposed to be good for you.'

'You still have to drink in moderation,' I said. 'Plus the French eat a mostly plant-based Mediterranean diet with lots of vegetables, fruit, herbs, fish, and whole grains. Also most of the saturated fat comes from dairy and vegetables – not meat.'

'Are you telling this or am I telling this?' Eli asked as Quinn nudged me.

'Sorry.'

'So after this report came out, *Sixty Minutes*, the CBS News show, did a story on it and – bam. It opened the floodgates and all of a sudden America started drinking red wine like there was no tomorrow because now it was good for you,' he said. 'All of a sudden it was a health food.'

Sasha turned to my grandfather. 'Is that true?'

'It is, though it has been debunked in some places,' he said. 'But being a Frenchman, I'm convinced that wine and good food have excellent health benefits.'

'Do you drink wine every day?'

'But of course,' he said, 'including tonight. However, before we get to the wine, we must have champagne to celebrate two engagements, *n'est-ce pas?*'

'Another family tradition you'll get used to,' Quinn said to Sasha. 'Champagne goes with everything.'

'I do know something about champagne,' she said. 'According to Napoleon, in victory you deserve champagne, in defeat you need it.' She gave my grandfather a beguiling smile. 'I love champagne.'

He threw back his head and laughed. 'Eli,' he said, 'where did you meet this delightful woman who quotes Napoleon? She is someone after my own heart.'

Until the champagne arrived we made small talk about the menu, Pépé's flight, how was everything in Paris, the weather. As family reunions go, it had its moments of silence, especially because Pépé and I still hadn't gotten over the visit to Cricket and my blow-up with Harry. Everyone else sitting at the table knew something was amiss. It was only a matter of time before we ended up talking about the elephant in the room.

'How was your visit with Cricket?' Dominique asked, nailing it perfectly. 'Every time I've been to Mon Repos to discuss the party and the art gallery reception, all she talks about is you, Pépé.'

'Has she paid you for anything yet?' Eli cut in before my grandfather could answer.

Dominique looked surprised. 'I told her I'll bill her when it's all over and I know the final numbers.'

He shrugged. 'You might want to ask for some money now.'

Quinn and I exchanged glances. I avoided looking at my grandfather.

'What are you saying?' Dominique asked.

'I'm still trying to get paid for renovating an upstairs bathroom because of a leak in the roof. I sent a bill two months ago, then two reminders. Plus I've had a couple of conversations with Harry,' he said. 'So far, *nada.*'

'*Mon Dieu,*' my cousin said. 'What did she say?'

'She'll get around to it.'

'I heard the same story from a woman whose daughter comes to therapy for spina bifida,' Sasha said. 'She's a single parent and owns a flower shop in The Plains. Usually she lets Harry and Cricket run a tab because they order flowers for the house from her every week. All of a sudden she's not getting paid, either.'

'That doesn't sound good,' Quinn said.

'I've heard that rumor, too,' I said. 'That there are money problems.'

Our waiter returned with our champagne and took dinner orders, and we dropped the subject. Pépé chose a bottle of Clos de Vougeot for the red wine and a Picpoul from Languedoc for the white. After the waiter left and we made our toasts, my grandfather set his glass down.

Here it was.

'The rumors about Geneva's financial problems are true,' he said. 'She told me before I left France that there's not much of the money Édouard left her remaining. I offered to help her manage her finances years ago after he died and she turned me down. Now she said she wishes she had accepted my offer. Plus she has Harriet, who constantly asked for money while she was living overseas.'

'Wasn't she working while she was overseas, as in *making* money?' Quinn asked. 'Seems there was always talk at the General Store about her latest assignment. Either she was running with the bulls in Spain or she was in India during Holi, that festival where everyone throws colored paint all over each other.'

'She was,' he said. 'And she did make money. Unfortunately she spent more than she made.'

'Which is why Harry was so happy to have signed a book contract for seven figures to finish Jackie Onassis's book,' I said. 'They need the money.'

Eli whistled. 'Maybe I'll send another invoice now that she has some cash coming in.'

Our dinners arrived. Filet of trout with mushrooms, crabmeat, and toasted almonds for Quinn and me, Dover sole with lobster for Pépé, veal scallops with Virginia ham for Sasha, and rack of lamb for Eli.

'There's something else,' Pépé said and set down his fork and knife. 'And I would like you to hear it from me before you find out about it elsewhere.'

'Very mysterious,' Sasha said, with a grave smile.

'What's it about?' Dominique asked.

'Jackie,' he said, 'and me.'

'What the . . .?' Eli began but Sasha laid a hand on his arm and he shut up.

My grandfather explained then how he'd met Jackie in Paris, describing their blossoming relationship in a matter-of-fact way, but there was something in his voice – a catch, little pauses and hesitations – that made it obvious there had been a lot more between the two of them than my grandmother's journals had alluded to. Jackie had always possessed a piece of his heart and maybe she had even broken it, because it seemed to me as I watched his face and listened to his voice that the pieces must have never fit together quite the same way after she went back to America.

Eli and Dominique looked stunned; Sasha's face was composed and nonjudgmental; and Quinn kept looking at me because he could tell none of this was news to me. And he probably wanted to know not only why I hadn't told him, but also how and when I'd found out. Pépé hadn't said a word about my grandmother's journals, which I'd moved back to their dark corner of the attic.

So what was I going to tell Quinn?

'You said we would find out about this elsewhere,' Eli said when Pépé finished his story. 'What did you mean by that?'

'Jackie wrote about the two of us in a journal Harriet found. It was with the notes and the outline for the book Jackie planned to write. I was with her the day she bought the paintings that are going to be on display in The Artful Fox.'

'Harry's going to write about your . . . relationship?' Dominique asked. 'Why? It doesn't have anything to do with Jackie's book.'

'A previously unknown romantic relationship involving Jackie Onassis is going to sell a lot more books than one about Marie Antoinette and the woman who painted her portrait,' I said. 'Jackie might be dead, but Pépé is not. Can you imagine how many journalists and tabloids would love to know his side of the story?'

'You've got to be kidding me,' Eli said.

'Harry also asked Pépé to help her, to explain more about his romance with Jackie, when we were over there this afternoon,' I said.

Dominique turned to him. 'What did you tell her?'

'I told her no.'

'Is this subject going to come to light in some way when the paintings are on display at The Artful Fox?' Sasha asked.

'Harry is using excerpts from the journal that will explain how Jackie happened to buy the paintings,' I said. 'They'll be a kind of teaser for the book. Her publisher is handling it.'

'Damn,' Eli said. 'So, Pépé, your name will come up since you were with her?'

'That is correct.'

'What are you going to do?' Quinn asked.

'Right now? Finish my dinner,' my grandfather said. 'And tomorrow I'm going to mend fences with Geneva. We have known each other too long to let something like this come between us.'

'What about Harry?' Eli asked.

'She is determined to finish the book and she needs the money,' Pépé said. '*They* need the money.'

'In other words, you won't do anything,' my brother said.

'I will have a word with Harriet as well,' he said. 'But in the end, I think we all know she is going to do as she pleases.'

Our waiter, who must have been hovering just outside the dining room, chose the stunned silence – which he probably interpreted as a momentary lull in our conversation – to return and refill everyone's wine glasses, ask if we were all right and how our dinner was, and whether we needed anything else.

My phone buzzed quietly with a text. I fished it out of my pocket. 'It's from Bobby,' I said to Quinn. 'He says the vineyard is no longer a crime scene and that he's sorry he didn't let me know sooner but he's here having dinner with Kit.'

'Invite them to join us,' Dominique said. 'Maybe there is some news about Parker's murder investigation.'

'I doubt he'll say anything if there is, but I'll invite them. They were both looking forward to seeing you, Pépé,' I said and texted Bobby.

Five seconds later he wrote: *B right there.*

Quinn pulled up two more chairs from another table as Bobby and Kit walked in holding hands. He looked more tired than usual and his eyes were hooded. I reckoned Parker's high-profile murder had been keeping him up nights. Kit looked worn out, too, but in her case it was her worrying about Bobby worrying about Parker's high-profile murder. Still, their faces lit up when they saw Pépé.

'You'll join us for dessert,' Dominique said to them as the waiter returned with seven dessert menus and Kit squeezed in next to me while Bobby took the chair next to Pépé.

Kit's hand went to her ample stomach and I knew she was thinking about the diet going all to hell, but she said, 'We'd love to.'

The first subject that came up was, not surprisingly, Parker.

Bobby shook his head. 'Nothing to report that I can talk about, though we're narrowing our list of possible suspects,' he said. 'However, we did release Parker's body so Ash can begin making funeral arrangements.'

I leaned closer to Kit and said in her ear, 'There's really nothing new?'

'Nope. Like he said, he knocked a few people off his suspect list, but he's still working the case pretty hard.'

'Any idea who he's focusing on?'

She raised an eyebrow. 'Are you kidding me? I'd be the last to know – he doesn't cut me any slack. There's still a lot of media interest in Parker's death and the public relations office is being deluged, but Bobby won't say one word until he's sure he's got something solid.' She opened the dessert menu and groaned. 'I want one of everything. What's new with you?'

I told her about dropping by Cricket's earlier and Harry using Jackie's journal for her book and the excerpts for wall text, but left out mentioning Pépé's affair with Jackie and the stormy conversation between Harry and me. Kit would find out everything soon enough.

'Harry,' Kit said, 'is sort of full of herself.'

'A seven-figure book contract, Kit. Of course she is.'

'Yeah, well, wait until her publisher reads the finished manuscript.'

'What do you mean?'

The waiter asked for our dessert choices. I chose *crème brûlée*; Kit asked for Fitz's legendary Died-and-Gone-to-Heaven Double Chocolate Cheesecake.

'The diet starts tomorrow,' she said. 'What I mean is that Harry spent her whole life as a freelancer, hopping around the world writing stories on spec for anyone who would buy them. She lived off her father's trust money until that ran out, then Cricket started financing her. She makes it out to be an incredibly glamorous life, you know, sunning herself on a beach in Juan-les-Pins, on safari along the Zambezi River, skiing in Kitzbühel, all that happy crap, but the reality is that in the business it's known that stringers – freelancers – are wannabe journalists who aren't really good enough or talented enough to land a full-time job.'

'Seriously?'

'Yup. I always know I'm going to need to spend more time editing a piece from a stringer than I would from one of our correspondents. It's just the way of the world.'

'So you don't think her book is going to be a blockbuster?'

'It depends on whether Harry is merely completing the book that Jackie left behind, or going rogue and doing her own thing.

She worked for the *Trib* for a while, you know. Years ago. They finally cut her loose. Her work was sloppy and she didn't double source her facts. It got her in trouble. Actually it got *us* in trouble.'

'I didn't know that.'

'It's not widely known and it was before my time – but I heard about it from the horse's mouth. Prescott Avery himself,' she said, naming the late head of the dynasty that had founded the *Washington Tribune*. 'Cricket and Édouard used to socialize with Prescott and his wife and the four of them palled around with Katharine Graham, Ben Bradlee, and Sally Quinn from the *Post*, along with all the other Washington journalism royalty back in the day. So the whole Harry thing was sort of swept under the carpet because no one wanted to embarrass the Delacroixes, who were such generous philanthropists and so well loved for all their charitable work. You know how it is. "How do you solve a problem like Maria?"' She hummed the tune from *The Sound of Music*. 'Or Harry, as the case may be.'

In other words, Harry got a pass about her journalistic abilities because of who her parents were.

'Did Prescott tell Cricket or Édouard the real reason Harry was let go?' I asked.

'Good God, no. He didn't even tell them that she *was* let go. Prescott let the official version be that Harry decided to leave. For all I know – and knowing Harry – that was the story she sold her parents as well. They adored her – Cricket still adores her – so maybe nobody pushed too hard to find out what really happened. It's tough when someone has a total blind spot for their kid.'

'And the "kid" is in her sixties,' I said.

'Old habits.'

'I guess so.'

Our desserts arrived, along with espressos and decafs, so the conversation shifted to what had happened in Atoka and Middleburg since Pépé's last visit. My grandfather asked for the bill, but the waiter told him it had already been taken care of. There would be *Sturm und Drang* between my cousin and my grandfather because of it. Her restaurant. He was the family patriarch.

We left them to it as everyone gathered up their coats and belongings.

'Hey, how come your sister and her boyfriend aren't here for the family reunion along with everyone else?' Bobby asked me when we were by ourselves.

I really didn't want to get into the whole thing about Mia and Pépé and the tension that existed between them over my mother's death. So I gave him the reason Mia had given me.

'She's got a lot of work at the moment and Sergio has a deadline for a client.'

His eyes narrowed. 'Is that so?'

'Yes. Why?'

'No reason,' he said, but a small shiver ran down my spine.

He knew I hadn't told him the truth. Bobby always knew a lie when he heard one – his cop's sixth sense. And then there was this: he never asked a question just for the hell of it. He always had a reason, even if he didn't tell you what it was.

But he gave me a sober-eyed look and I knew then that Mia wasn't one of the people who had been eliminated from his suspect list. I wondered if he'd learned some new information in the last twenty-four hours and, if so, whether it was related to something that had happened while my sister and Sergio were living in New York.

If that were true and Bobby was working flat out to solve the case, as Kit said he was, then it was only a matter of time before I'd find out, too.

I just wasn't sure I wanted to know what it was. Mia didn't have any reason, any possible motive that I knew of for murdering Parker. Besides, it just wasn't in her DNA to do something like that.

Unless there was something else I hadn't reckoned on: she did it for Sergio. The man about whom she knew next to nothing but loved to distraction. She wanted to help him cover up whatever had happened in New York.

And it was something Parker Lord had known about as well.

That would be justification enough for Mia to dump a fatal dose of tetrahydrozoline in something Parker was drinking, maybe in a moment of out-of-control anger or fear that Parker was going to reveal their secret and she needed to do something, *anything*, to stop him.

Love. Blind love.

It was a good motive. People have killed for a lot less.

NINETEEN

Pépé, the most nocturnal human being I have ever known, surprised me by showing up at breakfast early the following morning, already dressed in a suit and tie. Even Quinn wasn't downstairs yet, which meant I had made the coffee, but because Pépé would want his *café au lait* I'd brewed it strong, the way Quinn liked it.

'What are you doing up so early?' I asked. 'Why don't you sit down and let me fix your *café au lait*? There are slices of Persia's homemade sourdough *miche*, some Irish butter, and a jar of last year's strawberry jam on the table.'

He nodded yes to coffee and held up his phone. 'A text from Geneva, quite early,' he said. 'She asked if I can come to Mon Repos this morning. She wants to talk, to straighten things out between us.'

My grandfather always took his coffee in a cup and saucer because he thought mugs were for barbarians, so I heated his milk in a saucepan, whisked it, and added it to the strong coffee.

'Is Harry going to be there?' I asked, setting it down in front of him.

'*Merci, chérie, pour le café* and I believe she is not.'

'Good.'

'Lucie . . .' He sounded reproachful.

'She was horrible to you yesterday.'

'I know, but I still need to make things right with Geneva. I'm ninety-three, *ma belle*. Every day is a gift. I don't want to die holding a grudge against someone or with an argument that is unresolved on my conscience. Especially with such a dear friend, someone I've known almost all my life.'

'Mom always used to say "Never let the sun go down on your anger",' I said.

Her other rule had been that no one left the house in the morning without being told they were loved. Because, she'd explained, you never knew if it might be the last time you had a chance to say it – and you wouldn't want to live with that regret. As a teenager with the arrogance of presumed immortality I couldn't imagine someone just up and vanishing from my life, so sometimes I'd slip out of the house for the day before she got to say it.

The day she died I hadn't seen her when she left to go riding with Mia, but as I sat numb with grief at her funeral, I was profoundly grateful that my last memory was of her kissing me goodbye that morning and telling me that she loved me very much.

'Your mother was right,' Pépé said. 'After I get back from Mon Repos, I was wondering if we might visit her.'

'Of course.'

It was our tradition every time he came to stay that we would take flowers to my mother's grave in the family cemetery and then go out to pay respects at the small wooden cross Eli had made and Leland had erected where she died. Not far away was a wooden bench under an *allée* of cherry trees, a place Mom loved, where Pépé and I would sit for a while and talk about her.

'I can drive you to Mon Repos,' I said. 'Or ask one of the guys to take you, depending on when you need to be there. Josie Wilde is getting here at ten thirty. I just need to be back before then.'

'I am invited for ten.'

'Then I'll drive you.' I sat down across from him. 'I'm glad you're going to fix things with Cricket. But what about Harry? Doesn't it bother you what she's planning to do with Jackie's journal?'

'Of course it does,' he said. 'But I have no control over her, do I? You know what they say – everyone is entitled to a private life, but living a secret life will get you in trouble. This secret has finally come out in the open after all these years.'

'It's not Harry's secret to tell.'

'It's rare someone reveals their own secrets, isn't it? Usually someone else outs them; that's the way it works. Unfortunately I think Harry is going to turn my relationship with Jackie into one of your American television dramas – those soap operas Thelma loves so much – and that I don't like at all,' he said, showing a small flash of anger. 'I'm going to ask her not to do anything to cheapen or make vulgar what was a very special friendship.'

'Do you think she'll go along with it?'

'I hope so. Especially since I will assure her that if she does go through with this, it's going to involve her mother as well. My hope is that Harriet will want to spare Geneva all the unflattering interest and attention her book will cause.'

'You might have some leverage bringing Cricket into it,' I said. 'That's what made you such a successful negotiator in your diplomatic days. You always knew how to get what you wanted.'

He smiled. 'I'm not so sure about *always*. And on the subject of diplomacy, *chérie*, there is one other matter I must put right.'

'What?' I said, but I had a feeling I knew what he was going to say, especially after what he'd just told me. Mending fences. Putting his life in order. Preparing for . . . the end.

'My relationship with Mia.'

'Why are you doing all this now?' I asked.

He stared at me without speaking and I felt a lump rise in my throat.

'I'm glad,' I said, after a moment.

His eyes were grave. 'So am I. We have lost a lot of years. I know your sister wasn't the same after your mother died. She became such a rebel, got into so much trouble. I remember when Dominique made the decision to leave France and move to America to help take care of her since she was too much for your father.'

'Mia is just like Leland,' I said and told him about her being questioned by Bobby after he found eye drops with her art supplies at Mon Repos. And about the mysterious Sergio.

'You don't like him?' Pépé asked.

'It's not that,' I said. 'I think he's hiding something and I think Mia knows what it is. Parker told me the last time I saw him that he thought he'd met Sergio in New York years ago.'

'But Sergio is not a suspect,' he said, 'because he didn't see Parker the day he died, whereas Mia did.'

'Right.'

We stared at each other again and I knew we were thinking

the same thing. Had Sergio dragged Mia into some ancient business between him and Parker? Could she . . . *had* she . . . put those eye drops in something Parker drank? I still didn't want to believe it was possible.

And then there was this: just because Sergio said he hadn't seen Parker – even though Parker had driven right by his cottage – it was Sergio's word against Parker's.

And Parker was dead.

Josie Wilde met Quinn and me at the winery just as I got back from Mon Repos. I had asked my grandfather to call or text me after he and Cricket were finished with their visit so I knew whether he needed a ride home.

Josie, aka Doctor Grapevine, was smart, no-nonsense, don't-waste-my-time-efficient, and drop-dead gorgeous. This morning she wore skinny jeans, Wellingtons, a Kelley-green quilted sleeveless vest over a cream-colored sweater that set off her long, flame-colored hair, English rose complexion, and dark green eyes. I got a hug from her; Quinn – or 'Mr California', as she called him – got a firm handshake since the two of them hadn't quite found their modus operandi. I trusted Josie totally. Quinn, on the other hand, still wasn't ready to hand over the reins to her and let her tell us what we needed to do in the vineyard. It was only after I'd assured Josie that he would fall in line that she'd agreed to take us on. But the two of them still danced around each other like boxers in the ring trying to figure out who was going to throw the first punch.

Quinn drove our four-seater all-terrain vehicle out to the Merlot block and parked next to the dying vines. The middles – the area between the rows – looked trampled where Bobby's deputies had been searching.

Josie noticed right away. 'Is this the place?'

'It is,' I said.

She half genuflected as if she were saying a quick prayer and blessed herself. As she walked over to the withered vines I saw her take a swipe at her eyes with the back of a hand.

After a moment, she cleared her throat, but her voice still came out ragged. 'You've got scion rooting.'

'Oh, God,' I said. 'Are you sure?'

Josie knelt and brushed away soil from the graft union of one of the vines. 'Do you have a shovel? Or a hoe? This looks like phylloxera decline.'

Quinn groaned. 'That's all we need.'

'Damn.' I knelt next to her.

Phylloxera is an aphid that feeds and breeds on the roots of grapevines. It is so small it can barely be seen with the naked eye. What you do see are tiny, tiny yellow specks. It is deadly serious and usually fatal because by the time you find out you've got it, it's too late to do anything but rip out the vines.

In the 1860s, a botany exchange program that was sending native plants across the Atlantic to Europe unintentionally sent grapevines infected with phylloxera, wiping out millions of acres of vines with a scorched-earth swiftness that stunned the wine world. As phylloxera raced around the globe through Europe, across the US to California, and eventually to Australia, New Zealand, and South Africa, it destroyed world-class vineyards planted with *Vitis vinifera*, the noble European wine grapes. The irony was that the American vines that had caused the devastation – such as Isabella and Catawba, or *vitis lambrusca* – were the only vines that could save these decimated vineyards. And the only way to do that was to graft American phylloxera-resistant rootstock to Old World *Vitis vinifera*.

It was exactly what we had done here since Merlot was one of the noble grapes that wasn't resistant to phylloxera.

But there was a catch, and it's what had gotten us in trouble now: the graft union of the two vines – European and American – had to always remain above the soil line. Because if it didn't, the Old World scion would start sending out its own roots, bypassing the American rootstock.

Quinn left to get the shovel.

'It might not be too late,' Josie said, trying to reassure me. 'If we cut the vinifera roots and the rootstock is alive, the graft will still work.'

Quinn came back with a shovel. 'Should I dig?' he asked.

'Go ahead,' she said.

He dug a few inches down and moved the dirt away from the vine. Then he knelt next to Josie and me.

'Take a look,' Josie said and traced her finger along the trunk

of the vine. 'See there? These aerial roots from the Merlot
follow along the trunk of the vine and took root under the
surface so you wouldn't have noticed them if you hadn't been
looking.'

'We still should have realized the graft was not above ground,'
I said. 'That's on us.'

She shrugged. 'It happens. When you disc to break up the
soil or use mechanical cultivation to expose weeds so you can
kill them more effectively, the soil can mound up around the
vine and *voilà*, the graft is suddenly below the ground. Or if
you planted your vines with the graft too near the ground to
begin with and the vine settled, it can happen that way.'

She dug a little deeper and brought up a Merlot root, removing
a jeweler's loup that hung around her neck so she could take
a closer look. 'Yup, kids. I'm afraid it's phylloxera. You need
to get on this right away. Check the grafts of all the other vines
and cut off the aerial roots if the rootstock is still healthy.'

I glanced at Quinn. 'Now you know why she's the best,' I
said.

'Doctor Grapevine,' he said. 'I'm impressed.'

Josie grinned. 'I prefer my other nickname. I'm not a PhD,
you know.'

'What is it?' I asked.

'The Julia Child of Grapevines,' she said and we laughed.
She brushed the dirt off her hands on to her jeans and stood
up. 'Let's take a look and see how extensive the damage is.'

'There's something else we're worried about,' I said as the
three of us walked up and down the rows of grapevines, pausing
to kneel and check for grafts.

'Let me guess,' Josie said. 'We didn't have a single snowflake
all winter. Everything's blooming early and it's not going to be
long before the sap starts running.'

'Good guess,' Quinn said.

It was happening way too soon. Especially if Mother Nature
threw us a curve ball and decided we needed another hard freeze
later in the month, or even in April. Maybe more than one,
which would kill any bud that decided to show its tender head.

'Climate is what you wish for,' Josie said. 'Weather is what
you get. Plus it's not only Virginia. I just came back from

France. Do you know what's happening there? The winemakers in Bordeaux are asking to reclassify grapes grown in southern France and Spain as Bordeaux grapes because they're realizing the grapes they've grown for centuries are going to make different wines now that they've got a warmer climate.'

'We read about that,' I said. 'I still can't wrap my head around it.'

Bordeaux, where some of the most famous, most romantic wines in the world came from. Legendary vintages drunk at state dinners, coronations, and celebrations meant to be remembered for a lifetime. Wines – *French* wines – that would never be the same if they were made from a grape that came from Spain.

'So now what?' I asked.

'If we keep having this extreme weather – and we will – I think you're going to have to start planting hybrids or multi-Vitis varieties that have both American and European genes. Hardier grapes that will grow when there's too much rain or we have an exceptionally cold winter or a blistering hot summer.'

'We grow Seyval,' Quinn said. 'We already have a hybrid.'

'I know, and that's a good thing, Mr California,' she said, 'but I'm talking about newer crosses like Chardonel. It's a combination of Seyval and Chardonnay and holds its acidity much better. Then there are other French-American grapes like Chambourcin or Traminette, which has Gewurztraminer as one of its parents – they're better adapted to Virginia's climate. You need to think about them.'

Chardonel had been crossbred by the New York State Agricultural Experiment Station at Cornell. Traminette was born in the 1960s at the University of Illinois.

'In other words, genetically modified grapes,' Quinn said. 'Frankengrape. Something that will live in any kind of climate.'

'Absolutely not,' Josie said and I almost thought she was going to stamp her foot. 'The grapes I'm talking about were created either in nature or with human intention by old-fashioned pollination that occurs with the birds and the bees, or in this case the stamen and the pistils. There is a *huge* difference between GMOs and hybrids. Hybrids are created from nature.'

'Fair enough,' Quinn said.

'Look,' she said, 'the Europeans have already begun creating new multi-Vitis varieties and they're planting hybrids that are better suited to current and changing conditions. It's not either/or, you know – pure vinifera grapes or crosses.' She reached out and snapped off a dead vine, dropping it to the ground. 'It's a crapshoot when we're going to get the next crazy season. And you know it's not if, it's *when*. Do you really want to play Russian roulette and hope you can tough it out?'

Quinn and I looked at each other. 'We need some time to think about this,' I said to Josie. 'We're known for these grapes, these wines. Downgrading to hybrids is going to hurt our brand.'

'At least you'll have a brand,' she said in a tart voice and her words hit like a physical blow. 'I know this is tough to swallow, but I'm trying to help you plan for the future. That's why you hired me. So I'm not going to sugarcoat it. You already know it's going to be years before you'll make wine if you decide to plant new and different varieties – and longer before you actually sell your first bottle. There's at least a two-year wait before you can even get the custom-grafted rootstock – unfortunately – and then three years after you plant before you get a harvest from which you can make wine.'

'OK,' Quinn said. 'We're listening. But we need to crunch numbers and see how much we can afford to lay out without getting a single penny back on our investment for six years.'

'I know,' she said. 'If you want to make a small fortune running a vineyard, right?'

'Start with a large one,' I said. It was a tired old joke and right now it seemed DOA.

'When you're ready,' she said, 'I can help you order the vines. I've got some sources that might be able to get it to you a bit sooner than two years. Not by much, but anything would help.'

'In other words, we wouldn't order from Seely's?' I asked.

'Uh, no.'

'Any particular reason?'

'I don't know if you heard, but Gabriel was terminated at New Dominion U,' she said. 'They pulled the plug on his post-doc research work. It's affecting the nursery as well and business has been falling off. Apparently they're trying to triage and reach out to as many of their clients as possible, assure them that what happened at NDU has nothing to do with the integrity of the plants the nursery sells. And to answer your question, they aren't one of the places on my list. Even before everything happened.'

'Have you spoken to him?' I asked.

'Gabriel? No, not since Parker died. I gather he's still a suspect in Parker's murder investigation because of their argument. He's been told not to leave town.'

'Do you think he did it?' Quinn asked.

She glanced over at the trampled grass. 'I don't know. Somebody did it.'

My mobile rang in my back pocket and I reached for it. 'Sorry,' I said to her, 'this might be my grandfather. He's at Mon Repos and he's probably calling to ask if I can pick him up.' I glanced down at the display. 'Actually, it's not Pépé.'

'Who is it?' Quinn asked.

'Speak of the devil,' I said and hit the green button. 'Hello, Gabriel. What's up?'

TWENTY

Josie left to visit to Ash – a condolence call – after our meeting ended and Quinn and I drove over to Seely's Garden Center. Her final pronouncement to Quinn and me about our future had left us both subdued, as if we'd already lost a battle in a war we weren't ready to fight. Plus we had our work cut out for us with the serious problem of scion rooting and phylloxera if we didn't want to lose any more vines.

Gabriel had called with the pretext of asking if we still planned to order the list of plants and seeds for our garden that Ash had given him last week – before everything happened. I didn't know the current status of his relationship with Ash, considering the fact that, one, Gabriel was a prime suspect in the murder of Ash's husband and, two, Ash had just lost a lot of money now that Gabriel's research program had been terminated. So reading between the lines, what Gabriel really wanted to know was whether the deal was still on or were we taking our business elsewhere.

I suggested having the conversation in person and told him we'd be right over. He sounded pleased that we wanted to come by and see him so promptly, but I could also hear the apprehension in his voice that maybe we were going to tell him that after nearly forty years and hundreds of thousands of dollars spent on grapevines, plants, seeds, bushes, flowers, trees, fertilizer, gardening supplies, and our annual Christmas tree, we were through.

Seely's Garden Center was located at the intersection of Sam Fred Road and the Snickersville Turnpike on the outskirts of Middleburg. It sprawled across five acres with half a dozen buildings surrounded by beautiful display gardens that changed with the seasons and were connected by flagstone walks and footbridges crisscrossing a meandering man-made stream. The offices, help desk, and checkout counters were located in a spacious, airy building that looked like something resembling a log cabin crossed with a hay barn. It smelled of the tang of mulch and fertilizer as well as the vaguely tropical odor of indoor plants and flowers from an adjoining greenhouse. Out back the shade-growing potted plants were located under a covered pergola. Further back were sun-loving plants, bushes, and eventually the saplings and trees, lined up in neat rows like soldiers.

The first day of spring was tomorrow. Daylight savings time began two Saturdays ago. Our guys had already mowed the lawn twice. People should be leaving here with pallets crammed with pots of annuals for bedding gardens, seeds, bags of mulch, and flowering plants like azaleas or camellias or rhododendron. In other words, the joint should have been jumpin'.

It wasn't.

'How do you want to play this?' Quinn asked as he pulled the Jeep into a spot in the not-too-crowded parking lot.

'I'd like to hear what he has to say about why he faked his results and what happened when he and Parker argued that last day. Mia is still on Bobby's list – I'm almost certain of that,' I said. 'She didn't do it, Quinn.'

'And you're thinking what, exactly? That Gabriel's going to cop to murdering Parker – confess to us – and get your sister off the hook?'

'Of course not,' I said, indignant. But he was right. It was called grasping at straws. 'Okay, why don't we just wing it?'

'Probably a good idea,' he said. 'Since the truth is we don't have a plan.'

We went inside the main building and asked a young cashier at one of the counters if he knew where we might find Gabriel.

'I'll page him,' he said and spoke into a walkie-talkie. A moment later we heard a squawk and then Gabriel's distorted voice asking us to meet him in the back next to the azaleas.

'Tell him sure,' I said to the kid, who complied.

We walked outside to the pergola, which was flooded with warm light diffused through the canopy. Two women wearing bright yellow Seely's Garden Center tee shirts were watering the bedding plants, which were arranged on stepped shelves by color and varietal or spilled out of planters hanging from the rafters. Any other day I would have lingered to chat and ask about the latest arrivals and what was new this season, but today Quinn and I just waved and kept walking.

Gabriel, wearing a Panama boater over long dark curls, a white polo shirt, and jeans, was deep in conversation with a dark-haired, dark-skinned man in a Seely's tee shirt when we caught sight of him standing at the end of a row of barely budding azalea bushes. It looked as if Gabriel was either giving the guy instructions or the third degree since he kept jabbing his index finger on the clipboard he was holding to make his point. The man cut a glance our way and Gabriel followed his gaze. Whatever he'd been saying, he toned it down once he saw us.

When we reached the two of them, Gabriel said, 'Okay, we're done here. Are you all set, Orlando? You know what you've got to do?'

Orlando nodded, acknowledged Quinn and me, and left.

'Everything OK?' Quinn asked when the man was out of earshot.

Gabriel pushed up the brim of his boater and scratched his head. He was in his late thirties, but today the weariness in his eyes after everything he'd been through made him look older and a bit beat up. 'I just found out one of the supervisors on a big job we have out in Clarke County isn't giving the guys breaks and is working them pretty hard. They're building a huge fieldstone wall plus mulching and cleaning up garden beds on a ten-acre estate and the rather wealthy client is one of those people that makes you want to start drinking after breakfast she changes her mind so often,' he said. 'I told Orlando to lay down the law, make sure the guys are treated right.'

'It's tough when you have an employee who abuses the crew just to look good finishing jobs on time,' Quinn said. 'We had someone like that once. Got everything done, but a miserable human being.'

'What'd you do?'

'Fired him.'

Gabriel nodded. 'The supervisor's wife is expecting a baby in five weeks. He needs to shape up. I don't want to fire a guy with a kid on the way. At least not right now.'

'That's good of you,' I said.

'You need to give people a chance,' he said, settling his hat back on his head and tugging the brim so it shaded his tanned, lined face and hid the dark circles under his eyes. 'See if they can straighten up and fly right once you warn them.'

I wondered if he was talking about the job supervisor out in Clarke County or himself. NDU hadn't given him much of a chance at all. From one day to the next he was booted out the door. At least he'd given us an opening, though.

'We heard what happened at New Dominion,' I said. 'Parker came down on you pretty hard.'

'That's right,' Gabriel said with an edge in his voice. 'He did.'

'Was he right?' I asked.

'I can back up everything I wrote in that paper. It wasn't wrong.'

'Then what was the problem?' Quinn asked.

'Let's walk,' he said. 'I need to check out some dogwoods. We've got a commercial job coming up and the landscaper wants a dozen Bradford pears on either side of their entrance. I'm trying to talk them into dogwoods instead, even if they are more expensive.'

He hadn't been subtle about changing the subject – or avoiding the question. Hadn't Ash said that Gabriel went around Parker's back a few times to persuade a client to alter his design plans and choose different plants? And that the article in the *Trib* was partial payback for Gabriel undermining Parker's reputation and relationship with his clients?

'Why are you changing what the landscaper recommended?' Quinn asked, reading my mind.

'Because Bradford pears are beautiful, but one, they're invasive, and two, if you get close enough they stink. The smell attracts the right kind of pollinator but the trees smell like a combination of rotting fish and semen.'

'Point taken,' Quinn said.

'Do you do that often?' I asked. 'Change the plans of a designer?'

'When I think there's a better option or someone will regret their choice down the road – and they're spending a lot of money – I make a suggestion,' he said.

We walked down the dirt-and-gravel road toward a forest of

slender young trees. The nursery was just too quiet. Somewhere in the distance a tractor rumbled, but there weren't many people around except for the occasional employee in a yellow tee shirt.

'Are you guys still planning to go through with your order for the garden Ash is supposed to put in for you?' Gabriel asked.

I glanced over at Quinn who said, 'We are.'

'Excellent. You've been long-time clients, so if there's ever anything you need or you've got some problem, you come straight to me, OK?'

This was the triage Josie was talking about.

'We appreciate that,' I said. 'Look, we know business at the nursery has suffered because of everything that went down at NDU. But our families have known each other for decades, Gabriel. So what happened? I don't believe you're the kind of person who fakes data to get the results you want. Or expect.'

We reached the block of trees where the dogwood were located. Some were beginning to bloom, just as they had been at the Goose Creek Inn last night.

'Thanks for that, Lucie. I appreciate it. Come on, let's take a walk down here,' he said and we followed him down one of the rows. Dappled sunlight sifted through the branches above our heads, making a mosaic pattern of light and shadow on the ground.

Gabriel tugged on a white plastic tag on one of the trees. 'It sounds like you know Parker took offense when I suggested changes to his plans,' he said, peering at the information on the tag and writing it down on a paper attached to the clipboard. 'As if I were suggesting God should do some rearranging about what went where in the Garden of Eden.'

Quinn suppressed a smile and I said, 'But that isn't the only reason Parker wrote that piece in the *Trib*, is it? He found something that bothered him about the results of your experiments.'

'I can back up every result with absolute proof.'

'You said that already,' Quinn said.

'You didn't report all your findings,' I said. 'You cherry-picked the best data and made the results look better than they were. Am I right?'

Gabriel gave me a look as if he were about to step off a cliff and knew what was at the bottom. The abyss.

'You don't understand.'

Jesus Lord. Bobby always said that was the very last line he heard before a suspect finally gave it up and confessed. And it was always someone who genuinely believed they were a good person but got stuck between a rock and a hard place, in a situation they didn't ask for. *I didn't mean it. I didn't have a choice. It wasn't what it seemed. I had a good reason for doing it. I'm not a bad person.*

Quinn folded his arms across his chest, a troubled look on his face, and I said, 'Do you want to explain so maybe we will understand?'

I tried to keep my voice light and friendly but Gabriel looked at the two of us as if he knew we'd already made up our minds about him anyway.

'Yeah, I do.' He sounded combative. 'Because so far, no one seems to care about my side of the story. They just see it as black and white.'

Which meant he was operating in the gray shadows located next door to the slippery slope. What had Ash said? Even Gregor Mendel had massaged his famous green and yellow pea experiment results – and he was the father of modern genetics.

'Tell us,' I said. 'We care. Honest.'

Gabriel gave a rough laugh. 'Thanks.'

He deadheaded a spent dogwood blossom as though he were stalling for time or trying to figure out where to start. Then he looked up and I could see just how angry he was. The stalling was to get himself under control.

'If my project succeeded,' he said finally in a tight voice, 'do you have any idea what the consequences could be for farmers, vineyard owners like you – anyone who works in agriculture, horticulture, forestry, agronomy . . . I could go on. The data from my experiments strongly suggested that glutathione – which is a detoxifier and an antioxidant – plays a significant role in a plant's defense against a whole range of pests and stressors.' He threw up his hands. 'Jesus. Do you know what it would mean if we could manipulate a plant's glutathione so it would save itself instead of dying?'

'It would be huge,' I said. 'We'd be able to resuscitate plants that are grown for food, preserve wildlife habitats, maybe even mitigate the impact of climate change.'

'Exactly,' he said.

'Except "strongly suggests",' Quinn said, 'isn't the same as "is". In other words you still haven't proved it can be done, have you?'

Gabriel banged his clipboard against his thigh. 'Dammit, it *can* and I have. OK, not consistently, and there's still a whole lot I don't know. It's only the beginning. Baby steps. But I am dead-bang *sure* I'm on the right path.'

'You falsified your data to make your results look better than they were,' Quinn said. 'Parker wrote in the *Trib* that they were too good to be true.'

'I didn't falsify anything,' Gabriel said. 'But Lucie's right. I just didn't use data from results that didn't match my expect-ations. Let's just say I was a bit selective.'

'*Why?*' I said. 'Why did you have to cheat? Couldn't you have waited until you had better results? Or more results that proved you were right?'

He pulled off his hat and ran a hand through his wiry black hair so it stood up as if he'd been electrocuted. 'Do you have any *idea* the pressure in the science world these days to publish some new, exciting finding? Or just to publish in a prestigious scientific journal? Science isn't a big priority in the US these days – which is stupid and a damn shame – so we're hemor-rhaging talent and our smartest people are going elsewhere. Do you know what that means for the rest of us who face cut-throat competition for dwindling grant money?'

He didn't seem to expect an answer to what were clearly rhetorical questions so he went on.

'The really bad guys are the scientists who invent or fake data. You can send future researchers working on the same problem down the wrong path for decades with phony informa-tion, waste a hell of a lot of money and time,' he said. 'That's inexcusable.'

'And that's not what you did?' Quinn said.

'No,' he said, 'it's not. I took a short cut and I admit I shouldn't have done it. I painted a rosier picture than what really existed because I needed the early success to attract more money to continue. Parker decided to take a chainsaw to what I'd done and destroy everything. I don't think the punishment fit the crime.'

'You must have been angry when you saw him the other day,' I said.

'Damn straight,' he said. 'I didn't kill him, though, and if I had? Look around this place. A nursery. There are plenty of pesticides and chemicals and toxic substances right here that I know about and could have used. But tetrahydrozoline? Eye drops? My eyes are fine. I don't even wear glasses.'

'Any idea who did kill him?' Quinn asked.

Gabriel deadheaded another blossom and dropped it to the ground. 'Nope. I admired Parker for writing *The Angry Earth*, but he pissed off a hell of a lot of people and he wasn't shy about calling things as he saw them. My money's on someone he pushed too far because of that book.'

'You don't think it was someone from around here?' I asked.

'Look, I know I'm prime suspect number one, and Ash is second on the list because he and Parker argued the day he died. I didn't do it and I'll bet you any amount of money Ash didn't either,' he said. 'So who's left?'

His phone buzzed. He pulled it out and looked at the display. 'Sorry, do you mind? I gotta take this. It's the Bradford pear guy. I need to talk him into dogwoods and we need this job.'

'We know the way out,' Quinn said.

'You'll get our order for the garden in the next few days,' I said.

He nodded, mouthed 'thanks,' and punched his phone. 'Hey, Tommy. Can we talk?'

Quinn and I walked back to the Jeep in silence. Gabriel said he didn't murder Parker and he'd stake his life that Ash wasn't guilty either. Bobby's two prime suspects. So, he'd said, who did that leave?

I knew the answer to that question.

My sister.

TWENTY-ONE

My grandfather was in a somber mood when I picked him up from Mon Repos a few hours later.

'How did it go? Is everything OK?' I asked as he got in the Jeep.

'I'm worried about Geneva,' he said. 'I didn't realize she was as frail as she is. Harriet and I spoke about her after she went upstairs to lie down. I think our conversation exhausted her.'

I pulled out on to Mosby's Highway. 'You talked to Harry? How did *that* go?'

'Harriet is going to stay home and take care of her mother, which is a great relief to me,' he said. 'That's the reason she came back to Mon Repos.'

I thought the reason Harry came back to Mon Repos was because she'd run out of husbands and money. 'That's good of her.'

Pépé cast a sidelong glance at me. 'Sarcasm doesn't suit you, *ma belle.*'

'Oh, come on, there's something in it for her, you know that. That's why she's doing it.' I signaled for the turn on to Atoka Road and gave him a defensive look. 'She's spoiled and an opportunist. If she wanted the moon hung somewhere different, Cricket would figure out how to do it for her.'

He looked amused. 'That's probably true.'

'Did you talk to Harry about the book and Jackie's journal while you were at it?'

'I did. Not only did we talk, but I proposed a compromise.' He gave me a pleased look. 'That she accepted.'

'What kind of torture was involved?'

He smiled in spite of himself. 'I made it clear it would not be in her best interest to turn my . . . friendship . . . with Jackie into something that would end up on the cover of *France Dimanche* or the front page of *The National Enquirer.*'

'And how did you do that?'

His smile deepened. 'I reminded her that I have an excellent memory and that she, also, knew Jackie because of her mother's close friendship with her. So I said I'd respect her privacy concerning her relationship with Jackie if she would respect mine.'

'Blackmail?'

'I prefer to think of it as a mutually beneficial agreement,' he said. 'As for the excerpts from Jackie's journal that are going to be used with the paintings at The Artful Fox, there will be no mention of me – at least not by name.'

'That's a good thing.'

He shook his head. 'Not exactly. It was her publisher's idea. They already have a title for the book – even a cover design – though Harriet hasn't written a single word. It will be on display at the art gallery.'

'The gallery exhibit is going to be a promotional teaser for the book,' I said, disgusted. 'It's going to be about Harry, not the paintings.'

I wondered if Marilyn Gilbert Bernard was aware of this and whether she'd manage to convince Cricket to follow through with her donation to the National Museum of Women in the Arts once the exhibit at The Artful Fox ended.

'I suppose you know what the title is,' I said.

'*The French Queen, the American First Lady, and the Artist Who Captivated Them.*'

'Catchy. It will sell books.'

'I believe that's the intention.'

I made the final turn on to Sycamore Lane at the entrance to the vineyard.

'You didn't say whether everything was fine with you and Cricket.'

'I am going to be her escort at the gala on Friday and at her party on Saturday.'

'That sounds like it might be a yes?'

He nodded, but I wasn't entirely convinced. Maybe they'd only settled on a truce.

We reached the turnoff for the house.

'I thought we might go visit Mom,' I said, slowing down, 'unless you'd like to have a rest. You look a bit tired.'

'I'm fine,' he said, 'I'd like to see her. I can rest another time.'

I stepped on the gas pedal. 'Then let's go.'

Ever since my Scottish ancestor Hamish Montgomery received the land for Highland Farm as thanks for his service to America during the French and Indian War, everyone in my family – beginning with Hamish – had been buried in a small cemetery on the flattened crest of a hill not far from the house. Hamish chose the location for its breathtaking view of the Blue Ridge so he would always be able to enjoy looking out on his beloved mountains. My father was the last to be laid to rest here; my mother had preceded him by eight years. I had no doubt I would join them someday as well.

I came here often as my mother used to do, to sweep out fallen leaves and debris, clear up branches, and generally take care of the headstones and graves of my ancestors. On the patriotic holidays I left small flags at the markers of those who had fought in all of America's wars; other times, I brought flowers.

I parked at the bottom of the hill and Pépé and I – both of us with our canes – slowly climbed it together, to the creaky wrought-iron gate at the entrance. He opened it so I could go through first, and then followed me inside. A low redbrick wall surrounded the cemetery; it was high enough for privacy, but not so high to obscure the view. The weather had warmed up and a fresh breeze that smelled of spring blew through the branches of the still-bare trees around us. A few drifting clouds left checkerboard patterns of sunlight and shadow on the mountains. One of the pair of Mr-and-Mrs cardinals that had staked out the cemetery as their territory sang from the bushes outside the wall.

'It's peaceful here,' my grandfather said.

'It is.'

I had cut a bunch of bright-yellow daffodils from one of the gardens near the summerhouse and put them in water in a Mason jar. Now I gave it to Pépé so he could place it at my mother's headstone. I always left him to do this alone, to spend time with his daughter and to talk to her. And to grieve.

'*Merci, chérie,*' he said and turned toward her grave.

I had been here only last week to make sure it was ready for him, wiping the winter grime off the granite marker chiseled with her name, her birth and death dates, and the epitaph that had seemed so appropriate when we lost her. *I will go before you and light the way so that you may follow.*

I took off my jacket because it was warm, hitched myself up and sat on top of the wall, closing my eyes and tilting my face to catch the slanted sunlight. Pépé seemed to spend longer than usual talking to Mom and my heart skipped a couple of beats when I remembered our conversation from this morning: on this visit he wanted to make amends, put things in order, and that this was probably his last trip to America. I had counted on him coming to our wedding in May, just *assumed* he'd come – it was unthinkable that he wouldn't be here – but now I wasn't so sure.

I opened my eyes and watched as he bent to kiss my mother's headstone and pat it gently a couple of times. His eyes were moist when he joined me at the wall.

I slid down and slipped my arm through his. 'Shall we go visit her memorial now?'

He nodded without speaking, but as I closed the gate, which groaned in protest, he turned around for one last look and took a deep breath.

We walked back to the car in silence.

Eli had made a small cross out of two thick branches from a nearby oak tree, which he had cut, planed, and sanded smooth. The longer one was the base and a shorter one became the crosspiece. He notched them together and then burned the Greek letters for the beginning and the end – alpha and omega – at each end of the crosspiece and Mom's name, Chantal, down the length of the base. Leland erected it on the spot where she died. We planted rose bushes on either side, including her two favorites, a yellow Michelangelo rose and the beautiful red Victor Hugo. And because it was the national flower of France, we planted irises, which were a few weeks away from blooming.

I had brought two more daffodils to leave here; Pépé and I

each laid one in front of her cross. He never wanted to stay long in the place where her life had ended so he bowed, since I was fairly sure he could no longer kneel, and whispered to her in French while I waited a respectful distance away to give him privacy.

Then he turned and said, '*Allons-y*. We can go.'

It had been my mother's idea to plant the *allée* of flowering cherry trees on either side of the road, which was an offshoot of Sycamore Lane, in the south vineyard. It was not far from a footbridge over Goose Creek, which ran diagonally across our land, and had been one of her favorite places because of how beautiful and peaceful it was here. Eli, Mia, and I had chosen a redwood bench with curved wrought-iron arms that we placed under one of the cherry trees so we could come here whenever we wanted to remember her, or just get away. A brass plaque engraved with her favorite gardening quote from Thomas Jefferson – gardening had been her passion and she had been a devotee of Jefferson – was affixed to the bench: *No occupation is so delightful to me as the culture of the earth, and no culture comparable to that of the garden.*

Pépé and I had been to two memorials that commemorated my mother's death; this place celebrated her life. My grandfather seemed to exhale and grow calmer as we sat down on Mom's bench.

I reached over and laid my hand on top of one of his. 'If you're tired, I can take you back to the house. Just say the word. We can come here as often as you like, you know.'

'I know,' he said. 'Thank you. Let's sit for a few moments and then I believe I would like to take a little rest. I think the jet lag must be catching up with me.'

That was new. On other visits he had never complained about being jet lagged.

'This hasn't been an easy trip.'

He knew I wasn't talking about the flight. 'No, but as I told you, I needed to put some things right. With Geneva and Harriet . . . and also with Mia. She is picking me up at three at the house. We're going someplace for a coffee and then she wants me to see her studio at The Artful Fox.'

'That's good. It's good you're going to talk.'

He nodded and leaned back against the bench, closing his eyes. For a moment I thought he had fallen asleep.

'I wish I were going to be here when the cherry blossoms are in bloom because then it is paradise. Your mother missed France terribly, but she was happy here,' he said, murmuring, eyes still closed. 'She grew to love Virginia. After Eli, you, and Mia were born, it really became home for her.'

'Except she wasn't all that happy with Leland. He didn't make things easy. There were times I was afraid she might leave.' I had never told him that before.

He opened his eyes and looked at me. 'She stayed because of you three, *chérie.*'

'I know she loved us to death – she made sure we knew that we were the center of her world. As for Leland . . . I don't know. Every child wants to believe that their mother and father loved each other,' I said. 'I guess I never really wanted to look too closely at the cracks in their marriage because if I did, I was afraid I might cause everything to fall apart.'

'People get married for certain reasons and stay married sometimes for other reasons,' he said. 'Convenience, companionship, money . . . necessity.' He paused. 'Children.'

'You forgot love.'

'I didn't forget it. Love is important, but it is not always essential.'

Cricket had said something like that the other day when we were talking about Pépé and his relationship with Jackie – and my grandmother.

'Jackie didn't marry Ari Onassis for love,' he added. 'She wanted protection and he could give it to her, after what had happened to Jack and Bobby. She was scared.'

And it hadn't seemed like a particularly happy marriage, either, based on what I'd read about it in the many articles and stories about her life after she passed away.

'I can't imagine marrying for any other reason,' I told him. 'I'm marrying for love.'

'I know you are.'

'Did you? Did you marry Grandmama because you loved her? Or was it because she was waiting for you after Jackie left?'

He had been focusing on the two rows of trees with their swollen buds. Now his head swiveled around so he was staring at me again. 'You mean was your grandmother my "second choice" because I couldn't have Jackie? Is that what you believe, Lucie?'

'I don't know. Except I hope it's not true.' I couldn't keep the desperation out of my voice.

You couldn't *force* people to love each other. You couldn't *make* it happen. My grandfather had left love off the list of reasons people got married. Talked about Jackie making a second loveless marriage out of necessity. He and my grandmother had seemed happy and they cared deeply about each other. Wasn't that enough? Did it matter if my grandparents *loved* each other?

'It is *not* true, Lucie,' he said. 'I loved your grandmother with all my heart. I miss her every day. There hasn't been anyone else in my life who could take her place after she died.'

'But?'

'There is no "but". Except I believe it is possible to love more than one person in a lifetime. Love is not a finite thing – you don't only have a certain amount to give and then you can't give any more.'

Which, I think, was his way of saying that he also loved Jackie.

'We should go,' I said, 'and get you back to the house so you can rest before Mia picks you up.'

He didn't protest and he even let me help him get to his feet. I took his arm as we walked back to the car.

As we were leaving he said, 'I brought you something from Paris. I put it in the study off your bedroom before I left for Mon Repos this morning.'

'Oh? I haven't been back to the house all day. What is it?'

'It will be waiting for you. You'll see.'

My mobile rang and I looked at the display. Quinn. I wanted to – *needed to* – talk to him after this unsettling conversation with my grandfather.

I connected and before I could talk he said, 'I'm afraid there's a problem.'

'What is it?'

'Where are you now?'

'Dropping my grandfather off at the house for a nap before Mia picks him up in a little while. Why?'

'Can you meet Antonio and me at his place in five minutes?'

'Sure,' I said, glancing at Pépé who was shooting worried looks at me like darts. 'What's going on?'

'I'll tell you when you get there. Look, don't alarm your grandfather, OK?'

'OK,' I said, but he'd already disconnected. I turned to Pépé. 'Is it all right if I drop you at the front door? There's something we need to take care of at Antonio's cottage. Quinn asked me to meet him there.'

'What's wrong?'

'Antonio and Valeria have been having problems with flooding in their basement after it rains. We need to get it sorted out once and for all.' I pulled up in front of the house and he got out.

'Wish me luck with Mia,' he said before he closed the passenger door.

'Good luck.'

'And Lucie?'

'Yes?'

'It hasn't rained since I've been here. I hope everything is all right.' He closed the door and went inside the house.

When I pulled into the driveway in front of the farm manager's cottage a few minutes later, Quinn was waiting outside.

'What's going on?' I asked.

'Come on.' He put his arm around me and we walked up the steps to the front porch. 'Antonio and Valeria are inside waiting for us. There's something she wants to show us. Actually, she *doesn't* want to show it to us. Antonio told her she has to do it.'

'*What* are you talking about?'

Antonio opened the front door before we could knock, worried lines creasing his forehead.

'Lucita, Quinn. Please come in.'

We stepped into the cozy, compact living room. The aromas of cumin, garlic, and onions simmering on the stove drifted in from the kitchen where Valeria was speaking Spanish to her six-month-old daughter and the baby was babbling replies.

'Is everything OK?' I asked Antonio.

The first thought that raced through my mind was that we were here because of something to do with ICE. Both Antonio and Valeria were citizens – but maybe something had happened to someone else. It wouldn't be the first time. Or the last. At Christmas one of their friends had rented a cheap motel room in Sterling so he could wrap his kids' Christmas gifts and keep them as a surprise. Somehow ICE found out about it and the next thing we heard, he was on a bus to Mexico. I still felt like I'd been punched in the gut every time I thought about that story, wondering if the children ever got those gifts from their father, the very last thing he did for them, his punishment for loving them.

'There's something you should know,' Antonio said, turning toward the kitchen. '*Ven aquí, mi amor. Lucie y Quinn están.*'

Valeria walked into the room holding a wide-eyed baby who had a thatch of jet-black hair and wore a pink onesie that had *Snuggle Monster* written across the front. She was young, pretty, and utterly terrified. Her eyes went straight to her husband, who gave her an encouraging nod. He walked over to take the baby, who was chewing on a teething biscuit.

'It's OK,' he said to Valeria. 'Don't worry. Show them.'

She fished into the back pocket of her jeans, pulling out her phone.

'Antonio bought this for me the other day.' She spoke so softly that Quinn and I had to lean forward to catch her words. 'So I have been taking videos of the baby to send *mi mamá.*'

'She's adorable.' I gave her an encouraging smile. 'She's gotten so big.'

Valeria acknowledged the compliment but she was still tense and rigid, shooting another apprehensive look at Antonio, who had given up on the soggy biscuit and was letting his daughter gnaw on one of his knuckles.

'It's OK,' he said. 'You have to tell them, *trésor.*'

She took a deep breath. 'On Monday I was outside – right here – because we had just come back from a walk. I had the camera on video since the light was good – it was around five o'clock and the baby was *muy mona*, you know, so cute, sitting in the stroller – when I heard voices. Men, two of them shouting. It was coming from Mia and Sergio's place. So I walked over to see what was happening and forgot to turn off the video.'

She turned on her phone and flipped it around so Quinn and I could see. 'I got this.'

A minute of Valeria cooing to her daughter in Spanish, trying to coax a smile. Then voices, as she'd said, raised in anger. The picture shifted and now she was filming the ground, which was moving with vertigo-inducing speed as the voices grew louder and she came closer.

'Who were they?' I asked. 'The voices are muffled.'

'Sergio. And Parker Lord. I saw them, but they didn't see me. They were too upset.'

I froze. Sergio had told Bobby he was in his studio in the back of the cottage wearing noise-canceling headphones when Parker drove up, which was why he'd neither seen nor heard Parker's car.

So he did lie.

'Do you know what they were arguing about?' Quinn asked.

'No, not really. But before I left I heard Parker shout at Sergio, "I know what you did." Then Sergio told him to go and, um, do something to himself. I turned and left so they wouldn't see me and the next thing I heard was the sound of a car leaving – it wasn't Sergio's Fiat so I knew it was Parker. I didn't realize he drove into the vineyard. I thought he left. If I'd known someone was out there . . . the way he was . . . sick . . .' She stopped talking.

'It's OK,' Quinn said. 'You didn't know.'

'If I *had* known,' she went on, 'I would have told Antonio. He would have checked . . . we would have found Parker sooner and he might not have died.' She looked as if she were going to cry. 'I don't want to get anyone in trouble. *I* don't want to get in trouble.'

Antonio walked over and put his arm around her, pulling her tight. 'I didn't know about this when Bobby talked to us the other day. So I don't want no trouble, either. I didn't know about the argument and we didn't know Parker was still here at the vineyard. Valeria just told me this morning.'

'I'm so sorry,' Valeria said. 'I was really scared.'

I couldn't blame her. In her place I'd be scared, too. Citizen or no citizen, she didn't want a run-in with the Sheriff's Office.

'What you did now was very brave,' I said. 'If it helps, even if you'd found Parker right away, you probably couldn't have saved him. And neither of you has anything to worry about. We'll see to that.'

'So now what?' Antonio asked as the baby started to squirm.

Valeria held out her arms. 'I think she's hungry.'

'Go feed her,' I said. 'Can you leave us your phone, please?' She tossed it and Quinn caught it.

'Who are you calling?' Antonio asked as I pulled out my phone.

'Bobby Noland,' I said. 'He has to know about this.'

Maybe I'd been right after all in suspecting Sergio. There was only one reason for him to lie to Bobby. Not only saying he didn't know Parker, but also claiming he didn't see him arrive at the vineyard Monday evening.

Because he'd killed him.

TWENTY-TWO

B obby pulled into the driveway twenty minutes later in an unmarked car. I had already told him over the phone about Valeria's video, so the first thing he did was watch it and then send it to himself.

'Are you going to tell Sergio how you know he was with Parker?' Antonio asked. 'He's gonna know it had to be either Valeria or me who made the video. I don't want anything to happen to my wife or my daughter. The guy lives a hundred yards from us. I got a gun, but I can't be here all the time to protect them.'

Valeria had returned to the living room after feeding the baby and putting her down for a nap. At the mention of the gun, she laid a warning hand on Antonio's arm and whispered to him in Spanish. He muttered something to her under his breath.

The five of us were sitting together in a circle in the tiny living room; Quinn and me on a navy-blue sofa just purchased from Ikea according to Valeria, Bobby on a ladder-back chair with a brilliantly colored Mexican wool blanket hanging over the back, and Valeria and Antonio on chairs they'd brought from the kitchen.

'Don't go getting all vigilante on me, Antonio,' Bobby said. 'Those things never end well. I mean it.'

'I'm worried about my family, Bobby. You would be, too, if you were me.'

'I know,' he said to Antonio, but he was looking at Valeria, 'except you can calm down because we've had our eye on Sergio for a couple of days.' Now he shot a glance in my direction. 'He was part of an art forgery ring in New York City thirty-five years ago. He did some jail time for it back in the day. He was twenty-four, just became a citizen, too. Welcome to America, buddy. What a dumbass.'

He'd cleaned up his language for the benefit of Valeria and me, but it felt as if he'd just dropped an anvil on my chest.

Mia knew about Sergio doing time for art fraud. Of course she did.

'Sorry to be the bearer of bad news, Lucie,' he said. 'Nothing popped on your sister, but Sergio's currently wanted in New York for questioning concerning another ring of art forgers.'

'That's why they came here,' I said in a hard, flat voice.

'That would be my guess.'

'So he's hiding out here so the New York City police don't find him?'

Bobby gave me a rueful smile. 'Nope, nothing so neat and tidy. The extradition notice only goes as far as any contiguous state. Virginia is not contiguous with New York so he's safe here. They're not going to go after him unless he returns to New York, New Jersey, or Connecticut.'

'You're kidding. Why not?'

Bobby shrugged. 'No sheriff's office or police department has the resources and money to chase down a guy like Sergio who is, frankly, a two-bit small-time swindler. If he was a serial killer? Yeah, it would be different. But art forgery?' He snorted. 'New York City is not going to waste the money and manpower to send a team to Virginia to haul his sorry ass back to Manhattan. It's just not worth it. Simple as that.'

'So he came here because it's safe,' Quinn said.

'Yup. New York won't touch him here in the Old Dominion. And we're not going to do anything about it, either. Our hands are tied.'

'That stinks,' I said.

'Welcome to my world.'

'Now what?' Quinn asked.

'Now I go have a little talk with Sergio,' he said. 'His car's here and there's another unmarked car out of sight keeping an eye on him, making sure he's still at home.'

'Are you going to arrest him?' Antonio asked.

'Depends, but I'm definitely going to invite him to accompany me to headquarters so we can get to know each other better. He doesn't need to RSVP because he's going whether he likes it or not.'

'What about us?' I asked.

'You two take off,' he said. 'And Valeria and Antonio, you

sit tight here. If I need to do it, I'll have a patrol car outside your house later, but I don't think it's going to be necessary.'

Quinn, Bobby and I left together and Bobby waited until we got into our cars. I rolled down my window to say goodbye.

'Hey,' I said. 'I just heard something. Like a car door closing.'

I barely got the words out of my mouth when Bobby's car roared past me. By the time Quinn and I reached Sergio and Mia's cottage, Bobby and the other unmarked cruiser had Sergio's Fiat pinned between them so he couldn't leave. Bobby climbed out of his car, went over, and yanked open the driver door to the Fiat.

'Get out,' he said.

Sergio obeyed and looked over at where Quinn and I were now standing together about twenty feet away. Bobby almost certainly didn't want us as an audience, but right now the pile-up of cars was blocking the road and there was no way around them. We stayed where we were.

Sergio looked at Bobby and the two other deputies, both of whom had drawn their guns.

'What's going on?' he said to Bobby. 'What is this all about?'

'It's about Parker Lord,' Bobby said.

'I didn't kill him.'

'I thought we could talk about that over at headquarters in Leesburg,' Bobby said. 'Maybe you could explain why you lied to me about knowing Parker. And what you two were arguing about right before he died, which you also lied about. Something about noise-canceling headphones and concentrating on some project so you didn't hear or see anything, wasn't that what you said?'

'I want a lawyer.'

'Fine,' Bobby said, 'you want to play it that way, go right ahead. Your right to be represented by counsel is guaranteed by the Sixth Amendment to the US Constitution. Lucky you, you're a citizen. But before you make any hasty decisions, we know for an absolute fact you were arguing with Parker Lord practically right here where we're standing. It's already not looking too good for you, buddy.'

Sergio turned pale. 'I told you. I didn't kill him. He didn't look well when I saw him, but he was fine when he left.'

'How long did he stay? Did you serve him anything to drink?'
Bobby asked.

'No. He never set foot inside the house,' Sergio said.

'And why would I believe you?'

The sound of another car turning off Sycamore Lane and
heading our way distracted everyone. I recognized the engine
and I knew Sergio did, too.

Mia.

She must have finished her talk with Pépé and dropped
him back at the house. Wait until she saw the Welcome Wagon
committee, all of us here with Sergio who was surrounded by
cops.

'It's my sister,' I yelled to the two deputies who still had
their guns drawn. 'She lives here, too.'

'Stand down, guys,' Bobby said to them. 'Let her through.'

To her credit Mia did the math pretty fast once she saw
what was happening. I had been afraid she was going to fall
apart. Instead she was at Sergio's side instantly, arms wrapped
around his waist as if she could protect him and keep him
safe, all five-feet-nothing of her. Unfortunately she came up
with the wrong answer. She didn't realize this was about
Parker.

'He doesn't have to go anywhere,' she said, eyes flashing, as
she glared at Bobby. 'He doesn't have to answer any questions.
You have no jurisdiction over him here in Virginia. And he's
done nothing wrong – it's all a mistake.'

'*Cara*,' Sergio said in an urgent voice, 'hush.'

'It's OK, Sergio,' Bobby said, in a warm, conversational way
that I knew meant the hammer was about to come down. 'I
know what she's talking about. I've already had a little chat
with a good friend of yours in New York. A Detective John
Kowalski? Manhattan division of the New York City Art Fraud
Squad. Ring a bell? He'd like to have a word with you
about a couple of paintings that he says weren't painted by
the artists who really *did* paint them. And how they got sold to
people who believed they were the real deal.'

For the first time Sergio smiled. 'I don't have to talk to anyone
in New York, Detective Noland. Not Kowalski, not anyone. I
don't even know what he's talking about.'

Mia turned big eyes on Sergio as the light started to dawn. 'What's going on, baby?'

'It will be OK, *cara mia*,' Sergio said. 'Now it's my turn to be questioned about Parker's death.'

'You said you didn't know Parker,' Bobby said. 'That's lie number one. Plus you saw him right before he died. That's lie number two. We know that. Third, you were heard arguing with him – and you've got no alibi for the time of his death. We know for a fact that Mia was at Mon Repos.'

'She's lying,' Sergio said. For the first time he was rattled. 'I wasn't arguing with him. He started it.'

'Who's lying?' Bobby looked confused. 'Mia?'

Now Sergio was even more flustered. 'No one. Never mind.'

'Answer the question.' Bobby's voice was hard and mean. 'Or you can cool your heels in a jail cell while we get you that lawyer. It might take some time so you'd have to wait, but you've been down that road before so you know the drill.'

Sergio wavered, glancing down at Mia who was watching him, her eyes dark with confusion.

'Give me a name,' Bobby said, still in that tough way. 'Last chance.'

'Harry.' Sergio practically spat it out. 'It was Harry.'

'Harry . . . Delacroix? *Harriet* Delacroix?' Bobby looked stunned as Mia's face crumpled.

'Yes.'

'Harry was *here*?' Mia said to Sergio in a strained, incredulous voice. 'While I was over at Mon Repos working on her goddamn mural that she told me I needed to stay late and work on? The two of you were together here?'

He nodded again, but she barely noticed, her anger mounting.

She pointed at the cottage. 'This is *my* house. Mine. Whose idea was it? Hers or yours?'

I felt as if I were watching a slow-motion train wreck that I couldn't look away from even though I didn't want to see the crash and the ghastly wreckage.

'I'm sorry,' Sergio said and it sounded as inadequate as it was.

'Now I know why the maid kept coming to check on me so

often, making sure I was still there.' Mia's voice kept rising and now she was shouting at him. 'Did she warn Harry when I was leaving so you could . . . finish . . . what you were doing? *Did she?*'

'Yes.'

She slapped him hard across the face.

'All right.' Bobby pulled Mia away from Sergio. 'That's enough. You, Sergio, you're coming with us right now, riding with the two deputies. Lucie, you look after Mia, OK? Get her a drink. Get her a couple of drinks.'

One of the deputies handcuffed Sergio and helped him into the back seat of their cruiser. Mia watched, looking as if the world had just come to an end.

I went over and caught her as she sagged against me. Quinn was right behind me, picking her up in his arms.

'Come on, kiddo,' he said. 'Let's get you back to the house for that drink and something to eat.'

He set her in the passenger seat of the Jeep. She closed her eyes and massaged her temples as tears ran down her face. Quinn came around to my side of the car.

Before I got in he said, 'I'm going to talk to Antonio and Valeria. Let them know they're off the hook for as long as Sergio thinks Harry ratted him out and it wasn't either of them.'

'He'll figure out eventually that it wasn't Harry,' I said.

'We'll cross that bridge when we come to it.'

'What a mess. I wonder if he did it.'

'Bobby'll find out,' Quinn said. 'Lawyer or no lawyer.'

'My money is on Sergio.'

Quinn's eyes met mine. 'Mine, too.'

It took a lot of alcohol to get Mia calmed down. And it took Eli.

After Quinn spoke to Antonio and Valeria, he met my brother leaving his studio on his way home and filled him in on what had happened with Sergio. I met both of them when they walked into the house.

'I'll talk to her,' Eli said. 'She'll listen to me. She needs to get rid of that guy.'

I didn't say it, but I thought it: *Especially if he's a murderer.*

'She used to listen to you but that was more than ten years

ago,' I said. 'If you can get her to pay attention to you now, you're a miracle worker.'

'Right now if Jesus Christ himself tap danced across the room in front of her, I don't think she'd notice,' Quinn said. 'She's pretty far gone.'

'Some things never change,' Eli said. 'Let me see what I can do.'

When Mia had been younger – a lot younger – any time she had a boyfriend problem, which was often, she went to Eli for the Protective Big Brother Talk. I knew the script by heart. Eli would tell Mia he would punch the guy's lights out if the boyfriend du jour ever went near his sister again. Then he'd suggest that maybe Bozo or Gonzo or Whoever wasn't good enough for her because who wants to be with a jackass that's just going to keep breaking your heart and, as night follows day, the relationship would sort of peter out after that.

To Quinn's amazement, Mia fell into Eli's arms the minute she saw him. Even I was surprised.

'Come on, honey,' he said to her. 'We need to talk.'

He gave us an I-told-you-so look over Mia's shoulder, while Quinn poured Mia a glass of wine big enough to swim in and a normal-sized one for Eli. Then she and Eli went out to the veranda.

Pépé was still upstairs resting, so Quinn and I had our own drink in the parlor.

'Do you think Eli is going to be able to talk her into dumping Sergio? I didn't think she listened to anybody any more,' Quinn said. We were sitting on the sofa together, me with my legs draped over his knees, his hand resting on them.

'I hope so. She feels completely betrayed. I don't blame her. Plus there's Sergio's stellar résumé – jail time for art fraud. He just cheated on her. And now maybe murder. What's left to love?'

'I don't know,' Quinn said. 'I guess there's no accounting for why someone falls in love with the wrong person. You can't help it. You can't stop it.'

I thought about Pépé and Jackie. Mia and Sergio. My parents.

'No,' I said. 'You can't. The heart wants what it wants. Even if it hurts.'

Cricket had said that to me just the other day. It was true.

Quinn reached over and found my left hand, touching the antique diamond engagement ring that had been his grandmother's. 'I love you. You know that, don't you?'

'Yes. I love you, too. You *do* know that.' I twined my fingers through his. 'Tell me what made you fall in love with me?'

He smiled. 'I don't know. It was sort of gradual – remember how we were always arguing over how to run the vineyard? How we were always arguing over everything?'

'You mean our courting days? Who could forget?'

'After a while I started realizing that it wasn't that I couldn't live with you, but that I couldn't live *without* you. And that I didn't want to.' He leaned over and kissed me.

When I could catch my breath I said, 'I love you for saying that.'

'What about you? What made you fall in love with me? My magnetic personality? My charm and good looks?'

I laughed. 'Oh, yes. All those things. But something more. I don't want to be without you, either, because when we're together I feel complete. I've always loved the line from *Winnie the Pooh*: "If you live to be a hundred, I want to live to be a hundred minus one day, so I never have to live without you." That's how I feel about us.'

He bent to kiss me again and by the time Eli showed up, catching us off-guard, we were both more than a little undressed.

He cleared his throat in an exaggerated way and said, 'Alright you two, get a room. Actually you *have* a room. Why aren't you using it?'

Quinn got up off me so fast I nearly fell off the sofa. He grabbed my hand to steady me, but at least he had his back to Eli while I . . . didn't. There are some things siblings just shouldn't know about each other. Or see.

'Sorry,' I said to my brother, my face bright red as I tugged down my sweater and figured I could hook my bra later. 'We were talking. I guess we got a little carried away.'

Quinn fastened his belt and started buttoning his shirt, exchanging a knowing boys-will-be-boys wink with Eli. 'One thing sort of led to another,' he said. 'You know how it goes.'

Eli shook his head. 'I will never be able to unsee what I just

saw. I'll leave you two horny teenagers and go home to my
fiancée and kids now, if that's all right. Mia crashed on the
veranda after we finished talking. I got a quilt from the quilt
rack in the library to put over her but don't let her stay out
there too long. She's four sheets to the wind.'

I had recovered most of my dignity. 'Is she going to be OK?'

'The good news is that she's mad as hell at Sergio. Plans to
throw him out for lying about Parker, but especially for cheating
with Harry. Hell hath no fury, etcetera.'

'I wouldn't be sorry about that,' I said.

'Me, neither,' Eli said.

'I'll help him pack his bags,' Quinn said.

'You won't need to. The way Mia was talking, his things
will be scattered all over the front lawn by the time he gets
back from his little visit with Bobby,' Eli said. 'Of course, she
may not have to throw him out if he's arrested for murder. He'll
get a brand-new place to live and a whole new wardrobe, cour-
tesy of the Commonwealth of Virginia.'

'Either way, she's in no shape to do anything tonight,' I said.
'She ought to spend the night here and sleep it off. There will
be plenty of time to throw out him and his things tomorrow, if
it comes to that.'

'Well,' Eli said, 'in that case I'll leave you two to . . . whatever. I'll check in tomorrow and see how she is.'

'Tomorrow,' I said, 'is the gala at The Artful Fox. I wonder
how long it's going to take for word to get out that Harry was
fooling around with Sergio when Parker showed up at the
vineyard right before he died. And that Harry made sure Mia
stayed at Mon Repos to work on her mural.'

'Someone ought to give Willow a head's up,' Quinn said.
'Mia and Harry shouldn't be in the same room together right
now. Hell, they shouldn't even be in the same town.'

'My turn to talk to her,' I said. 'She ought to sit this one out,
stay home tomorrow evening. Willow will understand. Especially
once she finds out what happened.'

'If you need help with your technique,' Eli said, giving me
a superior look, 'feel free to call an expert.'

'Do you know one?'

'Below the belt, Luce. Yours, by the way, is still undone.'

I glanced down before I remembered I wasn't wearing a belt and he grinned.

'Truce,' I said. 'And thanks, Eli. Seriously.'

'Any time. Now I've really gotta go. I'm late.'

'Kiss the kids for me.'

'Yup.' He was gone.

A moment later the front door closed. Quinn turned to me and ran his finger along my cheek, tilting my chin so our lips were almost touching. 'We'll finish what we started in bed tonight.'

'I'd like that,' I said and pulled his mouth down on mine.

Quinn and I got Mia, who was drunk and half-asleep, off the veranda and upstairs on to the bed in Dominique's old bedroom, since Pépé was using her bedroom while he was staying with us. I covered her with the quilt, closed the curtains, and tiptoed out, though a marching band wouldn't have woken her.

Dinner was quiet, just Pépé, Quinn, and me. We filled Pépé in on what had happened with Sergio and he told us that he and Mia had a heart-to-heart talk about their relationship, Mom's death, and the matter of blame and whose fault it was.

'She has been carrying around a lot of guilt,' he said. 'I told her it was time to let it go or it would destroy her. It was an accident. No one blames her and she shouldn't blame herself.'

'What did she say?' I asked.

'She said she would try.'

After dinner, Quinn and Pépé went outside to the veranda to smoke cigars and I went upstairs to get ready for bed, remembering as I started to get undressed that my grandfather had brought me a gift from Paris that he left in the study.

I found it next to the framed photograph of Mom, Jackie, and me. It wasn't a gift in the way I expected, and the moment I realized what it was, I understood this was about his plan to put his life in order, make amends, and right wrongs. Leave no loose ends.

He had brought me Jackie's letters.

TWENTY-THREE

I had not been expecting such a voluminous collection of letters from Jackie to my grandfather. There were at least a dozen from the year she spent in Paris and many more from the years that followed – though there was a lapse before she began writing to Pépé until she was First Lady and he was the number two at the embassy in Washington. The first post-Paris letters were on White House stationary. Later, less formal and more personal notes in her bold scrawl documented where she was at the time: Red Gate Farm on Martha's Vineyard; her Fifth Avenue penthouse opposite Central Park; Skorpios, Aristotle Onassis's private island; and finally letterhead from Viking and Doubleday when she'd worked there as an editor.

What all the letters had in common was that they were written in French. Pépé had kept them in chronological order, from her note thanking him for the drink at the Brasserie Balzar after they met at the Louvre, to a letter dated a few weeks before she died. I set the fragile pile of papers and the Wedgwood-blue grosgrain ribbon that had been tied around them next to me on the bed, picked up the first letter, and started to read.

A few paragraphs in I realized how delightful and charming her French was; if she didn't know a word or how to express an idea she was clever enough to figure out another way to say it, almost like a written game of charades. Her interest in art history and literature, which she'd studied that year in Paris, was evident; her comments about this artist or that painting or a gallery or museum she'd visited with my grandfather were astute and thoughtful. She also seemed intent on absorbing everything she could about French life and culture, hungry to explore the beauty and history she found in a sophisticated, cosmopolitan city – but aware, as well, of the recent devastation of the war and the impact it had had on everyone she met.

What I hadn't expected was how alive she would become to

me through her letters: her keen artist's eye and way with language that revealed intelligence, wit, curiosity, and – another surprise – a strong sense of mischief. And then there was her romance with Pépé, which had clearly blossomed into something special. She loved the flowers he brought her and how he complimented her on what she wore. Before long, I knew for sure that she loved him, too.

If their romance had taken place today, I wondered if what she'd written would have been nothing more than a series of text messages traded back and forth that would have vanished into the ether, instead of these lovely, lyrical letters I held in my hands. No wonder Pépé had saved them; no wonder my grandmother had been just a teeny bit jealous. Jackie was incomparable. No woman could hold a candle to her.

By the time Quinn came upstairs to bed, I had read all of the Paris letters and was starting on the ones Jackie had written while she was living in the White House. I looked up and smiled as he closed the door.

'What are you reading?' he asked. 'Your grandfather just went to bed and I checked on Mia to make sure she was all right, you know, still breathing and everything. She's out like a light. And she's breathing.'

'Thanks for being so thorough,' I said and he grinned. I held up a letter on White House letterhead. 'Jackie's letters to my grandfather – written from the time they were together in Paris in 1949 until just before she died in 1994. Forty-five years of correspondence. He saved all of them. The only people who knew about them besides Jackie and him were my grandmother, my mother, Parker, and Cricket. Now I know and so do you.'

'How'd Parker find out?'

'He and my mother were drinking one day when Leland was out hunting and she told him,' I said. 'Parker and I talked about it that last day I saw him. He also told me that Jackie edited his very first book – kind of a Southern memoir – when she was at Doubleday and wouldn't take any credit for it. He said it sold copies in the tens.'

'That's rough,' he said.

I watched him get undressed. He didn't bother putting on his usual T-shirt and sweats. 'You look good,' I said.

He pulled back the covers and got into bed next to me. 'You're naked, too. And you look *very* good.'

'Thank you. I was waiting for you.'

'As fascinating as they are, maybe we could talk about those letters and Parker's book another time.' He kissed my shoulder and then he moved so his lips were between my breasts.

I picked up the letters and set them on my nightstand.

'What did you have in mind?' I ran my fingers through his salt-and-pepper hair and twisted one of the curls.

He lifted his head. 'Unfinished business from earlier this evening.'

I snapped off my bedside lamp as his hands roamed over me and he pulled me down so he could move on top of me.

'I'd like that,' I said and slid under him.

'Good,' he murmured. 'Now that we've got a room, we can take our time, do whatever we want.'

Cricket and Pépé were wrong. Marriage without love would be empty and hollow; it would be an arrangement, useful for certain reasons possibly, almost like a business deal. I couldn't imagine spending my life with someone under those circumstances – without giving all of myself to that person and that he would give all of himself to me.

Aristotle once wrote that love is composed of a single soul inhabiting two bodies. I wanted that kind of love.

'Tonight I want everything,' I said to Quinn.

'So do I,' he said. 'I always have.'

The less said about Harry Delacroix's party at The Artful Fox on Friday evening, the better, if you ask me. To begin with, Bobby had questioned Harry that morning about being an alibi for Sergio the night Parker came to the vineyard, so she knew the word was out about the two of them and that the source had been Sergio.

Pépé behaved like a consummate gentleman as Cricket's escort, but he was distant and a bit frosty with Harry, which was better than I thought she deserved. Quinn and I went along to support Pépé – we weren't going to leave him there on his own – though Quinn mostly went as my bodyguard, not to protect me but to protect Harry from me and make sure I

wouldn't do anything that would earn me a visit to the inside
of one of Bobby's cells.

Sergio had been released after Bobby questioned him, though
Bobby cautioned him not to leave town. As Bobby said to Quinn
and me when we met at the bar that had been set up near the
cash register, 'That boy is going to run out of country to hide
in if he's not careful. He'd better not piss me off by bolting or
he can add Virginia and our contiguous states to his list of
places with a "Do Not Enter" sign at the border.'

As for Harry, she kept her distance and instead hung on the
arm of someone from her New York publishing house that
looked as if he'd recently been able to start growing facial hair.
She also kept her champagne flute topped up, surprising me by
how well she could hold her liquor, though I noticed her laughter
growing louder and shriller as the evening went on.

I caught sight of both Dominique and Willow, who were busy
making sure things ran smoothly, as well as keeping an eye on
Harry as she drank glass after glass of champagne. But it was
her party and she could cry if she wanted to . . . or drink as
much as she liked, so I knew they weren't going to say anything
or try to cut her off.

The one bright spot was running into Marilyn Gilbert Bernard,
wearing a black satin tuxedo pantsuit and a stunning layered
gold and jade necklace made by an artist whose jewelry they
sold in the museum's gift shop. Kit was with me so I introduced
them.

'Lovely to meet you,' she said to Kit. 'Your newspaper has
been very good about writing about NMWA and, of course, we
welcome any chance for additional publicity. My door is always
open if there's anything I can do for you or the *Tribune*. Assist
with any story you're interested in.'

'Are you pitching me?' Kit asked, but she was smiling.

Marilyn batted her eyelashes, feigning innocence. 'I would
never be so crass, so brazen, so . . . Why, yes, actually, I was.
Did it work?'

We laughed and she added, 'Lucie, I met your grandfather
when I was speaking with Cricket earlier. He's absolutely
charming. I was completely smitten.'

'Get in line,' Kit told her. 'Every woman of a certain age

around here and even some of the younger women have their eye on him. Starting with Thelma Johnson, who owns the General Store.'

Marilyn grinned. 'I can see why.'

'Speaking of charming,' I said, 'have you charmed Cricket into keeping her word about donating the paintings to the museum?'

She looked down into her champagne glass. 'I don't know,' she said. 'It seems as if neither she nor Ash are going to make any decisions until Parker's murder is solved.'

'My husband is working on that,' Kit said.

Marilyn stared at her and her face cleared. 'Of course. Kit Noland. You're Bobby Noland's wife. I haven't read or seen much about the investigation in the media lately. Any news? How is it going?'

'Not as well as he'd like, unfortunately, since he doesn't have a suspect in custody.'

One of Bobby's suspects was Ash, who hadn't shown up tonight. Another was Mia, who still wasn't off the hook.

'Hopefully he'll find out who did it soon,' Marilyn said.

Kit gave me a sideways glance and I knew she was thinking about Mia. 'Yes,' she said, 'that's the plan.'

Marilyn caught the glance and I had a feeling she figured out we might have just stepped into landmine territory. 'So tell me, ladies, what do you think of Jackie's paintings?' she asked, unsubtly changing the subject. 'And the wall text Harry chose to go with them? I hadn't realized Jackie was with a male friend when she bought them. Apparently Harry will reveal more about that in her book.'

'Harry and her publisher really are promoting the book in a big way tonight, aren't they?' I said. The drinks coasters were book jackets; there were postcards, bookmarks, even pens scattered throughout the gallery.

'Just a bit,' Marilyn said with a what-can-you-do shrug. 'What about you, Kit?'

'I think the paintings are very nice,' Kit said with a polite smile. 'I hope your museum gets to keep them.'

Which, as Willow would have said, translated into 'not my cup of tea'. Marilyn knew it, too. She smiled back.

'Oh, we'd quite like to,' she said. 'I don't know if you knew that Élisabeth Vigée Le Brun was the highest-paid portrait painter in France by the time she was nineteen. She learned from her father and started painting at age sixteen. And she used to throw great parties.'

'Really?' Kit's eyes widened and she glanced over where a crowd was still gathered around the paintings.

'Yes. Unfortunately her husband – Le Brun, who was also the first curator of the Louvre – gambled away all her money. Plus she had to flee France or her head would have ended up on the guillotine because of her relationship with Marie Antoinette and the fact that she was a Royalist. So off she went painting portraits in every other royal court in Europe – except she didn't really like Catherine the Great of Russia. You know how it is; there's always one in the bunch, especially among the kings and queens of Europe. But Vigée Le Brun was known for painting such flattering portrayals of her subjects that she became very sought after.'

'If she was so famous and popular in her lifetime, why did she fall into such obscurity that Jackie Onassis bought those paintings for a couple of francs in a Parisian bookstall?' I asked.

Marilyn gave us her sweetest smile. 'She was a woman.'

'That's it?' Kit said. 'That's the reason?'

'My dear, it's the *only* reason. Why do you think Wilhelmina Holladay founded the National Museum of Women in the Arts in the first place?' Marilyn said, and then answered her own question. 'Because every other museum and gallery in the world was full of paintings by men. *Only* men. As if women had no talent.'

She opened her evening purse, and pulled out a business card, which she gave to Kit. 'Lucie, you already have my card. Why don't both of you come to D.C. sometime soon and let me give you a tour of the museum? I think you'd quite enjoy it.'

'We will,' I said. 'Thank you.'

'Excellent.' She squeezed my arm. 'And now if you girls will excuse me, Harry's toy boy has left, probably to get her more champagne. I'm going to take advantage of the chance to chat her up about the paintings before she gets totally potted. Back to work.'

She winked and glided away.

'I like her,' Kit said, fingering the business card. 'She's full of sass.'

'Me, too. I hope Cricket and Ash do the right thing and the museum gets their paintings.'

'If anybody can persuade Cricket, it's your grandfather,' Kit said. 'Cricket is totally gaga over him. Anyone can see that – especially tonight.'

'I know,' I said and wondered what Kit would think when she eventually read Harry's book and found out about the love affair between Jackie and my grandfather and that Cricket witnessed it first-hand that year in Paris.

Kit waggled her empty champagne flute. 'Well, I do believe I have drunk my quota of champagne for the evening. I want to take one more quick look at those paintings before I find Bobby – after what Marilyn told us about the incredibly talented teenager who painted them, plus threw great parties – and then we should go. This is the first break Bobby's had since . . .' She trailed off.

'I know. Since Parker died.'

She nodded, looking rueful. 'For the record – and as weird as this is going to sound – I don't think your sister did it.'

'Thanks. I wish Bobby were as convinced. I'm surprised word didn't get around about him questioning Sergio and the whole, you know, hook up or whatever with Harry,' I said. 'I expected to hear about it tonight. So far, not a peep. Did an alien spaceship kidnap Thelma and the Romeos?'

She laughed. 'Bobby's trying to keep a lid on as much information leaking out as he can. But it's like trying to stop gravity.'

'I know. See you tomorrow at the birthday party?'

She leaned in for an air kiss. 'We'll be there. And, Luce, take it easy. I'm not sure how this is going to end, but it is going to end. And things will be OK.'

Quinn found me after Kit left. 'Cricket is about to leave and she's got a car coming for her and Luc. What about you? Ready to go?'

I nodded. 'I've had all the Harry I can take for one night. I was ready to go before we got here.'

He grinned. 'Maybe we can skip tomorrow. Plead something

serious, like we might have been exposed to Bubonic plague and we shouldn't be around others.'

'Nice idea, but I want to be there for Pépé. I wouldn't put it past Harry to start blabbing about him and Jackie while he's still in town, just to get things stirred up. Generate more interest in her damn book.'

'OK, tiger.' He put his arm around my waist and pulled me close. 'Let's go. You want to thank our hostess for a fabulous evening?'

'No.'

'I didn't think so,' he said and we left.

I read a few more of Jackie's letters in bed with a glass of wine when we got home after the party until Quinn persuaded me that there were far more interesting things we could be doing. But now I knew for certain that in 1962 Pépé had been involved with the negotiations for the *Mona Lisa* to come to America after Jackie had charmed the French Cultural Minister at a White House dinner – and despite a news blackout in France and massive public protests that caused Charles de Gaulle to take what he called 'Moan Lisa' anxiety pills.

So after a long and satisfying lovemaking session, I fell asleep in Quinn's arms with mashed-up dreams of Mona Lisa (the girl, not the painting), Jackie, and a fiery teenager who painted portraits of kings and queens throughout Europe.

Pépé left for Mon Repos early Saturday morning – Cricket sent someone to pick him up – so he could be there to hold her hand and spend some private time with her before the rest of us arrived for her birthday party in the afternoon. After breakfast I took a cup of coffee and Jackie's letters out to the veranda where the sun had already warmed up the day and the sky was a sharp cloudless blue.

I had caught up to the years after Jackie left Viking and moved to Doubleday when one letter made me stop and re-read it. She wrote about editing a book for an unknown author named Parker Lord, whose writing she described as 'terrific, with a refreshingly unique voice.' A paragraph later, she mentioned that Harry Delacroix had wangled a meeting with her, bringing the manuscript of a novel she'd written and asking Jackie to read it. 'She played the you're-very-good-friends-with-my-mother card pretty heavily,' Jackie wrote to Pépé. 'So I took it. What else could I do?'

A couple of letters later, I found out in no uncertain terms what Jackie thought of Harry's novel. 'Utter rubbish, Luc,' she wrote. 'I wouldn't let this girl write help-wanted ads for the *Post.* She has no talent, no voice, and worst of all, she's arrogant. She handled me turning her down badly, took it personally, and said I'd "regret" my decision because one day she'd be famous in spite of me, rather than because of me. By the time she finished her tantrum and left, I was ready to open the bottle of wine in the bottom drawer of my desk that one of my authors gave me for Christmas. Fortunately Parker Lord – you remember I told you about him – came by just as Harry was leaving. He couldn't have been more appreciative and gracious, plus he was perceptive enough to realize how upset I was. We talked about the relationship between editors and authors and what to do with the ones who believe they have nothing to learn. I felt better after he left. It has been a day of opposites. I did have that drink after all, *cher* Luc, but at home. I opened the fabulous bottle of Margaux you brought me the last time you were in New York. Total bliss in a wineglass – and now I am homesick for Paris.'

There was one final letter mentioning Harry and her manuscript, clearly responding to advice my grandfather had given her.

'As usual, darling Luc, you are quite right,' Jackie wrote. 'I won't say anything to Cricket about Harry – I'll leave that to Harry herself, though the girl is so vain and spoiled that my guess is she won't have the nerve to tell her mother I turned her down. Instead she'll probably invent a story. Or maybe she won't have to, if Cricket has no idea her daughter wrote a book.'

I set the letter down. *Did* Cricket know that Jackie had once turned Harriet down – quite savagely – because in Jackie's opinion, Harry couldn't write her way out of a paper bag? And now what had happened?

Harry was writing *Jackie's* book. She would have been the

last person in the world Jackie would have wanted to touch her manuscript given that damning indictment of her writing ability nearly forty years ago. Maybe Harry had improved over the last four decades, but as Kit told me, someone works as a stringer because they're not good enough to get hired as a staff journalist. Even Prescott Avery had told Kit that Harry wasn't talented.

Was Harry appropriating Jackie's book – plus revealing Jackie's love affair with my grandfather – her way of getting back at Jackie for telling her she'd never make it as a writer?

Revenge is supposed to be a dish best served cold. It had been decades since Jackie turned down Harry and now here was Harry writing the book Jackie never got to finish – plus being paid a fortune because she planned to incorporate Jackie's private diary. If this was revenge, as I was starting to suspect, this dish would be very, very cold indeed.

And Harry was going to enjoy serving it. Oh, yes, she was.

TWENTY-FOUR

I called Mia before we left for the party to see how she was doing. She sounded subdued and said she was cleaning out what was left of Sergio's studio, getting it ready for him to pick up when he dropped by later in the day.

'Then he's gone for good,' she said with bitterness. 'Good riddance.'

'Where's he going? Bobby told him to stick around and not leave town.'

'I don't know,' she said with a weary sigh. 'Maybe Mon Repos, for all I know. I'm not going back there, by the way. Harry hasn't paid me a dime. I want my money.'

I didn't want to tell her that maybe there wasn't any money. 'Is the mural finished?'

'Are you going to the party?'

'As moral support for Pépé.'

'Then why don't you see for yourself?' she asked. 'Let me know what you think.'

'All right,' I told her. 'I will.'

On the drive over to Cricket's party I told Quinn what I had learned in Jackie's letters to my grandfather: that Harry had taken it badly when Jackie turned down her novel forty years ago and told her she lacked talent. And that Parker had arrived for a meeting on the heels of Harry's temper tantrum in Jackie's office.

'What are you saying?' he asked.

'I wonder if Parker confronted Harry about what happened between her and Jackie all those years ago. Now Harry is writing Jackie's book, so talk about irony. Or maybe it's payback. Parker would have known that Jackie never in a million years would have wanted Harry to take over this project.'

'How are you going to find out if he did confront her? Ask Harry today in front of most of Middleburg, Atoka, and

Upperville at her mother's ninetieth birthday party? Do you really think she'd tell you?'

'One, I don't know, two, I'll figure out something, and three, probably not,' I said.

'Good luck with that,' he said.

There was valet parking when we arrived at Mon Repos – your car was driven to an adjacent field by a couple of kids who had been hired for the event – so one of them took the keys to the Jeep and directed us to a flagstone walk that led around the side of the house. We walked through a wisteria-draped pergola and gardens blazing with tulips and daffodils, following the sound of voices and laughter and clinking china and glasses until we reached the terrace with its expansive view of the swimming pool, tennis courts, gardens, and, in the background, the lovely, layered Blue Ridge Mountains.

Because the weather was so spectacular, Dominique had moved the bar and buffet outside under a white tent set up on the terrace. By the time Quinn and I got there, it was so crowded people had spilled down the broad terrace steps on to the lawn where more chairs and tables were scattered around under turquoise and white striped umbrellas. Most of those were occupied as well. Today's crowd was older than the folks who had been at the gala last night. A few wheelchairs, lots of walkers and canes – I stood out only because of my age – and people moving slowly who needed a place to sit and rest.

I had assumed one or both sets of French doors leading from the solarium directly on to the terrace would be thrown open so people could not only see the mural, but also, with so many elderly guests, have access to one of the downstairs powder rooms. Instead, not only were the solarium doors closed, but the curtains were drawn as well. If you wanted to use the bathroom, a door leading to the library was open instead.

It seemed odd to not only lock those doors, but also to pull the curtains as if the room were some sort of secret.

'I'm going to check out the solarium,' I said to Quinn. 'I promised Mia I'd look at her mural.'

'I'll come with you,' he said. 'I'd like to see it, too.'

'Do you think you could check on Pépé instead?' I said. 'I'd feel better if you'd do that. I hope he's OK.'

'Of course. I'll meet you back here in ten minutes. Do you want a glass of champagne?'

'Yes, please,' I said. 'Champagne would be great.'

It took my eyes a moment to adjust to the interior gloom of the library after the bright sunshine outside. A handmade sign on the door indicated that the powder room was down the hall, first door on the left. The solarium was across the hall.

There was no one around so I tried the door handle. Unlocked. I opened it, stepped inside, and fumbled for the light switch in the darkness.

'What do you think you're doing here?'

I flipped on the lights and whirled around.

The Delacroixes' maid, hands on hips, looked at me as if she'd caught me stealing the family silver.

'Taking a look at my sister's mural,' I said, not apologizing. 'It's fantastic, don't you think?'

Mia had finished the wall she had been working on the other day, weaving together intricate floral patterns and geometric shapes. Instead of painting the rest of the room in a similar way, which I now could see would have been claustrophobic, she had continued a sinuous trail of leafy vines with flowers woven through them on the other three walls, adding a repeating geometric pattern that looked vaguely Moroccan above the baseboard and below the crown molding so it framed the entire room.

'It's beautiful,' the woman said, 'but you shouldn't be in here, Ms Montgomery. Miss Harriet said the room was strictly off-limits today.'

'Why? What better occasion than Mrs Delacroix's birthday to show it off?'

She looked surprised that I would challenge Miss Harriet's orders. 'I don't know, she didn't say. I suppose she wants the mural to be a surprise for the Garden Tour.'

'I won't tell,' I said, 'and I'm the artist's sister, so it's OK.'

She gave me a vaguely disapproving look and said, 'I'm sorry, but I should probably lock this door after you leave. Please don't tell Miss Harriet that I found you here. I don't want to get in trouble.'

As far as I could tell, she was the only household staff at

Mon Repos so she was almost certainly the person who spied on Mia at Harry's request the night Harry was with Sergio. In other words, this woman knew everything.

'I won't say a word. But before I go,' I said, 'do you remember the day Parker Lord came by to see Mrs Delacroix about a problem in her butterfly garden?'

She seemed surprised. 'Of course I do. I served them tea. The day before he passed, God rest his soul.'

Though I already knew the answer, I asked, 'Did he stop by and see my sister before he met Mrs Delacroix?'

She nodded. 'Mrs Delacroix hadn't come downstairs yet so he chatted with your sister for a few minutes.'

'And then what happened?'

'Miss Harriet showed up and found them together so she invited Mr Lord to the drawing room while they were waiting for her mother.'

'I see. Did you serve the two of them tea before Mrs Delacroix arrived?'

She looked puzzled at the question but she said, 'Yes.'

'And did you happen to hear what the two of them were talking about while you served their tea?'

The closed-down expression on her face told me I had crossed a line. She wasn't going to talk out of school.

'Please,' I said. 'It's important.'

'They were talking about Miss Harriet's book.'

'You've been with the Delacroix family a long time, haven't you?'

'Thirty-five years.'

'Long enough to remember when Mrs Onassis visited?'

Her face grew soft with memory. 'Of course I do. Those were very special occasions. Mrs D would always come into the kitchen checking and double-checking that everything was absolutely perfect. And then of course, Mrs Onassis was so lovely and charming.'

'I knew her, too, but I was much younger,' I said. 'She was a good friend with my mother – and of course with my grandfather.'

The maid nodded, warming up a bit, so I pressed on.

'Mr Lord wasn't happy about Miss Harriet finishing Mrs

Onassis's book,' I said. 'He told me so himself. Was that what he was discussing with her?'

Another hesitation. But she knew as well as I did that Harry held the not-uncommon attitude of those who employed house-hold staff and were used to being waited on: there, but not really there. Regarding the woman as she would a pet when she was in the room, or worse, invisible. Harry couldn't be bothered to be discreet or circumspect in front of the help.

'Please,' I said.

'Yes.'

'Were they quarreling?'

'I heard raised voices just as I was bringing the tea.'

'What did they say?'

'I shouldn't be telling you this,' she said.

'You can tell me,' I said and my voice hardened, 'or you can tell Detective Noland down at the Sheriff's Office. Your choice. Because I think you know something that's important.'

She gave me a despairing look. 'He told her that Mrs Onassis had told him years ago that Miss Harriet couldn't write her way out of a paper bag so she would be the last person who should be writing her book.'

'And what did Harry say?'

'She said, "You have no proof."' She looked uncomfortable. 'And he said, "I know your publisher, Harry. All I need to do is make a call. Don't think I won't do it."'

'Then what?'

'Then Mrs Delacroix came into the room and asked what all the shouting was about. She sat down and asked Miss Harriet to serve everyone's tea and tried to calm Mr Lord down. He left soon after that.'

So there would have been time for Harry to slip the eye drops into Parker's tea while he was distracted with Cricket's arrival, just before she served it to him.

'Thank you for telling me that,' I said. 'You've been very helpful.'

'I don't feel right about this,' she said. 'And now you should really go before Miss Harriet finds us here.'

'*What* is going on here?'

Harry's voice, shrill, behind us. She was dressed in a long

flowing red and white halter dress showing off bronzed shoulders and toned arms. Her honey-blonde hair was done up in a messy bun with tendrils framing her face and, as usual, she looked spectacular.

'Esme,' she said, 'why did you let her in here?'

She sounded as if Esme had let in a puppy that had just soiled the carpet.

'Esme didn't let me in,' I said, in a calm voice. 'She found me here and asked me to leave. I wanted to see Mia's mural is all, Harry. By the way, Mia hasn't been paid. I'm just passing that on.'

'She's not finished, Lucie, and Esme, you're needed in the kitchen,' Harry said to the maid in that same sharp voice. 'Now.'

Esme fled the room and Harry shut the door. 'I heard your conversation,' she said, folding her arms across her chest and moving so she stood in front of me. 'You were asking about things that are none of your business.'

'My sister is on Bobby Noland's short list of suspects because Parker was here the day he died. He found eye drops here among her paints and brushes,' I said. 'So I think it is my business because Mia didn't poison Parker.'

Her eyes hardened. Then she said, catching me off guard, 'Your grandfather told you, didn't he? I should have known he wouldn't keep his mouth shut, in spite of what he said.'

It came out of nowhere. She really had been eavesdropping. 'Told me what?'

'You know very well *what*.'

How long could we play this game?

Harry didn't know about Pépé's letters from Jackie, so she wouldn't know that's how I knew Jackie had shared her unfavorable opinion of Harry's novel not only with my grandfather, but also with Parker when he visited Jackie right after Harry left her office. There was no way in hell I was going to tell Harry about those letters.

'Sorry,' I said. 'I really don't know what you're talking about.'

'Never mind,' she said. 'He didn't keep his word. He'll pay for that and so will you. I need to shut you up, Lucie.'

She reached over and ripped a couple of leaves off a bush

growing in a large marble urn that looked like it belonged in the garden of a Roman villa. Oleander. Beautiful but deadly.

Before I realized what she was doing, she had grabbed me from behind, her arm, strong as steel from tennis and working out, wrapped around my throat.

'Open your mouth,' she said, trying to force the leaves between my lips.

I clamped my mouth shut and tried to pull her off me, slashing at her legs with my cane. She lifted her foot to kick it away before I did any damage. In the split second when her foot was in the air and she was off-balance, I yanked her arm off me and hit her hard across both shins with the cane. She yelped and swore, clutching at the oleander bush to keep from losing her balance. Instead she tugged it so hard as she fell that the heavy urn slid off the stand, crashing to the floor and pinning her underneath.

She lay on the floor moaning.

'I'll get help,' I told her because it didn't look as if she was going anywhere. 'Don't eat any of the damn leaves. They're poisonous.'

She threw me a murderous look.

I opened the door and collided with Bobby Noland who grabbed me with both arms. Before I could speak, he glanced over my shoulder at Harry, who was still writhing in pain.

'And I thought the party was outside,' he said. 'Hope I didn't miss much.'

'Harry will fill you in when she's feeling better,' I said. 'She's got a lot to say.'

TWENTY-FIVE

Harriet Delacroix was charged with the first-degree murder of Parker Lord. Esme, the maid, had lingered outside the door to the solarium after Harry dismissed her and the moment she realized what was happening between Harry and me, she ran to get help, finding Bobby, who had just arrived at the party with Kit. The rest of the afternoon – including Cricket blowing out the ninety yellow tapers Dominique had placed on a spectacular tiered lemon cake – had continued without anyone being the wiser about what was going on inside the house. I had persuaded Pépé to tell Cricket that Harry suddenly felt unwell and had gone upstairs to rest.

Cricket wasn't born yesterday – literally – so she knew something was up, but after nine decades her old-school politesse, elegant manners, and the strength of my grandfather's arm, which she leaned on heavily, got her through the afternoon and she carried on as if nothing had happened. Afterwards, when a few of us were in the drawing room and she finally learned from Bobby that her daughter had been accused of murder and why she'd killed Parker, she had clutched her heart, gave my grandfather a beseeching look, and collapsed. Later the ER doctors said the heart attack had been mild, but at ninety even a mild heart attack was something to reckon with.

Pépé changed his airline ticket and stayed on, visiting Cricket in the hospital every day for the ten days she was there. A great-grandniece, the granddaughter of Édouard's brother and a smart, pretty lawyer living in Raleigh, agreed to bring Cricket to North Carolina where she could convalesce, plus she would take care of putting Mon Repos on the market. Once it sold, it would take care of Harry and Cricket's substantial debts with money left over for Cricket to move to an assisted living home. On the day Cricket left for Raleigh, Pépé went over to Mon Repos to say goodbye. When he came home, he brought with

him the two boxes filled with Jackie's notes and papers for her
book – and the journal.

'Are you going to read it?' I asked him.

'I don't think so,' he said. 'Jackie never intended it to be
made public.'

'Aren't you the least bit curious?'

He shook his head. 'I knew the real Jackie. It's enough. I
don't need to read her private thoughts. And I have good news.
While I was at Mon Repos, Marilyn Gilbert Bernard was there
supervising movers from the National Museum of Women in
the Arts who were crating Jackie's paintings. They had just
come from Ash's place.'

'So the museum will get all the paintings that were originally
promised to them.'

'That's right.'

'What about Jackie's book?'

'Harry's contract is null and void, but apparently her publisher
is still interested in it.'

'Maybe Kit could write it,' I said. 'She's a journalist.'

But Kit said no, thanks, art books weren't her specialty, and
instead came up with the perfect solution.

'Ask Marilyn,' she said. 'I bet she'd do it in a heartbeat.'

Pépé had a late-night flight to Paris that would get him in to
Charles de Gaulle mid-morning the following day, so it would
be dark and quiet and he could sleep on the plane. The day he
left we had two more matters to take care of; the last of the
unfinished business concerning Parker's death and Jackie's book.

It was Willow Harper who suggested burning sage in the
vineyard to purify and cleanse the air in the place where Parker
had died. She also offered to perform the ceremony since she'd
done it many times for friends who wanted to banish evil spirits
or negativity that lingered in, say, a new home or an office. I
had heard about this spiritual ritual, which was also called
smudging, and knew it was part of the culture of certain Native
American tribes and had sacred meaning to them.

All of our workers and staff joined Willow, Quinn, me, and
Pépé in the vineyard that last morning he was with us when
there was still dew on the grass, along with Eli, Sasha, Mia,

Kit, Persia, Gabriel, Ash, Josie, Antonio, Valeria, and Marilyn
Gilbert Bernard. Bobby came too, though Kit told me that she
had to twist his arm about witnessing 'voodoo'. I told her that
Quinn had wanted to know if Willow was some kind of shaman
or maybe a good witch and asked what we were getting into.

'She's very spiritual,' I said to him. 'Please do this for me.'

So he agreed, though I knew he was only doing it because
I asked him.

Willow, who wore a flowing white caftan and had braided
flowers in her long silver hair, arrived with a fat bundle of sage
tied together with twine, which, after explaining what she was
about to do, she lit with a candle until it burned down to a
smoky torch. Then carrying an abalone shell – which she said
represented water – to catch the ashes, she began walking up
and down the rows of vines as the rest of us followed, waving
the smoky, smoldering bundle and calling out to the negativity
that had invaded this place and telling it that it had no power
here any more. When she was finished and we had returned
full circle to where we'd started, she extinguished what was
left of the sage in a bowl filled with sand.

I could feel Quinn squirming next to me, but when the
ceremony was finally over and after Willow left he said, 'It's
weird, but I feel better. Like I'm in a better mood.'

'You heard Willow. She banished the evil spirits with the
light of her grace. And sage does that to you. That's why you
feel better.'

He looked at me as if he couldn't tell if I was serious or
pulling his leg. Then he said, 'Maybe we'll have to try that
more often.'

The final ceremony – if you can call it that – was between Pépé
and me. He wanted to burn Jackie's letters and the journal in
a kind of funeral pyre.

'It's time,' he said. 'Except for your grandmother, you are the
only person who has read Jackie's letters, *ma chérie*, besides me.
Now you know everything and I can let them go. Let *her* go.'

There was an open fireplace at the Ruins, which was what
we called the old tenant house that Union soldiers had burned
while searching for the Gray Ghost. It was within walking

distance of the winery. A few years ago Eli had converted the first-floor shell into an open-air stage where we held concerts, plays, and hosted events and parties when the weather was warm.

I told Pépé we would use the Ruins' fireplace and that we'd have the place to ourselves.

I drove us there after he browsed our wine cellar to see what was left of the amazing vintages Leland had stocked it with and came up with a bottle of Châteauneuf-du-Pape. He had opened it earlier to allow it to breathe, then re-corked it and found two wine glasses in the dining room.

The sun was setting behind the Blue Ridge, providing a Technicolor sky of blazing reds, oranges, and purples as backdrop when we arrived. I started the fire with dry kindling I'd brought and it burned steady and bright.

Pépé poured two glasses of wine and gave one to me. 'To Jackie,' he said.

We touched glasses and drank.

'How do you want to do this?' I asked after a moment.

'The letters first, because they will burn quickly, and then the journal.'

I handed him the bundle of letters that I had retied with the grosgrain ribbon. He untied the ribbon and fed the letters into the fire one by one.

'At her funeral in 1994,' he said in a quiet voice, 'Teddy Kennedy said something I never forgot. He said, "Jackie would have preferred to be just herself, but the world wanted her to be a legend, too."'

He fed the last letter into what had become a small bonfire. I didn't speak. He was in his own world, bidding farewell to a woman he had loved for most of his life. My heart ached for him.

'She was happiest surrounded by friends and family she loved,' he said.

He refilled our glasses as we watched the fire burn down. When it was nearly out he set the journal on the glowing embers. The weight of the book almost extinguished it, but after a moment the brittle pages caught and with a noisy whoosh a flame rose up and began to consume the leather-bound book.

'Now we see but a poor reflection as in a mirror; then we shall see face to face,' my grandfather said, and I realized he was reciting the Bible passage on love from Corinthians that I wanted to be read at our wedding. He went on, 'And now these three things remain: faith, hope and love.'

He reached out and took my hand in his. We said it together.

'But the greatest of these is love.'

ACKNOWLEDGMENTS

As usual there are many people to whom I owe thanks for answering my questions and being generous with their time and expertise. What is not usual is that I'm writing these acknowledgments during week ten of social distancing, otherwise known as the coronavirus quarantine. Although writing has always been a solitary pursuit, the last few months have been especially solitary. To borrow a meme I've seen on social media recently, 2020 is a unique leap year: February has 29 days, March has 300 days, and April has 5 years.

Writing this in mid-May of 2020, it sure feels like it. I can't even begin to imagine the story for the rest of this already tumultuous year.

In the World Before Coronavirus I spent a fascinating and unforgettable afternoon after a pre-Christmas book signing at Slater Run Vineyards in Upperville, Virginia, discussing Virginia wine, climate change, and solving a major plot conundrum. My partners in crime and wine that afternoon were Chris Patusky and Kiernan Slater, husband-and-wife owners of Slater Run; Rick Tagg, winemaker at Delaplane Cellars in Delaplane, VA, and my indefatigable advisor for many years; and Lucie Morton, one of the country's top viticulturists and an internationally renowned ampelographer (look it up!), who is the inspiration for Josie Wilde and quite possibly responsible for me naming my main character Lucie Montgomery almost twenty years ago. Kiernan also shared her thoughtful and well-considered insights into what it's like being a female winemaker in a mostly male-dominated profession. Rick answered my many questions and continued my wine education with unfailing patience and humor as he has done for the last dozen years – plus the smudging ceremony was his idea. Lucie taught me the difference between climate change and extreme climate, genetically modified grapes versus hybrids, and told me everything I needed to know about scion rooting and phylloxera. We also both love quilting – and even though it has nothing to do with wine, we still spent a lot of time talking about it.

One of my last 'outs' before quarantine began and museums and art galleries in Washington, D.C., closed their doors was a visit to the National Museum of Women in the Arts with Rosemarie Forsythe, who is a member of the museum's Advisory Board and the Director's Circle, a gifted artist, and a dear friend. I owe her thanks for introducing me to the 'Old Mistresses', which she suggested might be an intriguing subject for a book; she also directed me to the paintings of Élisabeth Vigée Le Brun and plied me with lots of great reading material. At NMWA, she connected me with Lynora Williams, the Director of the Betty Boyd Dettre Library and Research Center, who sent me several information-filled emails, and Susan White, a docent whose intimate knowledge of Vigée Le Brun was the basis for the information Marilyn Gilbert Bernard shared with Lucie and Kit. Best of all, Rosemarie introduced me to Susan Fisher Sterling, the museum's Director, and Ilene Gutman, the Deputy Director; Ilene sat down with Rosemarie and me that afternoon and explained the duties and role of a museum curator, which was an enormous help in creating the character of Marilyn Bernard. I am so grateful to all of them – and highly recommend a visit to this beautiful under-the-radar museum the next time you're in Washington. The story of how it came to be is fascinating. (More information at https://nmwa.org)

Lucy Zahray, aka 'The Poison Lady', sent me information on tetrahydrozoline poisoning and answered numerous questions. Dr Tal Simmons, of the Department of Forensic Science at Virginia Commonwealth University in Richmond, helped with forensic information and explained the condition of a body that had remained outside overnight in March. Detective Jim Smith of the Fairfax County, Virginia Police Department told me about the laws and regulations of extradition between states. The director of a research laboratory in northern Virginia spoke to me about the consequences of falsifying data in scientific papers, why it's so damaging, and how someone who fakes data or forges results gets caught.

Thank you to Rochelle Zohn for bidding in a fundraiser for Arlington, Virginia indie bookstore One More Page Books (looking at you, Eileen McGervey!) to have her dear friend Marilyn Gilbert Bernard named as a character in *The French Paradox*. Marilyn passed away after a long battle with cancer just before Rochelle was able to tell her she had the winning auction bid, but the real Marilyn, whom I wish I'd known, was a beloved librarian in the Fairfax County, Virginia school library system for many years. A straight shooter, she really did own a Venus flytrap and really did tell her students, 'My plant hasn't eaten in two weeks.' According to Rochelle, many of those students stayed in touch with her after they graduated, crediting her with a lifelong love of literature.

I was already working on an early draft of *The French Paradox* involving Jackie Onassis who, indeed, often stayed in Middleburg to ride and hunt, when a *New York Times* travel story was published called 'A year in Paris that transformed Jacqueline Kennedy Onassis' written by Ann Mah, a fellow author, Francophile, and friend. Though my plot revolves mostly around Jackie's years as a book editor in New York, Ann's well-researched and charming article about Jackie's junior year in Paris was the inspiration for the fictitious long-ago romance between Jackie and Lucie's grandfather – and the serendipitous imaginary purchase of the Élisabeth Vigée Le Brun paintings.

Quinn's fascination with the red star Betelgeuse dimming and potentially exploding was an ongoing story I followed as I was writing this book. Nadia Drake's December 27, 2019 story 'A Giant Star is Acting Strange and Astronomers are Buzzing' in *National Geographic* was especially useful. I shamelessly stole from her the term 'splattered star guts' and the consequences of what would happen to our solar system if Betelgeuse really did perform star seppuku because she painted such a great, vivid image.

In addition to those articles, several books were helpful in my research. *Dreaming in French* by Alice Kaplan (University of Chicago Press, 2012) described Jackie's year in Paris in 1949 in wonderful detail. Greg Lawrence's *Jackie as Editor: The Literary Life of Jacqueline Kennedy Onassis* (Thomas Dunne Books, 2011) provided fascinating information and insight – since he was one of her authors – about, well, Jackie's years as a book editor. As a result of reading Lawrence's book, I knew I had to find a copy of William Howard Adams' book *Atget's Gardens* (Doubleday, 1979) so I could read Jackie's beautifully written introduction and love letter to the gardens of Paris and the photographs of Eugène Atget. Rosemarie Forsythe loaned me her copy of *A Museum of their Own: The National Museum of Women in the Arts* written by the museum's founder Wilhelmina Cole Holladay (Abbeville Press Publishers, 2008), bristling with multi-colored flags on pages she marked for my attention, which I returned after I took notes and bought my own copy. Thank you to Jilann Brunett and Kathy jo Shea of Second Chapter Books in Middleburg for introducing me to local author Linda Jane Holden's gorgeous book *The Gardens of Bunny Mellon* (Photographs by Roger Foley, Vendome, 2019) for inspiration about Cricket's gardens and also for information about the gardens at Oak Spring Farm, the Mellons' beautiful estate in Middleburg. I bought *The Last Great Plant Hunt: the Story of Kew's Millennium Seed Bank* by Carolyn Fry, Sue Seddon & Gail Vines (Kew Publishing, Royal Botanic Gardens, Kew, 2011) while in Britain visiting the Seed Bank in 2013 for research for *Ghost Image*, a book I wrote in a different series. This wonderful and fascinating book provided information (which I have greatly embellished) on research into how to possibly manipulate glutathione as a 'death trigger' so a plant would not self-destruct. Finally, I managed to procure a copy of *One Special Summer* (Delacorte Press, 1974) by Jacqueline and Lee Bouvier, an illustrated hand-written journal originally meant as a thank-you gift for their mother to describe a trip the two sisters took to Europe in the summer of 1951. Jackie's drawings are colorful, full of life, and utterly charming. Reading her account of a carefree summer in Europe – albeit probably omitting a few delicious details since she was writing to her mother – was insightful.

Every month without fail for the last ten years, Donna Andrews, John Gilstrap, Alan Orloff, Art Taylor, and I – affectionately known as the Rumpus Writers, or the plural, Rumpi – have met to read our latest works-in-progress to each other, to discuss craft and to talk about the writing business. Lately we're meeting on Zoom. As ever, I'm grateful to them all for comments and constructive critique on early drafts of this book – but mostly for their friendship and support.

Thanks to Kate Lyall Grant, publisher and my editor at Severn House Books, who fell in love with this book when she read it for the first time and who has been so wonderfully supportive. Also, thanks to Natasha Bell for overseeing the process of turning my manuscript into a book and to Claire Ritchie for copyediting. My oldest son Peter de Nesnera kindly redrew the map of Montgomery Estate Vineyard, adding changes and fitting this in during an exceptionally busy time at work in Germany – your mom is grateful. The following people read this book as a manuscript and made comments that improved it: Cathy Brannon, Rosemarie Forsythe, André de Nesnera, and Kathy jo Shea – thank you all.

Thanks and love to my agent Dominick Abel for seeing to it that this series continues, now with its third publisher. It has been a privilege to be among his 'family' of authors for the last fifteen years; no author could be luckier than to have a champion, friend, and sounding board who offers such sage wisdom and advice.

Finally, all my love and gratitude to André de Nesnera, my husband of nearly forty years, for so much love and for giving me the time, space, and unconditional support for my sometimes mercurial but always extraordinarily satisfying career as a writer. There's no one I'd rather spend every minute of every day during coronavirus lockdown with than you, my love.